BEFORE SHANNON DIED

Sydney Hope Archer

Published by Motina Books, LLC, Van Alstyne, Texas
www.MotinaBooks.com

Library of Congress Cataloguing-in-Publication Data:
Names: Archer, Sydney Hope
Title: Before Shannon Died
Description: First Edition. | Van Alstyne: Motina Books, 2022

Identifiers:
LCCN: 2021952513

ISBN-13: 978-1-945060-48-9 (paperback)
ISBN-13: 978-1-945060-43-4 (e-book)
ISBN-13: 978-1-945060-49-6 (hardcover)

Subjects: BISAC:
Fiction > Thriller>General

Cover Design: Diane Windsor
Interior Design: Diane Windsor
Photo of Chackbay Church: Rick Galvan (CC-BY)
Fog Image: Creative Fabrica

Praise for *Before Shannon Died*

"Heart-stopping and deftly-handled, *Before Shannon Died* will keep you
gripping the pages late into the night."
—A.J. Aalto, author of the thriller, *Closet Full of Bones*

"*Before Shannon Died* is a gripping tale of a family's desperation to
protect their reputation even if it means sacrificing one of their own. It
is by turns lyrical and devastating, inspiring and heart-breaking, and
readers will be thinking about it for a very long time after turning the last
page."
—Gordon Bonnet, author of *Descent Into Ulthoa*

"Heartbreaking and beautiful, *Before Shannon Died* fiercely,
unapologetically tells a complicated story of family, love, betrayal, and
religion. Archer hits on every emotional note. I was mesmerized by the
story, thought about the book when I wasn't reading it, was happy when
I returned. There's wisdom and grace in these pages, hard-earned but
lovely, and delivered with a sure hand. I'm glad *Before Shannon Died* came
into my life. I won't forget it."
—E.A. Aymar, author of *The Unrepentant* and *They're Gone*

PART ONE

EVIE

The room felt wrong.

Everything looked the same, but Evie knew something, somewhere had tilted. Inside Shannon Grady's tidy little apartment with its bowls of potpourri and shabby furniture, an oppressive *something* lurked, filling all the corners and every niche.

She knew if she moved, if she breathed, that malevolent something would drag her into a place of horror. Evie had faced down a lot of her own demons and troubles, but she'd never known real fear until that hour. Her gaze scoured the apartment from the compact kitchen to the spotless living room in which she stood.

Nothing was out of place, and yet it was. It was so out of place that Evie wanted to run for safety.

"Shannon?" The name came out tiny, almost a whimper.

No answer. No sound of movement, anywhere. And yet....

Evie gathered the ragged edges of her courage.

"Who's here?"

This time the strength in her voice fed her courage. Growing up on Chicago's south side, Evie had learned early how to street fight. At that moment she held nothing for defense—no gun, knife, ball bat or even a frying pan—but she would bite, claw, kick and punch until her bloody opponent cried for mercy—if she had to.

No one answered; no sound indicated any presence in the apart-ment other than her own.

"I'm dialing 9-1-1 on my cell phone right now." Evie could no more afford a cell phone than she could a new Lexus.

The thing was, in Shannon's apartment, just like all the apartments in the complex, there were only three rooms: the living room/kitchen combo, a small bedroom, and a miniscule bathroom that barely offered enough space for one person. An intruder could hide behind the shower curtain or the bedroom door, but that was it. No one could wedge beneath Shannon's low bed.

Evie charged across the small space, threw open the bathroom door and flung aside the shower curtain in one fluid motion.

No one there.

She snapped her head to the right, eyeing the bedroom less than four steps away. The door stood slightly ajar.

She moved, punched it open all the way. The knob crashed into the wall. The door shuddered like thunder before it bounced back toward her, but not before Evie saw her friend on the bed. She caught the rebounding door, clung to it as she stared and stared.

Take it back, take it back! Maybe she screamed it aloud.

Sweet, loving, disturbed Shannon, the woman who had given away so much of herself. The woman who had picked up the broken pieces of her life and was still about to give more. She had lost her way one last time.

OWEN

A cemetery in early summer is at its best with swept-clean green stretches of grass and polished headstones that gleam in the sunlight. In those times, a graveyard invites bittersweet memories and reverent hushes of whispered conversation. Visitors linger to pay tribute to those who've passed on or to discuss events of the day.

But on a day in midwinter, when bare branches clutch and rattle like brittle bones beneath the cold determination of a northeast wind, voices pour forth in a rush. No languid condolences while icy wind stabs the throat; no drawn-out accolades for the deceased when a need to find shelter and warmth consumes the mourner.

January 31st was such a day. Owen Grady stood with the last of his family by the graveside of their youngest sister many miles from the family plot. A tremor of lightness stole into his body as he finally laid aside the burden he'd shouldered too long. Shannon had lived thirty-four years, five months and eleven days.

Owen, thirteen years her senior, remembered clearly the day Mom brought her home from the hospital, a bright-eyed pink scrap who cried too often and too much. Born much later than her siblings, Shannon had been the unexpected baby, the "accident," the unwelcome little visitor who stayed.

Owen and his other sisters, Julie and Donna, had been good kids, always respectful of their mother and her needs. While Shannon consumed their mother's time and energy, they had to prepare their own sandwiches, make their own beds, think up their own games. In Owen's oft-voiced opinion, she clung to her mother like a briar. Somehow, as years passed and she grew older, it seemed Shannon never understood that she was not special, or darling, or necessary. To Owen, she lived in what always appeared to be a clueless disregard of others and what was important.

Though a bright morning sun pierced the eyes, its heat was as foreign as a carnival in this place of the dead, and the six who gathered beside the grave shivered in the relentless wind. Owen stood between both surviving sisters and stared at the small plain urn that housed Shannon's ashes. Frigid wind whipped the black fabric of their clothes and tore at their hair. Donna, the third born, sniffed and blinked only because the wind which slapped their cheeks and pinched their nostrils drew stinging tears to eyes that otherwise would be dry.

Julie, the eldest, didn't move. When Owen looked at her, it seemed she focused not on the dead sibling, but on something far away. She caught Owen's eye and smiled, then reached out to squeeze his hand with her gloved one. Donna duplicated the touch.

These are my real sisters, he told himself. Those two, who looked up to him, who recognized his place of leadership in the family after their parents passed away nearly seven years ago. Donna always sought his counsel and spiritual guidance; Julie lived in California and was generally out of touch with what went on back home, but at least she acknowledged his role. He hoped they trusted he always knew what was best for them.

These women were unlike Shannon, who had run her life on her own terms, ignoring his warnings and advice. She had refused to date the men he picked for her, or to attend the church of his choice, or to abstain from a multitude of activities in which no Grady should ever think about, let alone indulge. Shannon smiled right in his face, then always did as she pleased the moment he turned his back. It was as if he carried no authority with her at all.

His stomach clenched every time he thought of her obstinate indifference to his beliefs and wisdom. Above all, they were Gradys, and that name meant everything in Woodrow, Arkansas, from jobs to church leadership to city planning and management. The name carried influence and responsibility. It demanded respect. But for Shannon, the family name meant nothing but an easy meal ticket.

Owen gazed at the winter-brown grass at his feet. After all he had said and done for her, it was too bad that Shannon chose to discount the truth.

Now she reaped the harvest of the seeds she had sown, and she had only herself to blame. A smile of satisfaction settled into his features.

As the wind slackened, he lifted his head. On the other side of Shannon's grave, standing apart from the minister and his wife, was the only other mourner to attend the brief, obligatory graveside service. Shannon's friend, Evie Kendall, bore her dark and hostile gaze into his without flinching, as if she read his mind and knew everything he'd ever thought or done.

His heart fluttered, and he wiped away the smile, swallowing hard. He had never liked the woman, or any of Shannon's friends for that matter. They were drunks and druggies, low-life welfare cases. Every one of them had their hands out, or into pockets that weren't their own. You never knew what they were up to, but you could bet your bottom dollar it was no good.

Reverend Randall Yeager, minister of the Woodrow Worship Center where three generations of Gradys had faithfully attended, stood at the head of the grave, his back to the wind. The pages of his black leather-bound Bible fluttered. His wife, Patty, stood a couple of steps behind him. He weighted them down with the flat of his hand, cleared his throat, and began to read the short passage of scripture Owen had chosen.

"And I saw the dead, small and great, stand before God; and the books were opened: and another book was opened, which is the book of life: and the dead were judged out of those things which were written in the books, according to their works. And the sea gave up the dead which were in it; and death and hell delivered up the dead which were in them: and they were judged every man according to their works. And death and hell were cast into the lake of fire. This is the second death. And whosoever was not found written in the book of life was cast into the lake of fire."

Pastor Yeager looked up and met Owen's gaze. With his thumb and fingers flicking through pages, it seemed he might want to read from another passage, maybe something that offered hope. But it was a raw day, and the wind had long ago cut through the thick layers of their clothing. Everyone was shivering, including the minister.

Owen gave him a somber nod.

"Amen. Thank you, Pastor."

The preacher shifted, readjusted his coat, hesitated then said, "Very well. Let's bow our heads for a word of prayer."

The service neared its end, and his sister's remains soon would be placed in the small hole dug for the urn. Owen believed that prayers for the dead were a pack of nonsense. Tragic as it was, Shannon was beyond all hope now. The minister's prayer was for him and his living sisters.

Owen allowed the quick blessing and condolence to slide across his consciousness almost unheard. He opened his eyes too soon. Once again, he was looking straight into the piercing glare of Evie Kendall. A fresh blast of chilling wind reached his heart. He looked away, grateful when the prayer was over.

"Thank you," he said again, his deep voice carried the proper depth of somber reflection. "I appreciate you making the trip all this way."

"Bless you, brother." Briefly, lightly, the minister embraced him, a gesture that seemed forced and unnatural, as if the wind had pushed him into it. Patty's touch came more easily. Pastor Yeager turned quickly to the women, shook their hands, saying, "I'm sorry she missed out on heaven and its glory."

"My sister could have had better." Owen rocked forward on the balls of his feet and added, with conviction, "But she made her choice."

"Yes," the preacher said. "You did the Lord's work, brother. No man could have worked harder for her soul."

Owen tipped his head in a show of humility. "I did my best, Pastor Yeager."

"Yes," murmured the preacher again as his wife echoed, "Yes, oh my, yes."

Owen basked in their regard for a moment, letting the warmth of praise soak in, hoping for more, waiting for a benediction on his efforts.

Patty Yeager, the minister's wife, spoke. "We'll keep you in our prayers. All of you."

Owen looked at her, his eyes sharp, seeking a hidden meaning there. Finding none, he smiled sadly at her.

"I crave your prayers." Ignoring the bristling presence of Evie Kendall, he turned to his sisters and said in an undertone, "We'll stop at the Sizzler on the way out of town for lunch."

Standing on either side of their brother, the women tucked their arms into his, a show of unity against the glowering Evie, and prepared to plow through the blustery weather to his copper-colored Mercedes parked a few yards away.

With the end of the fiscal year fast approaching, Owen had an urgent business matter that needed his attention, but returning to the office after the funeral of a family member wouldn't look good. It would be mid-afternoon before they got back to Woodrow, but burying his sister in a cemetery full of strangers seemed more appro-priate than planting her with the family in the town where she was born and raised. Shannon had dragged their name through the mud long enough, and now it would take what was left of the Grady's to repair the family's damaged reputation. That restoration was of utmost importance, especially to him and Donna. He wasn't so sure about Julie; she didn't seem too much a part of things anymore. He'd have to talk to her, straighten her out, and he needed to do it soon.

The trio had taken a few steps toward the car when a voice called out. "Owen Grady!"

He stopped, inwardly cringing. Evie Kendall approached like a shabby sparrow, unbuttoned brown coat flapping in the wind, tresses of thin dark hair fluttering wildly around a chalky face. Faded flannel shirt, old jeans and stained sneakers. It was typical of Evie Kendall not to care how she looked at a funeral. Owen had never seen her decked in anything but thrift store casual. She was emblematic of the kind of people in Shannon's crowd. Thank God more of them had not shown up.

"What the hell was that?" She strode forward, pointing back at the small mound of earth where the urn would soon be out of sight.

Owen's spine stretched as he took in a deep, hard breath. He had never developed the fine art of debate. His thoughts always short-circuited each other so that a logical flow of words never left his lips. If a hard glare failed, and it rarely did, then he preferred avoidance to confrontation. In the Grady family, with the exception of Shannon and infrequently his father, his word was the last word, even the best word.

Donna, however, had no problem going head to toe with someone else. She spoke up. "Don't use your gutter language around us, Evie

Kendall. What's your problem?"

Evie stopped an arm's length from them. Her bare hands were curled into fists at her side. The wind whipped her slight body, but she didn't seem to feel its force or bite. In fact, the harder it blew against her, the stronger she seemed. She favored Donna with a dismissive glance, completely ignored Julie, and focused on Owen.

"My problem is this two-dollar service you just held for your youngest sister in a town a hundred miles from her home. No funeral, no memorial service, no visitation in the funeral home, a thing that looks more like a tin can than a burial urn. Hell, her obituary wasn't even in the newspaper—"

"I saw no reason—" he began.

"You didn't give anybody a chance to say good-bye to her!"

Owen's mouth tightened. "I saw no reason why everyone has to know."

Evie stared at him, shriveling him with a glare. Once again he was sure she tried to dissect the workings of his mind. He struggled to look away and could not.

"In your deluded way," she said, "do you think you can keep her death a secret? Just because you think she's no better than shit, do you believe everybody else feels that way? Do you think she has no friends? And where's Garrett? Does he even know she's dead? What is wrong with you?"

He attempted to quell Evie Kendall with his own glower, the one that worked so well on others. Evie either didn't notice or didn't care. His heart fluttered. He tugged his sisters' arms still linked to his own and attempted to go to the car.

Evie stepped sideways and blocked their path.

"Don't think you can brush me off the way you did Shannon," she said. "I'm not soft-hearted and forgiving like she was, and I'm not afraid of you. Don't think I'm as big a fool as these." She pointed to Randall and Patty Yeager as they approached, eyes wide, mouths open in the cold wind. "I heard you say how you'd done the best you could, how you worked for her soul."

Owen licked his lips and the wind dried them instantly.

"I did my best for her," he said and tried to move forward, but at his left Donna's sturdy body didn't budge.

"Our sister's welfare is no concern of yours," she told Evie.

"You are full of shit."

Donna jerked back as if Evie had kicked sand in her eyes.

"This is neither the time nor place for language like that," Pastor Yeager said, his face ruddy.

Next to him, Patty played nervously with the collar of her coat. She met and held Owen's glance then looked away quickly. Her wide gold wedding band caught the brittle sunlight and shot a hard beam straight into his eyes. He winced.

Evie ignored the pair. Her focus remained on Owen who mentally clambered to gather up the ragged ends of his wits. He took strength from his flanking sisters and from the ministerial couple nearby.

"Shannon did not deserve a funeral," he said, finding words at last. "She did not deserve to be honored with a service, to be memorialized in an obituary, or to be buried near our family. She chose to turn her back on us and on the Lord. She got what she deserved."

"That's right," murmured Randall Yeager.

"Exactly right," Donna agreed. Julie cleared her throat but said nothing. Owen shot her a look.

Her dark eyes flashing, Evie stared at all of them, each one in turn, as if they'd sprouted horns and tails.

"And you call yourselves Christians?"

Owen stretched his spine again.

"Yes," he said, as if she were deaf.

"Of course we are!" Donna snapped. Julie murmured something no one could hear. Owen hoped it was an affirmation of her faith.

Evie gave a little laugh that held no humor. She shook her head.

"Every last one of you is a fucking idiot," she said. "My God. No wonder Shannon blew her brains out."

EVIE

Evie flopped into a kitchen chair and reached for her smokes. She shook one out, fondled it like a lover, raised it to her lips for a moment, then placed it on the table next to her green Bic lighter. She slid out the rest of the pack and counted. Five cigarettes to see her through until her check arrived tomorrow. She craved a carton, wanted to light them up, one after the other, and let the nicotine ease the anger and hurt and helplessness that bore into her very middle.

"I'll never have another friend like Shannon Grady," she said to Toni and Dunn. She could ask them for a smoke, but their packs were as low as hers and they hoarded them like Scrooge with his gold.

"I know," Toni said. "She was great."

She tapped her fingertips on the table. The ragged red polish was worn halfway off her short nails. When her check came, she'd go to Dulcie's and spend a ton of money getting a new manicure. Toni Feeney liked to look nice, even if her clothes came from the Share Center, but Evie thought it was a foolish waste to have someone paint your fingernails and glue doodads on them.

Dunn Bradshaw, slouched in another kitchen chair, met Evie's eyes.

"We'd have gone to the service if someone would've told us." Not a challenge, exactly, more like a question.

"If I'd known in time, I woulda told you. As it was, I barely had time to get there myself. The whole thing lasted about three minutes."

Toni shook her head. Her short dark hair shone in the light from the overhead fixture.

"I don't get it. I thought the Gradys had lived in Woodrow for, like, forever, so why did they bury her way over in Champion? Why didn't she have a regular funeral?"

"Yeah, well, your guess is as good as mine. That whole clan is crazier than shit."

"The Gradys?" Toni's pitch said she didn't believe it.

"Oh hell, yeah." Dunn hooked one beefy arm over the back of the chair. "Think they're so all mighty pure and good. He makes a big deal every month at the warehouse meetings, tells us how we need to start going to church, stop living the way we do. If Owen Grady really wanted us to live better than we do, he'd give us more hours and better pay, not try to drag us to his church."

He reached into the pocket of his faded flannel shirt and took out a crumpled, half-empty pack of Lucky Strikes. He scraped a paper match across the bookcover and held the flame to the tip. He spoke around the filter.

"Take this two-week lay-off before Christmas every year for instance. Don't seem so Christian to me." He shook the match dead. "But it saves Grady Wood Products a ton of money. Old man Grady woulda never done things this way if he was still alive."

"Maybe the lay-off is Donna's husband's idea," Evie said. "Craig's the one who saved that company from going under right after Curtis died. Owen couldn't keep the plant going on his brains alone. He don't have enough sense to pour piss out of a boot. Of course, I suppose the company never did really recover. That fool nearly destroyed the town's only industry – and the town right along with it."

"Shannon tell you that?" Toni asked.

Evie gave in to her craving and lit a cigarette fifteen minutes before she'd planned to. She inhaled deeply, gratefully, then exhaled at leisure.

"She didn't have to. It was common knowledge. Besides, you know Shannon hardly ever said anything about her family. Critical stuff, I mean. She never complained. But sometimes, we'd get to talking and she'd say things. That time in the hospital after she'd cut her wrists, for instance. Probably the medication loosened her tongue."

"What'd she say?" Toni leaned forward eagerly. She loved gossip better than anyone Evie knew.

"I don't want to talk about it now. The fact that Owen and his sisters didn't give Shannon a proper send-off has just got me so mad." She smoked in silence for a few moments then shook her head. "I guess I need to call Garrett."

Dunn frowned. "You think they didn't tell him?"

"Are you kidding? He's as much of an embarrassment to them as she was. She did tell me about that, it upset her so much."

"Fuckin' idiots." Dunn scowled at his cigarette.

"That's what I said," Evie muttered. Then, "They blamed Shannon for her own illness, you know."

Toni glanced up from her fingernails. "They did?"

Evie nodded. "Owen stopped by a few months ago with some preacher, but they didn't stay long. After her folks died, the family never checked on her well-being or came to see her, except a coupla times a year when Owen tried to get her to go to a revival service or something. Not one of them ever asked her to their house for Thanksgiving or Christmas even though there'd always be some big family doings with Owen's bunch and Donna and Craig and their kids."

She inhaled deeply, held the smoke for a bit then blew it out noisily in an attempt to blow out her anger. She thought of Christmas two or three years ago, when Shannon baked a little canned ham she got from the Share Center. She'd made a pie from a couple of cans of Bruce's Yams.

"Just in case they ask me this year," she'd said, but the night before Christmas she'd told Evie, "Looks like it's you and me, kid."

Evie didn't mind this last-minute business. Her own dysfunctional family never met for holidays—or for anything else, and that was okay with Evie. But she knew Shannon's longing to be a part of a family who preferred her absence. What Evie failed to understand, and what Shannon seemed unable to fully explain, was why her friend yearned to be included in a tight little circle that choked off all the joy from life.

"They think it's a sin to smile," Evie had said to Shannon that Christmas afternoon as they watched *It's a Wonderful Life*.

"Oh, it's not that bad," Shannon responded lightly. "And it's not the smiling that's sinful; it's what they might have to do to produce a smile." Then she giggled, and the giggle turned into her infectious laugh and before long both women sprawled in their chairs, holding their aching sides.

"Dear Jesus, I shouldn't be so mean," Shannon said after a bit, wiping her eyes.

"How can you say that? You aren't mean; they are."

Shannon patted her friend's hand reassuringly. "No, they're just doing what they think is right."

But Evie wasn't reassured. Looking into Shannon's eyes, she saw pain, and she saw something else. Shannon had looked away before Evie identified it.

Now Evie pulled her focus off that day and reentered the present. She told Toni and Dunn, "The Gradys never understood Shannon. They never tried. If they were my family ...."

The pair across the table from her remained silent, but after a bit Toni said, "Did they even have music at her service? You know how Shannon liked music. They should have played something by Heart. Or maybe Blondie. You know how she loved Debbie Harry."

Evie just looked at her, then got up to refill their coffee cups.

"Guess they didn't," Toni mumbled as Evie sat back down. The other two watched Toni as she absently picked at her chipped nail polish. "I thought she was doing so well. I thought she was on meds."

"She was," Dunn said. "Told me she thought Copamin was her miracle drug. She'd been taking it for a few years."

"She told me the same thing," Evie said. "It didn't make her lethargic like Lithium did or jittery like Ritalin. That's why she stopped taking any of that shit in the first place. She wanted to function. You know, feel normal. But she's not been herself lately. Distant. Staying in her apartment. That worried me because she tried to ... you know ... a few times before ... once with an overdose of Xanax, once with a razor blade. But just the other day she swore up and down that she was all right, that she just needed a little time to herself."

Dunn gave her a narrow look through a blur of smoke. "And you bought that?"

"We all need a little space, Dunn. Shannon and I were friends, not lovers. We didn't own each other. And, anyway, I saw her every day. She was a little distracted, but she's been like that since Garrett was here. I didn't see anything that made me think she was heading for a crash."

Dunn crushed out his cigarette in the half-full ashtray on the table. The two of them stared at each other for a minute before he responded.

"Yeah. Well. I know she used to play around with her other meds, didn't take them like she should."

"She never let on, not for a minute, that she'd quit taking it. And the stuff stays in your system for a while."

Toni held out one hand and eyed her nails. She frowned, bit off a ragged piece of cuticle and spat it out.

"Then maybe she was. Taking her meds, I mean. Maybe it was something else that got her. Damn, look at that. I made it bleed." She popped her index finger into her mouth.

Evie frowned. "What do you mean, something else?"

"I dunno." She examined at the wound. "Like maybe she found out she had cancer or something and didn't want to go through all that." She glanced up, saw their faces. "Well, don't look at me like that. Some people can't take pain." She went back to picking off minute pieces of nail polish.

Evie took a deep breath and let it out slowly, almost painfully. She didn't want to talk but the words trickled out.

"Finding her ... that way … dead and cold ... " She lifted her coffee but the smell nauseated her and she pushed the cup away. "And later, after the cops and the coroner left, I stripped off the sheets because I couldn't stand to see them, but that mattress is still there, bloody and…." She took in a deep breath and fought back the rise of grief that threatened to take her down into a deep, dark hole. "And on the dresser…and the wall…." She swallowed hard. "You know what a meticulous housekeeper Shannon was. She'd not want something like that in her bedroom."

"Let the manager dispose of it," Toni suggested, but Dunn said, "I'll haul it off for you. I can borrow Pop's old truck tomorrow and dump the thing in the sinkhole on his place."

Tears stung Evie's eyes and she blinked, averted her gaze until she was sure she wouldn't cry in front of the others.

"That'd be great, Dunn."

The two of them smiled at each other, and Toni caught the edge of it. She and Dunn weren't married, or even dating anymore, but the other woman bristled at any perceived competition, no matter how benign. She stood and put on her coat.

"We need to go, Dunn. I'm almost out of smokes."

Dunn got up and opened the front door.

"Speak of the devil." He stared across the parking lot at the units on the other side. "Owen and his bunch are at Shannon's right now. That's some car he drives."

"Yeah. A new one. He buys one for himself and one for Sarah Jean every year or so." Evie looked out the window. "I can't imagine any of that clan cleaning out her apartment, but maybe I'm wrong. I'll go tell him you volunteered to haul off the mattress."

She shrugged into her coat and followed her friends out the door. They said goodbye and she headed into the north wind, steeling herself against the cold.

JULIE

Shannon's small apartment was warm for a day so cold. The three siblings stood in the tiny living room, coats, hats and gloves still encasing their bodies. Threadbare furnishings and cheap décor were softened by their cleanliness and a scattering of throw rugs and a knitted afghan. There was a certain atmosphere of hominess and welcome.

Underscoring the neat appearance, though, was an odor, metallic and foul. Julie chose not to mention it. Low-income housing always had its problems. God only knew what crept through the duct work and along rafters to breed, nest, or die.

"It's toasty in here," she murmured as she unbuttoned her coat. The walls seemed to press in, accentuating the compactness of the apartment. Or maybe she felt claustrophobic because of a sudden and overwhelming need to escape this place, these people, the calamity that had brought them together. She longed to close this chapter of her life as fast as possible.

"It isn't toasty. It's hot," Donna said. "I'm sure she never bothered to turn the heat down ... except in the summer when she probably ran the air conditioning full throttle. Shannon always had to be comfortable." She wrinkled her pug nose and sniffed. "And what's that nasty smell? She probably never cleaned the place." She brushed invisible dirt from her navy Donna Karan pantsuit.

Julie looked at her sister, at the shining brown chin-length bob, the carefully applied make-up, small eyes, and tight lips. Gaudy diamond rings on her short fingers caught the light from the overhead fixture.

Owen's rust-colored eyebrows matched his hair, and he had those brows drawn into a scowl as he studied the room. "The money for the heating bill in these low-income places comes out of the taxpayers' pockets. You know that? And the cooling bill, too. She didn't have to pay for it." He dipped his head toward a kitchen so tiny two people could never fit in. "She didn't have to buy her food, either, and probably ate better than most folks."

He probed the small spaces with his narrow gaze as if he sought dust or roaches, or even sin lurking in the corners, beneath the furniture, or on the shelves. He spotted a stack of books on an end table. The books had library labels on their spines.

"She had plenty of time to waste reading." He sighed. "Our baby sister had an easy life."

Julie knew if she held her peace, Owen would continue talking, and what he had to say about Shannon would be merciless or loutish. He and Donna seemed to delight in vilifying her.

"Doubtless her life was harder than you think," Julie told him. "How easy can your life be when you choose to end it?"

He fixed a look on her. "Whose side are you on, anyway?"

"I'm not on anyone's side. There are no 'sides' in this situation."

"Shannon had everything handed to her on a silver platter," Donna declared.

"That's right," Owen said. "She never had to turn her hand at anything. She never kept a job because she didn't want to work."

"Oh, come on. She—"

"Shannon had an easy life. She took the easy way out of it."

"That's cold, Owen," Julie said. "Heartless and cold. Maybe we did spoil her when she was born. I was fifteen years old. You were what, thirteen? Donna was ten or eleven—"

"Ten," Donna snapped. "I was only ten years old when she came along and don't think for a minute that Mom didn't have me running my legs off to get the bottle or a diaper or fetch the baby rattle ...."

"My point is," Julie said, raising her voice above Donna's shrill complaint, "that she was a baby in a houseful of older children and adults. Of course we petted her and made over her. She was cute and sweet."

"People don't stay cute and sweet," Owen said. "Shannon grew up and avoided responsibility like a deadly disease. She spent every last penny she got her hands on, and she wore a hole in Mom and Dad's wallet."

"Mom and Dad helped us all, and you know it. You got a lot of help from them. Both of you."

He narrowed his green eyes. "No more than necessary. I wouldn't take advantage of them the way Shannon did."

"She was sick!"

"She was lazy! They paid her bills and her rent every month. They even bought her that car."

"The folks made the down payments for you both on your first houses," Julie reminded them. "And they bought cars for your kids when they went off to college." Owen shifted his feet while Donna's mouth wagged for a moment.

"That was their way, to do things like that," Owen said.

"My point exactly. So when Shannon—"

"All that was a gift for us and the kids," Donna's voice as thin and sharp as a needle. "They would have done the same for you if you'd stayed here but you ran off the minute you graduated high school. You don't know what went on after you left, Julie."

She had known this diatribe was coming. It always did. This time she refused to rise to the bait. Instead she took off her coat.

"Didn't that woman in the housing office tell you she wanted the apartment empty and clean before the end of the month? I'm leaving day after tomorrow so if you want my help with this we need to get busy."

"You're leaving?" Owen asked, as if this surprised him. He hadn't moved from his spot in the center of the small room since they walked in.

Julie laid her coat across the back of the sofa and looked at him over her shoulder.

"Did you think I planned to stay in Woodrow? I told you I would come for the service and help get her affairs taken care of, but that's it."

"You need to come home and stay."

She gaped at him.

"Are you kidding? My job, my home, my life is in Los Angeles. I'll be glad to pack up Shannon's things, but beyond that ...."

She could see he had shut out her words, that he listened to his own voice echoing from somewhere in the corners of his brain. He gave her that smile, the one she hated, the one that said he was so much smarter than her.

"Listen," he said, spreading his hands and stretching his neck toward her as if to imbue her with his wisdom, "you need to be here. This is where you were born, where you were raised. Your family is here."

He narrowed his eyes again and gave her a look between his lashes. He used to do that when explaining game rules or telling her how to plant tomatoes in the vegetable garden. It was a look that sneered, "You know nothing!"

As far as Julie was concerned, Owen was an ignoramus. And Donna, too. They moved in only their small, tight social circle, and knew only the rigid grip of their religion. This pokey little town encompassed their world, fulfilled their needs, and provided their safe haven. Nothing existed beyond its borders. What Woodrow, Arkansas, failed to do for them, their church did. This safe, comfortable plane of existence, where all things in their lives orbited around them, fulfilled every need the Gradys could possibly dream.

She sucked in a deep breath, reminding herself of the resolve she'd made on the hurried flight out here to avoid foolish arguments.

"Looks like she kept her apartment clean. All we need to do is pack up her things. Owen, did she leave a will?"

Her brother stared at her, obviously clutching at the ragged ends of a conversation where the subject had changed without his permission. His mouth wagged a couple of times.

"She didn't have the sense to write a letter let alone write a will." Donna meandered to the shelf on the far side of the living room. "Who'd want this junk, anyway? I say throw it all away." She paused, then gasped as she grabbed something off the shelf. "Would you look at this!"

She held up a snow globe the size of a grapefruit on a dark wooden stand. Inside, a thin white church with a sharp spire stood on a hill dotted with evergreens. When she shook it, thick white flakes swirled briefly and settled.

"I remember that," Julie said with a slight smile. "Mom kept it on the table near the front door of the lake house at Christmas." She held out her hand to look at it but Donna clutched the ornament to her chest. Her gripping knuckles shone white and rigid.

"It was my very favorite thing!" Donna cried. "Look at it! What did she do to it?" She pointed to a small V-shaped nick in the wood. "Of all the keepsakes, I wanted this and I couldn't find it anywhere. Now I know why. Shannon stole it!"

Julie dropped her hand. "She didn't steal it. Mom and Dad's things were for all of us."

"She took everything else, so she didn't need to take the snow globe. I wanted it!" Her sister's shrill voice stabbed Julie's eardrums.

Julie glanced at the worn-out chairs and ancient television. She saw an old CD player, but nothing new or trendy. Although cute and well-tended, Shannon's decorations were strictly thrift store/bargain basement.

"Donna," she said, turning to her sister, "you have the piano, the folks' bedroom set, their antique desk and all their books. I believe you took Grandma's Grady's silver and her china, plus those imported table linens. Owen has Dad's gun collection and the grandfather clock. I took the quilts Grandma Biddle made and that oil painting of the woodland pool. But I don't see a thing in here that belonged to Dad and Mom except that old TV and Mom's mixer over there on the counter."

"She took Mom's mixer?" Donna said in dismay.

"She probably sold everything else," Owen said peevishly.

Julie gave her brother a look. "I thought you sold their things. And their house. And the lake house. You told me an auction was the quickest way to dispose of the estate. Didn't you?"

His face reddened. "Yeah. But still."

She picked up the soft blue afghan from the back of chair, rubbed the corner of it against her cheek. It smelled of the fabric softener that promised spring time freshness.

"What did you do with the money from the sale, anyway? I hope you shared it with Shannon since I never saw a penny of it."

Owen and Donna exchanged a guilty glance.

"There were needs," he muttered. "We worked hard taking care of the estate…." His face reddened and he broke off.

"Shannon would have just blown it on booze and drugs, anyway," Donna said. "And besides, she'd been sneaking their things for a long time anyway."

Julie gave them both the benefit of her scorn. "You two are something else. You make me sick. As I said a minute ago, I don't see anything here but the television and the mixer that belonged to Mom and Dad. Maybe Shannon hid all those things she stole from the folks—including both of their cars—in her bedroom. Think so? Shall I take a look?"

Disgusted, she crossed the room and opened the bedroom door. The smell that had greeted them upon their arrival in the warm apartment assaulted her like a punch in the gut. She took a rapid, instinctive step backward. She stared at the dark, rust-colored stain on the mattress, at the bloody spatters mixed with chunks of rotting tissue on the wall above the head of the bed and beyond.

"That stink is worse!" Donna cried. She shoved Julie aside, took one look and stepped back, gagging. The snow globe fell from her hands and hit the carpet with a soft thunk.

"Shut the door! Shut the door!" She fled into the bathroom and vomited violently.

Julie was unable to tear her gaze from the bed where her little sister had ended her life. Questions, both foolish and desperate, flooded her mind. What were Shannon's last thoughts? Had she prepared herself in some way, bathing and perfuming her body? Why had she chosen such a desperate final act? What had led her to that decision? Something must have propelled her. Didn't she know she could have called Julie or gone to her? Had she thought of Julie at all?

This had not been Shannon's first suicide attempt. One time she overdosed. On another occasion she'd slashed her wrists. In between, she'd been in and out of the hospital for taking too many meds or not taking them at all. She had "crashed and burned," as the nurse on the psych ward so unkindly phrased it the time she'd been forcibly institutionalized.

During it all Julie had stayed in California, a little concerned but mostly convinced that Shannon's actions were more a plea for attention than actual destruction. Julie's guilt fed and grew on the knowledge that, like her two siblings, she had chosen to believe that if her younger sister was going to throw away her life on worthless friends, drugs, alcohol, and poverty, she'd get what she deserved. Then, when she finally hit rock bottom, maybe she'd wake up and try to straighten herself out. Julie was prepared to offer a helping hand if Shannon would just snap out of it. But it seemed she was hell bent on wrecking her own life. Julie, fifteen hundred miles away, was powerless to stop anything. But even if she had she been closer, would she have intervened?

"Oh, God," she whispered, staring at the stain as truth seeped into her consciousness. *I would have watched her disintegrate, and I would have* done nothing to stop it.

Owen reached around her and pulled the door shut. His face was white and pinched. Maybe he was less unaffected by Shannon's death than he seemed.

"I thought the police would have cleaned that up…." he muttered.

"I watched a documentary on TV not long ago about crime scene and suicide clean-up." Julie heard her voice, so calm and controlled, as if it came from someone else. "The family, or the landlord, has to take care of it." She drew in a deep, shuddering breath. "I wish I had remembered that earlier."

"Yes," Owen said fiercely. "This could have been taken care of right away. Someone should have told me."

Donna emerged from the bathroom, mopping her face with a frayed washcloth.

"The police should do it," she said. "It's their job."

They stood in the living room in silence for a moment.

"Well, someone will have to—" Owen began.

"Don't look at me!" Donna snapped. She tossed the wet cloth into the bathroom where it hit the linoleum with a sodden plop. She picked up the snow globe from the floor, examined it briefly for damage then cradled it against her chest once more.

"I'm not touching anything else in this dump," she told them. "You two can scrub out that mess in the bedroom or you can let the housing people take care of it, but I'm going home."

As a child, Donna had been bossy and demanding, as humorless as her brother, cruel to animals and to the handicapped boy who lived down the street. The unattractive child had grown into an ugly woman, and expensive makeup and designer clothes were powerless to hide it.

"You won't have to touch anything," Owen assured her. "I'll call someone. Julie, put on your coat."

"But Shannon's things…we need to—"

"Whoever cleans the bedroom can take care of Shannon's stuff," Owen said.

"I want to go home now!" Donna cried. "That stench is making me sicker." She opened the front door and cold air rushed in. She gulped in two or three breaths, paused, turned and strode into the kitchen where she unplugged the white Mixmaster and grabbed it.

"Let's go, Owen," she said as she crossed to the front door with her plunder. "I think that awful friend of Shannon's is coming this way." They hurried out.

Julie glanced around, taking in what remained of her sister's life. She spotted two small framed photographs near the stack of library books. One was a picture of the four siblings that was taken years ago when Shannon was a young teenager. None of their smiles looked real. The other was a photo of Shannon and a young man who bore a remarkable resemblance to her. Julie had never met him, but she knew who he was. She slid both pictures into her coat pocket.

Outside Owen and Donna stood by opposite car doors while he fumbled with his keys then dropped them in his rush to avoid Evie Kendall. She was upon them by the time he punched the button to unlock his Mercedes.

EVIE

Evie rarely wasted time on refined small talk with idiots.

"Are you cleaning out Shannon's apartment?" she asked without preamble.

Donna looked at her across the top of the car. She clasped the old mixer and snow globe Shannon had bought at a garage sale last fall and held them as if they were priceless.

"What possible business is that of yours?" she asked Evie. "Get the car warmed up, Owen. It's cold out here."

She wedged herself and her plunder onto the front seat while Owen opened the back door for Shannon's other sister.

The woman was tall and slim and wore a blocky black pantsuit. Her green eyes were the same color as her brother's but did not hold the same coldness. She wore her graying brown hair in a short wash-and-wear style.

She smiled at Evie and politely asked, "Did Shannon have something of yours? Would you like to go inside and get it?"

Evie stared at her in surprise then shook her head. "I don't think there's anything of mine in there. But I'd like to be the one to clean up her place."

From inside the car Donna squawked like a chicken. "She'll steal everything that isn't nailed down!"

Julie ignored her. "Are you aware that the bedroom…well, it's really bad?"

"I know. I found her."

"I'm hiring a cleaning service." Owen avoided looking directly at Evie. "Let's go, Julie."

He got in the car, slammed his door, and started the engine. Julie rested her hand on the open back door, but she did not get in.

"We'd be happy for you clean it, if you're sure you want to."

"But she'll—" Donna shrieked.

"Be quiet, Donna!" To Evie, "Take what you want of Shannon's things. We don't want any of it."

"Our friend Dunn will haul off the mattress tomorrow."

"Oh, that will be a huge help. Thank you." Julie reached into her purse. "Let me write you a check."

Evie shook her head and allowed herself to smile at the woman, just a little bit.

"I don't want to be paid. Me and Shannon, we never had much money or nice stuff, but we took care of each other."

She glanced through the open back door at Owen and Donna. They sat as stiff and mute as mannequins. She swallowed hard and refused to let her voice break. "This is one last thing I can do for her. I'll treat her belongings with respect and make sure all her friends get a keepsake or two."

"Do that," Julia said warmly. Donna started squawking again and Julie slammed the car door, closing out the harsh sound. "And don't let those two stop you. They just want to throw her things away. Your idea is much better." She smiled again, and held out her hand. "Thank you for doing this for us."

Evie eyed the hand a moment, then shook it awkwardly and let go.

"I ain't doing it for any of you Gradys. I'm doing it for my friend." She paused, wondering if Julie was as big a fool as the others or if she just hid it better. "Shannon had a hard time of it, but it seems none of you Gradys cared. I don't understand that. I don't think Shannon understood that." She paused again, ran her gaze over the tailored woman facing her. "You seem like an okay woman, like someone with a little sense. So with all the hard times Shannon went through, why weren't you ever here for her? Didn't you care about her, even a little bit?"

The wind whipped against them while Julie seemed to struggle for words.

"I…I…." Looking sick, she shook her head, opened the car door and got inside. "Thank you," she said as she closed out the wind, the cold, and her sister's best friend.

The tinted windows blocked them from Evie's sight but she heard the rise and fall of their voices as they argued. In a moment, Owen's window slid down a couple of inches. Holding it by the very tip, he thrust out a key.

"Here. Turn this in at the office as soon as you've finished." He backed the car out of the parking space then screeched his tires on the cold pavement in his hurry to get away.

The next morning Dunn backed his pickup truck to Shannon's apartment door and parked with the rear wheels on the sidewalk. Evie stood aside and watched him lower the rusty tailgate. The day was raw and damp. Dunn cocked a glance toward the low hanging clouds.

"S'posed to snow this afternoon."

"Shannon always liked snow. Said there never was enough here." Evie unlocked the door and entered the apartment ahead of him.

"Geez," he said quietly as he glanced at the boxes Evie had packed then stacked along one wall. "This ain't her place anymore."

"No."

"It always had this…this nice feeling, y'know? Like you were home when you were here."

"I know."

Neither one said anything for a minute, then Dunn dipped his head toward the boxes and said, "What are they gonna do with her things?"

"Her family was gonna throw her stuff away, I guess. At least that's what one of 'em told me."

"Are you kiddin'? Just throwin' it out?"

"I guess. But when I said I'd take care of it, she said okay. The other two—Owen and the ugly one—they had a shit fit when she said that. You woulda thought I was planning to rob the whole clan." She pointed to a large box that sat apart from everything else. "Things in that box is for friends to take. Keepsakes. The clothes and dishes, stuff like that will go to the Share Center thrift store. I gave some of the food out of the 'fridge and cupboards to Mrs. Lawrence next door, some I kept." She glanced at the old sofa and arm chair. "You know anyone who could use the furniture?"

Dunn followed her gaze. "Maybe. My cousin's recliner gouges me in the ass every time I sit. He don't have a couch. He might like that one."

"How about the dinette set?"

He shrugged. "He eats in front of the TV."

"Well, I guess that'll go to the thrift store, too." She paused. "But the bedroom furniture…Dunn, I want it burned, the mattress and box springs, the dresser, too. It has…something on it."

He frowned. "What?"

She nodded, swallowed hard. "From the gunshot. It's on the wall, too."

Dunn opened the bedroom door, stepped in, halted.

"God."

Evie stood behind him, locked her gaze on his broad back. Funny how she'd never noticed, at least consciously, that Dunn was a burly bear of a guy. They'd been friends so long she'd just taken for granted that she could count on him. Not like she had Shannon, of course. But he was a good friend.

"Listen, Evie." He glanced at her over his shoulder. "If you'll hold open the front door for me, I'll haul all that out."

"It's awkward and heavy. I'll help."

"I'm awkward and heavy, and I don't need your help."

"Dunn."

"Evie."

He turned, stroked her face with one large, calloused hand. Not in a way that indicated he wanted to get into her panties or anything, just comforting and friendly.

"You've done all this for Shannon. Let me do something for you."

She saw in his eyes how much he needed to help, to be a part of this farewell to their friend. She gave in. She held the front door open as he lugged out the foul-smelling mattress and loaded it on the truck bed.

"At least let me help you carry those springs."

He grunted a reply. She trailed him into the bedroom, shoved aside every thought and hefted one end of the box springs. She saw the corner of a blue box under the bed.

"What's that?"

They shifted the springs. The box was the size and shape of a shirt box. Gray duct tape secured the lid along the width and another strip along the length.

In Shannon's neat printing were the words: "For Evie Kendall."

"Well, look there." Dunn rested the springs a moment and gazed down at the box. He lifted his eyes to Evie. "What's that?"

"I don't have a clue."

Dunn smiled. "Maybe it was a birthday present and she was hiding it till March."

Her eyes stung. I will not cry! she screamed in her head.

"Let's get these springs out of here," she said gruffly and pushed on her end until he complied.

"Don't you want to see what's in that box?"

"Not now. I…I…let's go."

After Dunn loaded the chest of drawers, he asked, "You wanna ride with me out to the sinkhole?"

She shook her head. "I need to clean the bedroom."

Dunn slammed shut the tailgate. "I'll help with that."

She started to protest. This was her responsibility, a commitment to one last act for her friend.

As if he could read her mind, Dunn said, "She was my friend, too, Evie. And so are you. Let me do this." Still she hesitated, and he added, "You need to get away for a bit. A ride into the country'll help you."

Another moment, then she nodded. "Okay, then." She got her coat and climbed into the cab. The seat was crusty with dirt, the rusty floorboard full of cigarette butts, McDonald's wrappers, empty beer and soda cans. Dust on the ripped vinyl of the dash was equaled only by the dust on everything else.

"Shannon ever ride in this disgusting thing?" she asked as she pulled the greasy seatbelt across her torso and fastened it. She lit a cigarette and so did he.

Dunn smiled, eyes unfocused for a moment as he looked into his own memories.

"Yeah, a few times. She rode out to the sinkhole with me when I dumped Mom's old refrigerator a couple of years ago. She stared at the junk in that hole and said, 'Dunn, haven't you ever heard of ground water pollution?'"

"And what did you say?"

"I told her my family'd been dumping stuff in that hole since 1926 and our well water hadn't killed no one yet." He looked at Evie and she saw a telltale wetness in his eyes. "She didn't know I loved her, did she?"

"She knew we all loved her."

"I don't mean that. I mean, I loved her. The way a man's supposed to love a woman."

"You never told her?"

He studied his cigarette for a moment. "Nah. She was way too good for me."

Her heart hurt for him. "Oh, Dunn." She couldn't think of anything else to say.

He turned and looked out his side window, fingers restless and drumming on the steering wheel. She knew he fought the weakness of tears and when he faced forward again to start the truck, his eyes were red.

By the end of the day, with Dunn's help, Evie finished her tasks in Shannon's apartment. With steely resolve they had cleaned the bedroom, Evie washing the carpet and Dunn scrubbing down the wall where the bed had been. His broad body blocked the gore from Evie's sight.

For the last time they walked out of Shannon's door. Holding the box that bore her name, she carefully turned the key and double-checked the lock. She rested her hand against the door, stood with her back to the world and stared down, unseeing, at the doorknob where the brass had been worn away.

"It just doesn't seem real," she whispered after a moment.

Dunn placed a hand on her shoulder. "I know."

Evie drew in a deep breath and released it, then drew in another and turned. She forced a smile.

"I need to take the key to the office and tell them the apartment's clean now. They'll want to paint it right away."

Dunn went to his truck and opened the driver's side door. He looked back at her, his warm breath pluming in the cold early evening air.

"If you need anything, Eve, call me. You hear?"

She nodded, unable to speak.

"Toni's home by now. Maybe you oughta stay with her for a while."

Evie liked the woman well enough, but Toni was self-absorbed and shallow. Evie would rather be alone.

"I'm fine." She cleared her throat and lifted her head to meet Dunn's eyes. "Besides, I want to see what's in the box."

She started down the sidewalk toward the office then veered off course to hug him quickly. "Thanks for your help, Dunn. I really appreciate it." She stepped back.

He gave her a little smile. "Let me know what she gave you, okay?"

"Right."

"Evie, here." He reached in, got something from inside the pickup and tossed it to her. A fresh pack of Luckys. "You haven't had any time to get to the store."

She wanted to cry again but didn't. His gesture was something Shannon would have done for her.

"Thanks, guy."

"You bet. See you soon."

She walked toward the office and just as she reached the door, something popped into her mind. Every gift Shannon ever gave her had been festooned with ribbons and bright paper, sometimes Mylar balloons. If her friend had the money, she always splurged.

Evie looked at the box, the snug strips of duct tape as if Shannon wanted to discourage anyone from revealing the contents. She shook it, heard a slight rustling but nothing else. She did not think this was a gift at all. Maybe this was something Shannon had placed in her care for safe keeping.

EVIE

The bottle with its smooth, cool glass and amber contents mocked her. Its solid presence on the table gave her more options that she wanted to embrace. Enhance the courage, smooth the stress, numb the pain, and lastly, blessedly, bring the escape. Let her forget this past week happened, let her go back in time. Then, maybe in a few days, when Evie climbed out of that blessed bottle, her friend would be alive, and the world would be right again. Evie hadn't had a drop of alcohol in three years, six months and twenty-eight days. Clear-eyed sobriety stunk.

She eyed the bottle again, the sealed cap, the Wild Turkey label. That bottle had been beneath her sink since the night she pledged to sober up. It stayed right where she could see it if she wanted to, could reach it if she needed to, could partake if she couldn't help herself. Until that moment she'd been all right. Those times of anger and frustration when she felt herself at the weakest level, Evie had called on Shannon who'd pulled her back from the edge. Even at her lowest ebb, Shannon had wanted Evie to be stone cold sober.

Evie remembered that time at the hospital when Shannon lay as white as the bandages on both fragile wrists. She clung to Evie with icy hands, her eyes haunted.

"Stay on the wagon, Evie Kendall," she whispered in a voice as ragged as the edges of fresh sawed wood. "If you go down, who'll hang on to me?"

That night, for the first time in her life, Evie had fully realized the depth of Shannon's need for a solid presence. Evie, who had never answered to anyone but herself, vowed to God, to Shannon, and to herself to accept the duty of true friendship, no matter what. She hadn't always been successful, but she'd tried. By God, she had tried! And she'd not touched a drop since the night of the party when Shannon had paid the price for Evie's foolishness.

But tonight, exhausted in body and spirit, she had reached the end of that responsibility and didn't know if she could make it through the night. She looked at the bottle but didn't touch it. Her ashtray, lighter and crumpled pack of Lucky Strikes lay next to the bottle. She reached for these and smoked two down to their filters.

On the table between her and the bottle lay the box from beneath Shannon's bed. A short-bladed, red-handled paring knife was on top of the box, ready to be used. Evie stared at the knife, its cheap plastic handle, the flimsy blade. Such a lowly, ugly tool for a momentous task. She took another smoke from the pack and held flame to the tip.

Evie feared the desolation that would descend once the box was open and its contents revealed. Her final connection with Shannon severed. She looked at the Wild Turkey then at the knife. Back and forth, back and forth. Release one friend, return to an old one. But she'd be damned if she'd open Shannon's gift drunk.

She viciously stubbed out the cigarette and grabbed the knife. She plunged the thin blade into the duct tape and yanked it through the adhesive fibers of every side. One, two, three, four, before she could lose her nerve. The top released itself, and with a deep breath, Evie lifted the lid.

She didn't know what she had expected, but not what she found—a sealed envelope and three thick spiral notebooks. Nothing else.

Before she battled with herself again, Evie tore open the envelope and took out two sheets of notebook paper filled with Shannon's neat block printing. She read the first line, "Dear Evie" and stopped. She tilted back her head and stared at the ceiling until her heartbeat slowed, then she lowered her head and read the letter.

"Dear Evie, If you're reading this then I guess something bad has happened and I'm so, so sorry to leave you. We always told each other that our lives must have been formed on a day when God either wasn't paying attention or someone had sneaked into the formula room and screwed with our DNA. Whatever it was, I'm glad we've been friends. You've accepted me, warts and all, and never once let me down. Your loyalty gives me an anchor to hold when the bad times come, and they sure come a lot, don't they?"

Evie stopped reading and struggled to breathe. Was she up to this? Could she read the rest and not collapse, not forget all the good things she'd learned to be? Maybe it was best to wait, just until she was rested, until her grief wasn't so new, her heart less raw and aching…but no. Shannon must have needed to share these things with her friend once more. Like an apology or something. An apology for having bad times, and for leaving this world too early.

Shannon and bad times. Her bad times always came swiftly on the heels of days filled with joyous abandon, days when she seemed ready and able to set the world on fire. She embraced her mania, plunging herself into it headlong, looking neither right nor left, but going full throttle.

"I have to do these things now," she gaily announced to anyone who noticed her tireless energy. "Dark days are a-comin' and I can't do anything then." She seemed indestructible.

In her good days, she laughed off the weeks of black depression which were sure to follow. Thank God she had more good days than bad.

Of course, on the good days she wrote checks on an empty bank account, slept with men she barely knew, slipped out of the house late at night to go joy-riding with Rex Jason if he was out of the clink. She got married on a good day to a man she'd known less than forty-eight hours. When the depression came creeping out of the night a few weeks later to lay hold of her, that drunken asshole beat the shit out of her and high-tailed it out of town. Evie never knew what happened to Teddy Stamp but she hoped he lay rotting in a shallow grave somewhere.

Evie looked down at the letter in her hand, at the precise printing, like a schoolteacher's. She wondered if the bad days had slipped up on Shannon with little warning this time and if she had written the letter before the depression humbled and humiliated her into hopelessness.

She'd been there so many times that maybe the dark days and their pain were too much to face. Maybe, this time, Shannon had decided she just couldn't go through it again.

"Why didn't you talk to me?" Evie said aloud. "We could have seen it through together like we did before. You know we could've, Shannon, damn you. Damn you for leaving me. What am I supposed to do now?"

The levee inside Evie broke open. Rage, confusion, and loneliness spewed out of her in tears and cursing. She fell to the floor and pummeled the thin carpet with her fists until her arms and shoulders ached. She cursed herself for not seeing the signs this time. She railed against God, the world, Shannon, and Shannon's family until she found herself spent and motionless on the living room floor. For what seemed like eternity she lay there while life went on without her.

At last her senses stirred, and she came around like someone waking from a deep sleep. Weak and trembling, she pushed to her feet, eyed the bottle, then stumbled into the bathroom where she drenched herself in a hot shower. By the time Evie had dried her skin and hair and dressed in clean sweatpants and T-shirt, she was able to pick up the letter again.

"You know every therapist I've talked to over the years has only wanted me to take my meds and play nice. The newest one—her name is Joanna—seems to have a brain in her head. Instead of ragging at me about replacing bad behaviors with good habits, she's been digging around inside my mind. Since I started seeing Joanna, I'm remembering things. Some good things. Some not so good. Mostly what I'm remembering right now is ugly, rotten stuff.

Evie, don't get mad at me for not telling you about this earlier, but I have a reason. It's all really confusing, and I didn't want to tell you about it until it makes sense for me. Besides, Joanna said I needed to write it all down as it came to me, so that's what I've been doing. Once I started writing it, I couldn't stop until I came to the end. And now I'm writing this letter."

Evie looked at the date at the top of the page. January 27. Two days before she had found Shannon's dead body. She continued to read.

"Here's the thing. I'm not sure if what I've remembered is real. It *seems* real. Maybe it's all in my imagination, but I don't think so. It's bugging me, driving me crazy. I need to find out the truth.

I don't know what the outcome will be and I hope you'll never have to read this, but if you're reading it, then my memories must be real. So I want you to read the notebooks. You're smart and logical; you don't have a brain that flares then sputters like mine does. I'm trusting you to do what needs to be done.

But you'll have to stay off the booze, Evie. You can't help me if you're wasted. And be careful. Don't tell anyone what you find until you're sure of the truth. Then go to the right people.

You've been there for me so many times. Be there for me this one last time. I need you, girlfriend.

Love, Shannon"

Evie read the letter three more times, but it made no sense. Why had Shannon chosen to play this game? Why hadn't she just come to Evie and told her whatever it was that this Joanna person had helped her remember?

She eyed the whiskey bottle and the old craving stirred, stretching its limbs, readying itself for full wakefulness.

I need you, girlfriend.

Evie closed her eyes tight against the sight of that bottle.

I need you, girlfriend.

She could taste it. Feel its warmth in her throat, its heat flowing into every cell as she took the alcohol into herself and became one with it. She needed that drink and that release. She needed to lose herself, just for tonight.

Evie reached for the bottle.

PART TWO

SHANNON

Before she met Joanna at the mental health clinic, Shannon Grady had only the foggiest memories of her childhood. She could always recall one event that often flashed and died in her mind like broken Christmas lights, but little else. A long ago Christmas…

Beneath a Christmas tree glittering with tinsel and glass balls and thin strands of silver icicles, lay bright packages her mother had promised held good things for her.

"Like the Happy Baby in the Wish Book?" Shannon had asked eagerly.

"Maybe." Mommy smiled and wiggled her eyebrows the way she did when she had a secret.

Donna grabbed a cookie in each hand and stuffed one in her mouth.

"Happy Baby Doll!" she scoffed. "The ugliest doll in the whole catalog."

"Donna, don't speak with your mouth full."

Donna stuck out her tongue and wiggled her hips. Mommy was taking another pan of gingerbread cookies from the oven and didn't see. Shannon thought about how naughty Donna was, but she didn't say a word. If she did, Donna would smack her. Donna liked to slap and pinch.

On a small table near the door, Mommy had arranged fluffy white stuff that looked like cotton candy except you couldn't eat it. In the center of the fluff, with small cedar boughs all around like a forest, sat a snow globe. Inside, a church perched atop a snow-covered hill. Shannon loved to gaze into the snow globe. She imagined tiny people inside singing Christmas carols and smiling at each other. She pictured greenery that looped from window to window and candles flickering while the people listened to the story of Baby Jesus. If she closed her eyes, she could pretend she was inside that church on top of the hill and a little girl who looked just like her was watching everything from far away.

Donna came up behind her, grabbed the globe and shook it hard. Shannon got to her feet and tried to see the swirling flakes settle, but Donna held it just high enough that the tiny snowstorm was out of Shannon's sight.

"The people inside are singing," Shannon told her.

Donna looked at her in disgust. "There aren't any people inside it, stupid. It's just a dumb old piece of glass with a plastic church and fake snow."

She plunked the globe down and stomped away.

Shannon leaned against the table and stared again at the church, at the tiny windows that seemed to have light coming out of them. Just because Donna couldn't hear the singing didn't mean there were no songs. She picked up the globe and rubbed Donna's cookie-smudged fingerprints off the glass then replaced it carefully on the table.

"I hear you singing," she whispered to the tiny people.

On Christmas morning, Shannon screamed with delight when she tore off the wrapping paper and saw the Happy Baby Doll with its bright blue eyes and silky yellow hair. Its little hands and round smiling face were soft as real skin. She hugged it to her.

"I love it, I love it!" she squealed, leaping around the room.

"Do you have to be so loud? Mom, make her quit squealing." Owen was scowling at a brand new leather-bound Bible. He ran a fingertip across his name stamped in gold on the cover. He had wanted a rifle, but their father said guns were inappropriate as Christmas gifts.

"She's excited." Julie, home for Christmas, laughed and watched her little sister dance around. "Look how her eyes shine."

"Remember how excited you were when you got that stereo last year?" Mommy asked him. "You hollered quite a bit, and no one asked you to be quiet."

Owen gave Shannon a dark look, but he didn't say anything else.

"I never got a Happy Baby doll when I was three years old!" Donna yelled.

"Don't think they had 'em when you were little." Daddy put another piece of wood in the fireplace and snapping red sparks shot out as he gouged the poker around in the fire.

"As I recall, you only liked Barbie dolls," Julie said.

Shannon looked at Donna. Her sister's face was splotched with bumps. Julie called them pimples; Owen called them zits. They looked angry and painful. Shannon hated to let go of her new toy, but Donna seemed so hurt and upset and her bumps were red. Shannon held out the doll.

She said, "You can play with my new Happy Baby, Donna. Do you want to hold her? She's real soft."

Donna glowered at her. Inside their buttonholes of skin, her eyes seemed small and hot. She looked at the doll, new in its pink pajama set.

With her lips hard and tight, she lifted her hand and smacked the doll free of Shannon's grasp. Happy Baby flew across the room and landed face down in the fireplace.

Shannon screamed as the flames claimed her toy.

"Donna Sue Grady!" Mommy hollered. "Why did you do that?"

"It's just an ugly, stupid doll!" Donna said, "Shannon gets everything she ever wants. All the time!"

"You're nearly fourteen," Owen said with a sneer. "Did you want a doll, too?"

Donna glared at him until he lost his smirk and looked down at his Bible again.

Mommy and Daddy were scolding Donna, but their voices seemed far away. In her head Shannon heard the doll shriek. It called her name. It cried and screamed. Daddy tried to scrape it out of the fire but it came out in pieces and kept screaming.

Over and over, she heard the sound. Shannon hadn't known if the voice that screamed was her own or her doll's.

Bits of unimportant happenings from the next few years flashed through her memory. The time Donna dropped Mommy's favorite pitcher on the kitchen floor and it shattered into a million pieces and Mommy cried for hours, or when Owen told her that something dark and rotten peeked into her window at night, or when Julie called to say she was going to get married then didn't. But all those things were snippets of recollections or dreams. They were gone in mere seconds.

Something else always lingered, waiting to be summoned. It frightened her when it slid into her thoughts. Quickly she shoved it away but not before she glimpsed a shape in the dark, closer and closer…eyes…and breathing…and…and….

She shuddered and told herself, "If I pretend it isn't there, the shadow will go away."

"You have the perfect little face and beautiful blonde curls," her teacher had told her the night Shannon was to play Cinderella in the fourth-grade assembly program at the end of the year. "Your dress is beautiful, just right. Every little girl should be a Cinderella like you."

Shannon smiled. "Thank you, Mrs. Massey."

"Are you nervous?"

"I don't think so. I know what I'm supposed to say."

"Yes, you've done a fine job to learn your part. But it's natural to be nervous, so if you feel a little scared, it's okay."

Shannon looked past Mrs. Massey toward the small stage where cardboard cut-outs made a fairy castle. Being in front of people and playing her part made her feel good. She liked to perform and sing and dance. But she was scared. She was always scared, and whatever frightened her possessed neither form nor name.

She spoke all her lines perfectly. The ugly stepsisters and the stepmother knew their lines, but the fairy godmother messed up and so did Prince Charming. Shannon whispered cues to them. No one in the audience heard so it was all right. Then, at the end of the play when the prince was supposed to take both her hands in his and the curtain was supposed to come down, he had kissed her instead. Right on the mouth. Hard.

Shannon had stared at him. Something black swallowed her, and she didn't remember most of that summer.

The periods of memory loss diminished by the time she reached high school.

That first year Shannon threw herself into her schoolwork. Only juniors and seniors could be cheerleaders, but she played with skill on the girls' basketball team, performed with enthusiasm on the drill team and gleefully joined the drama club. Her family name and money, blonde good looks, bright smile and adventurous spirit assured her place in Woodrow High's in-crowd. During their school years, her older siblings had achieved their own places of prominence. Athletic and strong, Owen played basketball. He'd also been student body president for three years. Donna had knitted a tight little clique around her that had focused on fad and fashion. Julie's straight-A average had earned her the valedictory title. Teachers fawned over the Grady children, students deferred to them, and the three oldest ones moved through high school like massive ships on the high sea.

But Shannon was different. Beautiful and vivacious, she also possessed a burgeoning wild streak that blossomed during her freshman year. The other three Grady kids had been easily controlled, so Shannon's behavior caught her parents completely unprepared. In attempting to redirect her boundless energy, Curtis and Melba Grady bribed their youngest daughter with gifts and attention. This indulgence infuriated Owen and Donna who were, by then, married with families of their own.

"She only acts that way so you'll give her everything she wants," Donna said.

"Lay down the law with that girl," Owen ordered his parents. "You want her going around making the rest of the family look like fools?"

Finally, when coaxing and coddling failed to tame their daughter, Curtis and Melba gave in to their older kids' advice and used firmer discipline.

"If you can't get home by curfew, then you're grounded for two weeks," Curtis told her one night when she'd brazenly come home three hours late. "Only two phone calls a night for ten minutes each. You decide who you want to talk to, but that's your limit."

"Shannon, you cannot have your friends over here all the time," her mother fussed. "You have homework, and you need your sleep."

This attempted intervention did not faze Shannon. She simply ignored the rules and did as she pleased. In desperation, Curtis and Melba tried to watch her every move, but they couldn't be with her everywhere at every moment. The one place they felt secure enough to relax their vigil was church.

The Woodrow Worship Center offered an expansive youth program that included everything from stage drama and music to athletics and overnight trips out of town to other Christian-sponsored youth activities. Shannon dove headlong into those church events with the same daring that she did everything else. Believing that God would watch when they could not, the older Gradys failed to recognize potential risks existing in what they naively assumed was a safe and holy environment.

Boys liked Shannon. Beyond the winsome beauty that charmed and flattered burgeoning male egos something untamed, almost feral roared to life. She met male eyes boldly, stood too close, laid perfumed hands against their chests. She laughed raucously at their dirty jokes. In her fourteen-year-old eyes smoldered the promised fulfillment of their needs. At school and at church, they craved her. They fought each other for her. They pursued her relentlessly, and she loved every moment of it.

"You absolutely are not dating until you're sixteen," Curtis and Melba told her.

She sneered at the order. "That's dumb, but okay. Whatever."

Her easy acceptance of their directive gave them a sense of security, and they relaxed. What they didn't know was that Shannon didn't need to see boys under the guise of "dating." She saw them whenever the notion took her, and wherever she chose. At church, no grown-up seemed to notice when she crept outside during youth services, or at school as she slipped, unseen by any adult, into the boys' room.

By the time she was fifteen, Shannon had the sexual knowledge and experience of a woman twice her age. The power she felt when a masculine body climaxed inside her gave her the feeling she could do, be, have anything, absolutely anything.

In the early autumn of her sophomore year, Shannon awakened in the middle of the night to a thick, smothering presence pressing her onto the bed. This was not the murkiness that had lurked in the periphery since childhood, that menacing outline which threatened her with hushed whispers and fierce demands. This presence did not seem to have being or movement, but simply descended, or rose, to envelop her in a terrorizing agony of loss and hopelessness. She tried to sit up, shove away the darkness, but she could not move.

Into her mind entered thoughts of the boys and men who used her, who fell at her feet in devotion, who hovered near, and she felt sick at the mere thought of them. Thoughts of her mother's soft eyes edged into her consciousness, her father's joking ways, Julie's absence, Donna's scorn, Owen's disapproving stare. The pastor's sermons, the Sunday school teacher's lessons, the Bible stories, the sacrifice of Christ, the expectations of the Holy Spirit.

"I can't," she whispered in the dark, barely able to push out the words.

Tears formed of their own accord, and they refused to stop. When her mother came to wake her for school the next morning, Shannon barely heard the beloved voice calling.

"Are you sick?" Melba Grady asked when the girl continued to weep.

A reply took more strength than Shannon held.

"Are you hurt?"

By mid-morning, Melba was beside herself. She stayed next to Shannon and called Curtis from the pink princess phone on the nightstand.

"I don't know what's wrong. She won't say. Please come home right now."

He was at Shannon's bedside in less than twenty minutes.

"Honey, are you sick? Shannon, please, you have to tell us what's wrong so we can help you."

Shannon heard their distraught pleadings but she could not respond. She felt lost, helpless, guilty for bringing them to this point, but she also felt as though she stood to one side, watching. The watching part of her was numb; it did not care what happened.

"Tell us what's wrong and when you're better, we'll go to Florida for a week. Would you like that?"

She simply looked at him as tears continued to leak.

"You can have a party. Invite as many of your friends as you want and we'll get Elsie to make her fudge surprise cake," Melba said with an eager, coaxing smile. Then, when Shannon did not respond, she said, "I'm calling Owen."

"What can Owen do?" Curtis replied. "Leave him out of this."

"He can help snap her out of whatever's going on."

"I said, leave him out of this."

"And he can pray!" Melba snapped.

"Don't call Owen. You and I will handle it."

Shannon was the only one who had ever heard her parents quarrel, and lately they quarreled a lot.

The sound of their angry voices felt like knives plunging into her soul and she moaned. They heard the small sound and looked at her, waiting for her to speak.

"Please…I want…." she began, but her voice trailed.

By that evening she had quit crying. Melba seemed so relieved that giddiness oozed from her. She laughed and talked, plied Shannon with all manner of treats and snacks. Shannon turned from the food and wished her mother would leave her alone so she could escape into sleep. At least Curtis and Melba weren't fighting right then.

School could be missed for a little while, of course, but missing church services was out of the question. The Gradys held a place of honor in the Woodrow Worship Center and it took more than sickness or strange moods to keep them away. Shannon attended the youth services. She looked at her friends, listened to the lessons, heard the music and longed to be home, in her bed, away from the sights and the sounds and the frenetic activity of her lively peers. Boys tried to get her attention, but she ignored them and the heated, lustful gazes they passed to her. A couple of times she tried to focus on the Bible study, but it was too difficult. God didn't care; He probably didn't even know she was alive. She was tired of it all.

On Saturday afternoon a week later, Owen and Donna left their respective spouses and young families at home to confront the girl who lay inertly on her bed. Shannon glanced at them when they walked into her room. She sighed and looked away, saying nothing.

"What's wrong with you?" Owen said in that hateful way he had.

Donna stood beside him. "You look like you haven't bathed in days. Or combed your hair."

"I haven't," Shannon said dully.

There was a small silence, then Owen said, "Well, you can't be this way."

She let out a shallow breath. "But I am."

"You're making the rest of us look bad."

She moved her eyes enough to take them both in. "I'm sorry."

"Sorry doesn't do it," Donna snapped. "Get up, get washed, get dressed and act like somebody."

"I'm tired."

"You're not tired!" Donna screamed. "You can't be tired. Mom says you've done nothing but lie in this bed for days." She eyed the plate of food on the night stand. "Mom has to bring your food in here? This is Elsie's day off, isn't it? The least you can do is take your dirty dishes to the kitchen so Mom doesn't have to come all the way up here and get them."

"You got Mom worried sick about you," Owen said. "You know that? She's at her wits' end. You need to get up."

Shannon sighed. "I know. I'm sorry, but I'm tired. And I don't think I can get up and do anything."

"You're lazy," Owen said.

"You're a slob," Donna added.

Owen told her, "Get up from there right now."

Shannon felt her eyes fill. Since the crying jag last week that had so upset her parents, she made sure they did not see her weep again. But every day the tears came. They stole up on her silently, burning her raw eyelids, streaking the chapped skin of her cheeks. She did not know why she cried; she knew she was helpless not to.

"Don't you start that bawling while I'm here, you big baby!" Donna descended, her fingers digging into the thin, tender flesh of Shannon's arm and jerking her to her feet. She dragged her into the small bathroom on the far side of the room. "I don't feel sorry for you in the least, and I am not putting up with this stupid behavior, you selfish little twit."

She turned on the water, yanked the wrinkled pajamas and underwear off Shannon and shoved her into the shower. The water was too hot but Shannon didn't care. Something about the pain of burning skin made her feel better. Donna grabbed a washcloth and bar of soap and thrust them into her sister's hands.

"Wash your nasty self."

Shannon lifted the wet cloth and moved it in a lethargic circle across her upper chest while Donna watched. After a moment, Donna jerked the washcloth from her grasp, lathered it heavily and reached into the spray to scrub her. Shannon winced, but she welcomed pain that, for a little bit, overcame her deep misery. Pliable beneath the rough scouring she allowed Donna to wash her body and her hair. When finished, Donna shoved a thick towel at her.

"Can you at least dry yourself?"

Shannon nodded and began blotting away the wetness while her sister watched.

"I thought Mom said you weren't eating much," Donna said after a minute.

"I'm not very hungry."

"I don't believe that. Looks to me like you're putting on weight."

Shannon wrapped herself in the towel and said, "I need pajamas."

Donna shoved her into the bedroom, saying, "You're getting dressed in daytime clothes. Who do you think you are, a princess?" She snatched away the towel and left Shannon bare in front of Owen.

Shannon gasped and tried to cover herself with her hands. Owen gaped in surprise but didn't turn away. She saw something familiar in his eyes, and she hated it. Rage filled her.

"Get out of here!" she screamed at him. "Get out of my room!"

He gave her a startled look, then glanced at Donna.

"I'll tell the folks we took care of her," he said.

SHANNON

By the end of the month Shannon began to crawl out of the depression that had gripped her for nearly six weeks. But she was not well. Her back hurt constantly, and the smell of food soured her stomach.

"It's all that lying in bed," her mother said when Shannon pushed aside Elsie's meatloaf one evening. "Maybe a nice bowl of chicken noodle soup. Or a baked potato."

Shannon shook her head. "I don't want any."

"But, honey, you're making yourself sick. Your face is white as a sheet."

Wanting to appease her mother, she said, "Well, maybe some toast."

Melba jumped up. "I'll fix it myself. And some tea."

A little later, as Curtis and Melba watched, Shannon nibbled the warm, buttery toast and drank sweet, hot tea.

"Let's go to the lake this weekend," Curtis said. "It's not so cold that we can't be out in the sun a little. Would you like that, honey?"

Shannon studied their expectant, almost desperate faces. She hated that she'd worried them, that she'd scared them. At least her parents were blessedly ignorant about the things she'd done with boys. Now, if she could only take away their anxious expressions….

"I'd like to go to the lake," she said with a smile. "Can we go out on the boat, too?"

They seemed to sag in relief, took turns hugging her.

"Maybe," Curtis said. "If we have a warm day or two."

"You don't want to catch a cold," Melba added. "You've been so weak lately."

Shannon nodded, gratified to see their worry lines decrease.

The lake house with its wood-paneled walls and wide-planked floors was small and snug, decorated with overstuffed furniture and a couple of comfy old rocking chairs near the stone fireplace. It had been in that very fireplace where Happy Baby had died.

The evening they arrived, Shannon stood wrapped in a well-worn nine-patch quilt and gazed out the huge front room window at Bull Shoals Lake. Daylight faded to a lavender smudge that deepened blackly across the water. Curtis had built a fire and the flickering flames valiantly chased the damp chill from the room. In the small kitchen, her mother's navy bean and ham soup simmered in a big pot on the ancient range while a pan of cornbread baked in the oven. With hired help to do it for her, Melba Grady rarely cooked, but when she did, her dishes were simple and comforting.

Shannon gazed over her shoulder at the woman who was taking soup bowls out of the cupboard. These days Melba looked old. She was old. Fifty-one this coming January, and Curtis would be fifty-four in April.

Shannon would never be that old. What do you do when you're that old?

"Do you see your father?" Melba asked.

Shannon cupped her hands around her eyes and pressed against the cold glass. A figure walked slowly near the lake's edge by the tree line, almost out of sight. She thought someone walked with him, but maybe not. Darkness was gulping down every bit of daylight.

"Yes. Shall I go get him?"

"No. You stay by the fire. He'll be in directly."

Something about her mother's voice, a tightness maybe, caught Shannon's ear. She looked at the woman, but Melba seemed focused on putting dinner on the table.

"You all right, Mom?"

Melba looked up. A thin sheen coated her eyes and the smile she gave seemed forced.

"I'm fine, honey." Shannon didn't believe her, but the older woman said nothing more than, "You want to pour yourself a glass of milk?"

Those days at the lake were quiet ones, some might them call peaceful. Curtis went on long walks every day. Sometimes Shannon went with him. She loved the crisp autumn breezes, the fishy smell of the lake, the easy camaraderie she shared with her father. Melba was by turns distracted, irritable, or sad. She chose to stay inside. Maybe she was tired. After all, being married to the wealthiest and most powerful man in town held considerable responsibility. Melba Grady was a force in her own right, heading committees in church and in the community. She managed the Grady household and kept the home running smoothly, and still she seemed to have time for hobbies and other interests. At the lake house, she focused on cooking, needlework, or reading.

Sometimes, it seemed to Shannon, her mother never slept.

As days passed and her strength returned, Shannon grew increasingly restless. Not the driven restlessness that had gripped her earlier in the year, but a need to be moving, doing something. The quiet pursuits of reading, knitting, or piecing quilts with her mother were not enough for a girl approaching her fifteenth birthday.

She began to clean. She emptied the cabinets and scrubbed the shelves. She scoured the old stove until it gleamed like new. The floors shone and the lamps glowed. In the bathroom, white porcelain fixtures sparkled. Curtis and Melba noted in considerable alarm that she worked with single-minded purpose. No amount of clucking and demands stopped her industry. As Shannon washed away dinginess to reveal the luster which hid behind dust and dirt, something inside her responded; she felt fresh and bright again.

"We're going home," Curtis said one day after dinner as he watched Shannon scour the pans her mother had used. "Maybe you'll rest more."

Shannon glanced at him over her shoulder. Her arms were elbow deep in suds. She'd had all the lake's peace and quiet she could stand.

"Yes, Daddy. Let's go home. I want to get back to school."

"All this work because you miss school?"

She dimpled at him. It was so easy to get her way with every man she knew, if she smiled.

"Well, no. I just felt like…cleaning. But if I had homework and…and a social life maybe I wouldn't be so bored."

Her parents exchanged a look. She glanced from one face to the other.

"What? Why are you looking like that?"

Melba took a deep breath. "We don't think school is the best thing for you right now, honey. We're hiring a tutor."

She whirled around in dismay, imagining a rigid dour-faced old crone who would force her to sit still eight hours a day.

"A tutor! I don't need a tutor. I'm not stupid. My grades have always been good." She threw her father a pleading look. "Daddy, I don't want a tutor. I'll die inside the house all day with an old tutor."

"We've already talked with a very reputable organization in Harrison; they'll send someone as soon as we let them know we're ready."

She stared at them in horror, seeing before her unfolding days of nothing but study and torment.

"I can't," she said weakly.

"You will," Curtis told her.

She pushed out her lower lip.

"This was Owen and Donna's idea, wasn't it? You two would never come up with something so mean and unreasonable."

"Honey, we aren't trying to be mean and unreasonable," Curtis said.

"Owen suggested it, yes," Melba said. "He thought you needed a more serene environment than school. And it won't be so bad. Just until the end of the year. You can catch up on all the lessons you've missed. Maybe even get a little ahead."

Shannon looked from one parent to the other. Something helpless rose inside and burst forth. She sank to the floor and began to sob like a young child. This was not the fearful, unending tears of earlier days but the wretched call of a young girl thrown into a situation she despised. Until that moment, Shannon had never cried just because she didn't get her way. She wasn't sure why she did so now.

The missed cycles, the weight gain, the sick stomach, the rounding of her flat belly. By the time she missed her period four months in a row, Shannon stopped telling herself she absolutely, positively could not be pregnant. She knew how to keep from getting knocked up, so how had she been luckless enough for it to happen? And how could she tell her folks? A big ol' belly on a tall skinny girl was impossible to hide. This was the worst thing in the world, the most awful situation she'd ever been in.

Donna and Owen would be fit to be tied, of course, and if Curtis and Melba had an inkling to be supportive, her brother and sister would quash that inclination in a heartbeat. Julie or Donna would never have gotten pregnant before they were married. Never!

"I'm the worst daughter in the whole world!" she told herself.

Even so, as she guarded her secret from everyone, she knew she'd have to tell her folks sooner or later.

To the Gradys and other devout churchgoers, the Lord's Day was sacred. Hearts should be tender and close to God. An attitude of forgiveness should blanket the pious Gradys on Sunday afternoons as they shared their weekly family meal. Shannon reasoned that after dinner, and after her siblings departed, would be the ideal time to break her news. But during the meal, as Shannon poured herself a second glass of milk, Donna watched her with eyes that glittered like a viper.

"You better drink lots of milk," she said.

The look in her sister's eyes panicked Shannon. She hadn't breathed a word of her pregnancy to anyone, not her best friends at church, or school. No one. Donna couldn't possibly know.

"I've always liked milk," she replied.

Sarah Jean, Owen's thin blonde wife, spoke up. "You seem to be putting on weight, Shannon. Maybe you should drink low-fat milk. Better yet, try the Rotation Diet. I've been quite successful with it." She patted her flat stomach.

Donna snorted. "Shannon shouldn't be dieting now. Craig, quit staring at her and pass the biscuits." Her husband, thin and balding, always quiet and meek, blinked and jumped a little, then handed her the breadbasket.

"Sorry," he muttered.

She knows, Shannon thought wildly. The urge to flee thrummed through her body, yet she was frozen in her chair.

Melba chuckled. "What a thing to be talking about. Shannon has put on a little weight from staying at home so much. She isn't wearing herself out with basketball or drill team like she would be if she was going to school on campus—"

"Oh, please," Donna said, slathering butter on her fifth biscuit. "Anyone with two eyes and half a brain can see she's eating for two." She bit into the bread and cast a smug look at the others.

"Donna," her husband murmured.

"Shut up, Craig," she said without looking at him.

Shannon felt the blood drain from her face.

No, no! Not this way!

She threw a desperate glance at her parents.

"What do you mean?" Melba asked.

"Mom, Dad, I … I … Donna, how could you …?"

Her food began to backtrack. She leaped from the table and ran into the powder room across the wide hallway.

As she bathed her face and rinsed her mouth with water from her cupped hands, she realized her family clustered just outside the bathroom door.

"Is it true?" Owen said. "Did you go and get yourself pregnant?"

Donna dug around in her teeth with the tip of one long fingernail and extracted a lodged bit of her lunch. She examined it and then sucked it off the end of her finger.

"Of course she did, the little slut. Look at her."

Curtis and Melba seemed unable to speak, but Sarah Jean shoved her way past her in-laws and stood in the doorway, hands on hips. She studied Shannon's midsection then shook her head in disgust.

"You should be ashamed!"

"What will everyone say now? Are you trying to ruin us all?" His lips thinned while his censuring gaze bore into her.

She stared at him, at Sarah Jean, at Donna, at Craig, and finally at Melba and Curtis, whose gray faces alarmed her.

"Daddy, Mommy, I'm sorry! I…didn't mean…."

"What will folks at church think of us?" Owen kept burning her with his angry eyes. "We won't be able to hold our heads up anywhere in town. None of us, and all because of you."

"She doesn't care what anyone thinks," Donna said. "She only considers her own spoiled self. Always and forever. That's why she got herself in trouble, to get attention. And now she expects Mom and Dad to bail her out."

"That's not true!" Shannon shouted. "I love Daddy and Mama; I didn't mean for this to happen...."

The shame she felt, the deep pain in the center of her heart, the sudden crash of her betrayal shoving until she slumped against the wall with nothing to grasp.

Curtis pushed away the others.

"That's enough," he said to them. He put his arm around his youngest daughter. She leaned against him, clutching the front of his clean white shirt with her shaking fingers and met his sad blue eyes.

"I'm sorry, Daddy," she whispered. "I didn't mean to...."

"I know." He stroked her head with one hand, patted her back with the other. "We'll work it out. Everything will be okay." He let her rest against his solid strength for a while, then he turned to the others. "Owen, Donna. Go home."

Silence met this command. Seldom did the mild-mannered Curtis Grady talk to his family as if they were his employees. The two siblings stood without moving, testing him.

"Get your coats and your kids, and go home. *Now*. We'll handle this."

"But, Dad, you don't seem to understand—"

"I understand perfectly. I said 'Go home.'"

"Now, Dad, you aren't—"

"Owen, let's keep this quiet and peaceful. Don't make me throw you out."

Shannon closed her eyes.

"Thank you, Daddy," she whispered. His embrace tightened, and he planted a warm kiss on top of her head.

"It'll be okay, baby girl."

After the others left—and they had left with no attempt to disguise their disgust, and Owen loudly voicing his opinion of what should and should not be done—Curtis and Melba sat with Shannon in the silent family room. Her guilt weighed so heavily that she could barely lift her head, let alone meet their eyes. She stared down at the sodden Kleenex in her hand and plucked it into tiny pieces.

Melba cleared her throat. "Do you feel all right now? Do you need some dry crackers or anything?"

Shannon shook her head. "I'm okay."

"Well."

A brief silence fell until Curtis spoke. "I guess we need to decide what to do about this…situation."

She nodded.

"We don't believe in abortion, Shannon," Melba said.

She flung up her head and her gaze locked with her mother's. "I know that! I'd never get rid of my baby."

"Of course not, honey," Curtis said. "Your Mommy only meant…."

"I know what she meant. Donna or Owen probably put that notion in her head. They hate me so much."

"They don't hate you!" Melba said. "They're just concerned."

Shannon rolled her eyes.

"Both of them would just as soon run me out of town and leave me to starve to death in a ditch somewhere, and you know it."

Shannon so rarely lashed out at anyone but herself that they regarded her in surprise.

"Let's forget about Owen and Donna for the time being," Curtis said. "We need to decide what to do about this trouble."

After a moment, Shannon released her mother's shocked gaze and transferred her attention to Curtis.

"Decide what? I'm going to have a baby. I can't unring this bell."

Melba cleared her throat again. "No, but you have choices."

Shannon said nothing.

"You can either put the child up for adoption, or you can marry the boy."

The silence that filled the room seemed to grow thorns and oversized brutal hands. In that painful, strangling stillness, she lost all ability to think. Cold seeped into the marrow of her bones.

"I want to keep my baby," she managed to choke out.

"You're too young to get married," Curtis said. He frowned at his wife. "Melba, whatever made you even suggest such a thing?"

"Owen said if she's old enough to … to get herself in trouble, she's old enough to face the responsibility."

"'Owen said, Owen said.' Your son is a fool, Melba. No fourteen-year-old girl is old enough to get married."

Panic raced unrestrained though every cell of Shannon's body.

"I don't want to get married!"

"Of course you don't," her father said. "And even if you did, I wouldn't allow it."

"Well, she'll have to let the father know!" Melba snapped. She turned to Shannon. "We thought we watched you so carefully. How could this happen? Who is the boy, anyway?"

The thin cords of Shannon's sanity stretch tighter and tighter. Any moment now, they would snap apart and so would she.

Her father seemed calm, but his carotid artery throbbed violently. Melba's eyes were wide and frightened. She cradled fists against her lips as if to keep from crying out.

"Who is he, Shannon? What boy did this to you?"

She felt her lips tremble. From one face to the other, and back again, she sought for the right words that would quiet her father's thrumming blood and soothe her mother's fear. But she could not. She had been a bad daughter, the worst that had ever been. She hated herself more than she'd ever hated any living thing in her life.

In the quivering quietness of their home, her kind and godly parents waited for her to reveal the name of some familiar boy on whom they could assign blame. The clock ticked. The furnace kicked on. A car went by on the street. They waited for her to turn into a good girl again.

The thin line that held Shannon together broke at last.

"I can't tell you who he is," she screamed. She looked wildly from one ashen face to the other. "I can't tell you because I don't know!"

They gawked wordlessly at her for the length of five heartbeats, then Melba asked in a strangled voice, "What do you mean you don't know? How could you not know?"

"Did someone force you, Shannon? Attack you?" Curtis's body bristled with wrath. "Were you raped?"

"No," she said hoarsely. "No one forced me to do anything."

"Then how…how could this happen?"

Words poured out of her, and she was helpless in their rush. "I liked it! All right? I liked how it made me feel, and I wanted them to do it to me, and they did. And now I'm pregnant, and I don't know anything else to tell you. That's it!"

She hid her face, but she could not hide her shame.

SHANNON

Melba took to her bed. Curtis moved through the next couple of days in stony silence. Shannon tried to talk to them, to explain that she did not always seek out boys, that something, someone out of control inside herself made her do what she did. She tried to tell them that crazy person was not the real Shannon Grady. But it seemed that knowing of her promiscuity was all it had taken for her parents to join ranks with Owen and Donna. They withdrew from her, and their distance opened an unlocked door.

Depression skulked through that opening and into her mind once more. Dark thoughts sought and found her. She relived her careless activities, her ungodly ways. She yearned to escape this bad place inside her mind.

And then, like an act of grace, unbidden new thoughts budded without preface, reminders of the fresh life growing inside her. As she pondered how a baby lived and grew, safe and oblivious of the world, hope stirred, faintly at first, then growing bit by bit. She imagined tiny baby hands, wee pink toes, little fat rolls on arms and thighs, soft kissable cheeks. Instinct told her she carried a son. Thoughts of that son kept her from being borne away completely in the smothering arms of despair. When the baby was born she would hold him close to her and love him more than anyone could ever love another person.

That winter the family spent Christmas at home instead of the lake house. With their cook Elsie gone for the day, Melba rallied enough to prepare the traditional Christmas meal. Fragrant and plentiful, everyone's favorites weighed down the dining table, but the mood was so bleak that an outsider could easily have mistaken the holiday for a wake. Even the grandchildren were subdued. When Shannon attempted to coax them into play later on, Sarah Jean and Donna ordered their progeny from her presence.

"Go play outside," Donna ordered them.

"But it's too cold!" said her oldest, seven-year-old Amy.

"Get outside!" she yelled. "I'll tell you when you can come in."

Sullen but submissive, they went into the backyard. Looking out the kitchen window, Shannon saw them near the empty swimming pool, huddled in a little clump, their breath a frosty cloud above their heads.

"Let them come back inside where it's warm," she told their mothers. "I'll stay away from them."

Shannon helped clear away the dishes and tried to clean the kitchen, but Owen and Donna stood in the middle of the room to rail and lecture, pummeling her mercilessly with their harsh words. Sarah Jean, who had never helped wash a dish or wipe a counter in that house, pleaded her customary headache and went to lie down in the spare room until the work was done. Shannon grew so tired of her siblings' harsh voices and their presence that she retreated upstairs to her bedroom, locked the door, and pushed a chair against it.

Even after Donna and Craig took their children and went to spend the remainder of the day with Craig's family, Owen continued to rant. His words seeped up through the floorboards and into her room. Shannon curled on the bed and pulled the comforter over her, trying to block the voice.

"She needs to get right with God!" he yelled. "It's her separation from Him that is causing all this. He's turned his back on her and that won't change until she repents."

"Don't you think we know that?" Melba cried. "Don't you think we've tried to pound it into her head?"

"How many times do I have to tell you people that she *does not care* about anyone but herself? She never has and she never will."

Shannon drew into a tighter ball.

It'll be different next year, she comforted herself. *Next year my baby will be here, all sweet and fresh, and when they see him, they'll forget their nastiness and will love him because he'll be an innocent little baby.*

The following morning Curtis tapped on the door of her bedroom and walked in before she had a chance to invite him. She sat cross-legged on her bed, staring at a game show on her small television. Her father held out an envelope and waited silently as she took it and extracted the contents. She held ten one hundred dollar bills and a plane ticket. She looked at him questioningly.

"We're sending you down to Texas to stay with your aunt Eunice until after the birth. There's an agency there that will take care of finding the baby a good home. You won't have to worry about it. Him. Her."

Her heart stopped. "What do you mean? I'm keeping this baby."

"Of course you can't keep a baby!"

"But, Daddy, I have to—"

He sat on the edge of her bed and regarded her solemnly. "Honey, you're too young to be a mother. You'll be barely fifteen when that child is born. Your whole life is still ahead of you. And I invite you to recall that just few weeks ago you couldn't even get out of bed."

"But he's my baby! I want him. I need him."

He drew in a deep breath. "Shannon, you aren't ready to rear a child. Your mother and I are too old to take on the responsibility. So…no. You are not keeping that baby."

She scrambled off the bed, the money and the ticket still clutched but forgotten in her fingers.

"Daddy, it's not right—"

"Shannon. You won't be a fit mother."

The echo of his words bounced through her brain until they shattered her soul and the shards pierced her heart. Those were the same words she had heard from Donna and Owen. The words she told herself in the deep hours of the night. To hear her father speak them filled her with a crushing misery.

As Shannon's spirit died by slow degrees, Melba slipped into the room, a thick, fuzzy robe wrapped snugly about her. Recently, she had taken to wearing her robe all day. Her usually neat hair was barely combed and sloppily arranged. It was as if she'd absorbed Shannon's despair.

"You can't raise a child," she said. "You don't…well, what I mean is, you aren't…." She looked helplessly at her husband. "Curtis, talk to her.

Explain this."

"You had relations with a boy…boys…without the benefit of the law or God's blessing or any good sense," he said. "The mere fact that you were so indiscriminate proves that you're thoughtless and careless." He paused, let that notion sink in. "That being the case, the baby will be given for adoption, and you will return to us next summer an older and, I hope, wiser young woman."

The pronouncement meant nothing, and she refused to accept it.

"But what if they mistreat him? What if they beat him or starve him? What if they yell at him and…and…I'll be so good to him. I'll be the best mother in the world. You'll see."

"No, honey." Curtis's voice was gentle yet iron hard. Melba remained silent, her mouth thin and firm, her expression unrelenting.

"Oh, but…."

She searched their eyes for a trace of softening, a tidbit of understanding but found none. They were right, of course. She didn't know anything about infants, their care, their needs. She thought of the last year, her reckless behavior, her uncontrollable fits of tears, and the dark gloom that gripped her mercilessly. Her parents were right. Owen and Grady were right. Shannon was bad, from the marrow of her bones to her skin. The sweet little boy growing inside her deserved better, and she knew it.

The dreams she'd so recently spun around herself and her child shriveled like fresh leaves in an icy gale. Grasping at the ragged ends of her strength, Shannon pulled in a deep breath, accepted her parents' decree and gave up.

She looked down at the ticket in her hand. It was a round-trip ticket to Austin, Texas.

"May I at least stay home?" she asked. "I don't know Aunt Eunice. I've never even met her."

"She's your father's aunt."

"But I don't want to live with a strange old woman in a place I've never been before. Please don't make me go there. Can't I please stay here with you and Daddy?"

"No!" Melba's voice cut into her soul like a razor; it reverberated with the echoing tone of Owen's influence. "We have an image to keep up in this town, and you've done a terrible thing, getting yourself pregnant. And the fact that you…that you…messed around with more than one boy…." Melba shuddered, then turned to leave the room. At the door she paused. Without looking over her shoulder, she added, "We tried so hard to raise you right, but this is the worst thing any Grady has ever done. You've nearly cost me my religion." She went out of the room and firmly shut the door.

Shannon stared at the door a moment then sat on the edge of the bed, her back rounded. Her actions and their consequences were far worse than she imagined.

"I had no idea I could hurt Mama so bad," she whispered, sinking down on the edge of the bed next to her father. "Only an awful person could cause her mother to lose her religion."

Curtis said nothing for a while, simply studied his daughter's face then smoothed back her hair. "You're not an awful person. You're a trusting young girl who has made a terrible mistake." He sighed and clasped his hands between his knees. "Your mother's state of mind is not your fault. She seems to have a lot of problems lately. I shouldn't say it, I guess, especially to you, but I've come to think she enjoys her troubles. Your brother's excessive sympathy just makes it worse." His voice trailed and his mind seemed elsewhere for a little bit, then he came back to himself and straightened. "She'll have to work those problems out for herself, I guess. In the meantime, it'll be better for you both if you aren't here where she can watch you…fill out." He made a rounded growing gesture with his hands

"Mama's been angry and nervous for a while now." She plucked at her bedspread, thinking of those times. "She bites my head off a lot. She didn't used to do that. I guess I get on her nerves, you know, the way I get on Owen's and Donna's nerves. I'm glad *you* still love me, Daddy." She leaned into him and wondered if she'd ever lose his love too.

Curtis smiled at her. "Of course I still love you. That will never change. And your mama still loves you, too. But right now you should give her wide berth, let her sort out her feelings. You know, honey, you might frustrate and confound us; you might make us angry. But you can never do anything to cause us not to love you."

Her heart swelled with relief.

"Daddy, if I can't stay here at home, then can I go to Julie's instead of Aunt Eunice's? I'd like to see California, and I'd still be away from Mommy and Owen and Donna and all them…couldn't I do that?"

He refused to meet her eyes. "I've already talked with Julie."

"You did? What'd she say?"

He paused so long that she pitied him and she answered her own question, "She doesn't want me. Do I embarrass her, too? Does she think I'm terrible? Did Owen make her hate me?"

"No, no, no. Don't think that way and upset yourself. Julie said she's away from home a lot and she thinks you shouldn't be left by yourself out there. And I agree. Los Angeles is a big city. Aunt Eunice said she'd be more than happy to have some company. You'll be leaving day after tomorrow."

Shannon looked up at him as he got to his feet. Although she hated the thought of being away from her parents, she understood the reason. Being here would embarrass her mother and cause her father to feel torn between them. And staying here would just invite Owen and Donna to be nastier than ever. Even though she'd never been to Los Angeles to see her sister—Julie actively discouraged family visits, saying her place was way to small for company—the thought of being alone in the apartment while Julie was away gave Shannon the creeps.

"All right, Daddy. I'll go away."

For as long as she lived, Shannon would love the smell of moth balls and peppermint. Those two disparate scents mingled in Aunt Eunice's small home and, combined with warmth and a good deal of laughter, gave Shannon the best memories of her life. The old woman was neither agile nor energetic, but the days Shannon spent with her were full of activity and purpose.

"Let's go through that old trunk, dumpling," her aunt said once. "Maybe you'll find some play-pretties to take home." Another time she suggested, "Let me show you how to make a good biscuit." Or, "Let's sit on the front porch while we mend these curtains."

Days that normally would have made Shannon scream from sheer boredom filled her with contentment. Woodrow, Arkansas, and her unhappy family seemed blessedly far away. Although she missed her parents terribly, she wished she could stay forever with her great-aunt, in the quiet security of that tiny, fragrant home. Maybe, under Aunt Eunice's tender regard, Shannon could escape the raging need for wild expression and the black fiend of depression which always followed it. But, watching the old woman move in careful steps around the house, Shannon knew that living with her indefinitely was as impossible as escaping the dictatorship of her moods.

At 10:42 on the morning of May 4th, after ten hours of labor, Shannon caught a glimpse of a tiny arm, a bloody wisp of dark hair on a small head, heard a soft mewling. She knew a rush of joy unlike any she'd ever experienced. A moment later a nurse whisked the crying infant to the far side of the room where she wiped him off, wrapped him snugly and carried him out of the delivery room.

"Wait!" Shannon called after her. "Let me see him. I want to hold him. Please!"

The doctor and nurses attended to post-birth details, but Shannon's focus was fully on the swinging doors through which her son had been taken.

"Please let me hold him!" she called out. Her words went unheeded.

Sobbing, she called for her baby, reached for him. Her empty arms were disregarded. The Bible verse from Jeremiah flooded into her mind: "…there a voice was heard, lamentation, and weeping, and great mourning, Rachel weeping for her children, and would not be comforted, because they are not." It echoed in her brain as loudly as if someone had shouted it in every corridor of the hospital.

She tried to get up. A nurse scurried to her bedside, silently fed medication into the IV drip. In a matter of moments Shannon slid away into unconsciousness.

"It's better that you never saw the baby," the adoption agency's social worker told her a couple of days later as Shannon prepared to leave the hospital. "In a month or two all this will be a distant memory, and you'll be free to resume a normal life." She smiled brightly.

Shannon stared at the willowy, well-dressed woman whose make-up was faultless and every strand of auburn hair had been lacquered in place.

"How can you say that?"

The woman laid a slender, perfumed hand on Shannon's arm. "Because it's true. Really, Shannon, you don't want a baby at your age."

"You've never had a baby. Have you?"

Something brittle shot across the woman's expression. She sniffed, straightened the sleeves of her tailored jacket, brushed away invisible dust.

"This is not about me. Now, if you're ready, I'll take you back to your aunt's house."

The baby's birth was not the promised distant memory, and resuming a normal life remained an elusive dream for Shannon Grady.

When Shannon returned to Woodrow the tension between Curtis and Melba virtually shivered off the walls. They spoke to each other only in cold clipped phrases or in a spate of heated words. Melba's distance from her husband and from Shannon stretched further every day. Curtis spent more and more time at his office in town.

"That's just like him," Shannon overheard Owen say to their mother one day when he had dropped in for fresh apple cake and coffee. He rarely visited unless Melba had prepared food for him. "Dad always spent more time and attention to Grady Wood Products than he ever did to his family."

"That's not true," Shannon said, coming into the kitchen where mother and son sat cozily at the breakfast table. "Daddy always tells me and Mama to call him at work if we need him. And he comes home right away if he needs to."

Owen gave her one of his serious, level stares but said nothing. Shannon doubted Curtis had changed between Owen's childhood and hers, but it seemed to suit Owen to believe in his father's indifference.

"Here, son, let me give you another helping."

Melba gave him an extra dollop of motherly affection along with more cake.

Six weeks later, Aunt Eunice died in her sleep. The girl mourned the old woman's passing with an intensity that amazed her family.

"She was good to me," she said, trying to explain in simple terms the depths of her loss.

"She smelled funny," Donna said during dinner the next Sunday.

"She was an old woman," Owen said dismissively. "I'm surprised she lived as long as she did. Pass the gravy, Mom."

In youth group at church and once school started, Shannon found herself left out of the inner circle. She overheard whispers and laughs and, knowing she was the target, she made few attempts to reestablish close friendships. Soon, though, she found herself drawn to others, the outsiders at school, the smokers and the punks, the ones with spiked hair who dressed entirely in black, or the ones with stringy tresses whose ill-fitting clothes came from the Share Center. These kids were unimpressed by her family name and fortune. If they knew about the baby or her mood swings, they didn't care.

Left out of all that was familiar, Shannon sought and found her survival skills by grasping the rebellion modeled by her new peers. She no longer hid behind the good-girl persona. Bit by bit she released the notions and hard-nosed dogma hammered into her head by the church and her family. Her new friends supported and championed the change. When the racing thoughts, heightened senses and need to soar through life gripped her again, she gave in to it. She relished her body's urges to seek fulfillment in fast cars or with boys and alcohol. This time, her companions were along for the ride.

Then, as it had done before, the hungry darkness came stalking, and overnight it swallowed her whole. From the belly of the beast shame and guilt returned and ate her every moment and would not be sated. During the previous black times, the only liberation from torment in her mind had been when Donna plunged her under scalding water. She yearned for intense pain again, like the pain of childbearing when birthing seemed to rip her body apart. But this time no seizures of childbirth rescued her, and a blistering shower wounded only for a short time.

Shannon needed something more, something that remained. Something she could look at later and remember....

She bit her left forearm.

As her teeth plunged into the flesh and bore down, she felt no release. She bit again, harder, but once more, the sensation was too mild. Teeth marks remained and would bruise her pale skin, but it wasn't enough. She wanted to feel, to bleed, to amend for her wickedness while proving life still coursed through her body.

She opened her bedroom door quietly, stole along the hallway and down the backstairs to the kitchen. Silently she took a small knife from the rack, examined the blade's thin edge, pricked her thumb as she tested its sharpness. She returned to her room. Sitting on the edge of her bed, Shannon looked at the bite-marks.

She smiled grimly. Then she took a deep breath and pressed the knife's tip between the bruises and sliced through. Pain shot through her senses as the skin split. Blood flowed but it did not gush.

The hurt was such relief, expiation for all she had been and all she still was. As pain increased, she dropped the knife, closed her eyes, and lost herself in the wound, the blood, the bliss of physical sensation and punishment.

Shannon had found a way to deal with the darkness.

SHANNON

When she was twenty-one, Shannon moved into a small studio apartment near downtown Woodrow. The cycles of highs and lows continued, but often she felt normal, able to work and function like anyone else. But during those bad times, she buried herself in a nest of blankets while her television ran day and night.

Small, regimented scars neatly lined along the inside of her forearms, like notches on the handle of a gunfighter's pistol.

She could pay most of her bills by working a series of low-paying jobs. For the first time, she was on her own, and this streak of independence thrilled and frightened her. If she could just make a success of herself, maybe Owen and Donna would see her for the person she was inside; if she fell flat on her face, they'd gleefully underscore every negative thing they espoused about her.

"And why do I care what they think?" she asked herself in the late night hours.

But she did care. In spite of everything and in a way that even she did not understand, Shannon loved her family. Curtis and Melba heartily disapproved of her lifestyle and her friends, and sometimes Melba was difficult and brusque. But she knew they loved her without compromise. She often thought about the child she'd given away. Where was he now? Was he happy? How had he celebrated his latest birthday? Did he know he was adopted? Would he ever want to meet her someday?

She was an adult now; she could look for him. But to what end? Her cycle of debilitating bad times and reckless good times proved she was poor quality mother material. Unable to provide well for herself, she could never provide well for a child.

There were those wistful times, too, when she thought about moving out of Woodrow altogether, go where no one knew her and make a fresh start of her life. Fear stopped her every time. She was terrified to be away from Curtis and Melba, the only security she'd ever known. Even though Shannon yearned for independence, she knew her weakness, her inability to survive on her own. She refused to go where she could not be caught in their arms if she fell. So she stayed in Woodrow and lived near her parents.

When her finances lagged, Curtis and Melba paid her rent. They bought her a new Corolla. Nothing fancy like the rest of the family drove, but fairly safe and reliable.

Shannon knew they tried to make up for Owen's and Donna's disregard and Julie's prolonged absence. She clung to her parents' unreserved love like a lifeline, even when the mania kicked in and she fed the unplumbed depths of her appetites.

A few days before Christmas, Melba called the apartment.

"Honey, can you take some things up to the lake house for me? Your dad drove up this morning but he left these canned goods and decorations right here by the door. I don't know what gets into that man sometimes. I don't have time to go myself. I would have called Owen, but his time is so valuable I hate to bother him."

Shannon had waited tables for the last eight days at the Dairy Diner and she was dog-tired, but her parents rarely asked her for anything.

"Sure, Mama. I'll be over in a few minutes."

"Do you need gas money?" Melba asked a little later as Shannon put the two boxes on the backseat of her car.

"No. The tank's full."

"Take this anyway." Melba pressed two twenties into her hand. "And don't let Owen or Donna know I gave it to you."

There were times Shannon thought her mother might relax Owen's grip on her actions. At that moment, Melba was again the warm, kind mother she used to be. More and more, though, Melba seemed weak, even helpless, without her son to direct her ways.

"I don't want your money, Mama."

She held it out but the woman stepped back.

"Just take it, Shannon, and no argument. Is your apartment warm enough?"

She had to spend money on gasoline so she could drive to work and her food supply had dwindled to half a box of saltines and three cans of chicken noodle soup, the store brand. Her paycheck failed to stretch far enough to keep her apartment warm, too, but she didn't say so.

"I'm fine. Really I am."

Melba sighed and chafed her arms in the chill December breeze. "If you'd just move back home, you wouldn't have to—"

"Mama. I mooch off you and Dad too much as it is."

"Why, you don't! You're our baby girl. We want to see to it that you're taken care of."

"I'm twenty-one now. Please don't worry about me."

"I'm your mama. I will always worry about all my kids." She shivered a little in the chilly air. "Honey, did you know there are government programs to take up the slack when you don't have enough? Go to social services; get some assistance. Please."

"I don't want to bleed the government, either. I can support myself!" But she wasn't sure she could, not if the bad time came again. No employer would keep her on the payroll when she couldn't get out of bed.

Melba took Shannon's hand in her cold fingers. "I wish you'd come back to church. You need the Lord." She squeezed tightly as she looked into her daughter's eyes. There. That was familiar. That was Owen's voice.

There was no way Shannon would return to the Woodrow Worship Center and be the target of gossip, rumor, and censure. Owen and Donna would be the ringleaders of it all.

Shannon held her mother's gaze and knew she could not speak these words to the woman.

"What would the Lord do with me if he had me?" she said, laughing slightly. "Really, Mama, I'm fine without church."

"Oh, honey." Melba sighed again and let go. They'd had this discussion too many times to count.

Shannon glanced at the sky. Watery gray underscored the pale blueness and promised an early end to the daylight.

"It'll be dark soon. I better get going."

The lake house was less than an hour away. Every year Curtis went a day or two early to check the fireplace, the toilets, sinks and stove. He always cut and brought in a perfectly formed tree for the family to decorate. The last few years, though, Christmas had been a tense celebration at best. Shannon hoped this year it would be different. This year she wanted something fun-filled, a traditional day with eggnog and fruitcake and candy.

A disturbance skipped through her mind, here and gone in a flash, but it left her feeling strange. It had something to do with the memory that she had never been able to grasp fully. She thought briefly of Happy Baby, then shuddered and shoved that remembrance away. Maybe it was best that she couldn't recall everything. Maybe other ugly events, like the burning of Happy Baby, occurred in those lost memories. If that was the case, she didn't want to dredge up any of them. That was why she never reached too deep inside her mind where darkness lingered. It was easily disturbed if she pushed too hard.

The sky grew laden with promised precipitation, and it was nearly dark by the time she reached the lake house. She got out of the car and breathed deeply. Fragrant smoke plumed from the big stone chimney. It heralded the Christmas season as much as carols and mistletoe. Through the big front room window, Shannon saw candle flames flickering in the house. The house seemed so cozy and welcoming, but candlelight when Curtis was there alone meant the electricity wasn't working. The family might have to spend Christmas at Owen's or Donna's. They'd been whining for a change of venue for years. They said coming to the lake was foolish and tiresome. It was too small to hold everyone. Too old, too far from town.

"And only two tiny bathrooms!" Owen's wife Sarah Jean always whined.

Shannon swore mildly at the thought of spending Christmas day at Owen's new mansion with its priceless antiques or at Donna's cold, cavernous house with its marble floors, ornate furniture, and pretentious appointments. Most of her friends could live for a year or two on what Donna had paid just for the décor in her living room.

Shannon sighed and took the boxes from the backseat. Balancing them in her arms, she walked the narrow stone pathway toward the front door. The muted music that greeted her as she neared was neither familiar Christmas carols nor the Southern gospel her family preferred. Instead, smooth, sultry jazz slid from the speakers. Seductive; sexual. Luther

Vandross, maybe. Curtis must have broadened his tastes, and she smiled at the notion. Owen would pitch a fit if he could hear that saxophone played just that way and know their father listened to it. She nearly laughed out loud.

She glanced inside, through the shining plate glass, past the homey front room with its multitude of shimmering candles, beyond the breakfast bar and into the kitchen. She froze in bewilderment. Her father stood at the range, stirring something, his back to the room. A few steps away stood a slender woman in a silky dark blue robe. Her thick, wavy dark hair hung past her shoulders. She was smiling tenderly, head to one side as she watched him cook. Then, to Shannon's amazement, the woman closed those few steps and wrapped her arms around him. Amazement transformed into disbelief as her father turned, pulled the woman even closer, then kissed her.

The boxes in Shannon's arms slid free of her grasp. She fumbled to hang onto them and lost the battle. Cans thudded as they hit the earth and rolled free. She shot another look at the oblivious couple inside then squatted and blindly groped for the scattered items. She shoved the cans back into the box, stayed crouched in the semi-darkness for what seemed an eternity. Finally, with great deliberation and by slow degrees, she stood. Her gaze found proof of what she'd hoped was imaginary. The couple in the kitchen stood, arm in arm, she with her head on his shoulder, and he resting his head on hers. The casualness of their pose, the easy intimacy, the carelessness with which they had left the curtains open, exposing their affair to the eyes of the world, all of it said this relationship was a settled one.

For a moment Shannon thought she would be sick. Should she go in and confront them? Should she steal away unseen? Her mother, back in Woodrow, was working like a horse to prepare for the big family Christmas celebration, while her father was here, taking his ease with some ... some strange woman ... .

Shannon strained to see her more clearly. With a start, she realized the woman was Nancy Wright who had lived on the property next to the lake house for as long as Shannon could remember. Nancy was neither young nor ripe; in fact, she was probably Melba's age. But she was slim where

Melba was plump, stylish where Melba clung to drab, modest apparel. She stood where Melba should be; caressed Melba's husband with a careless grace that alleged she owned such privilege.

Inside Shannon's brain, sudden shadows flashed and silent screams filled her ears. She left the boxes on the porch and fled to the car. Blindly she drove back to Woodrow, ignoring the speed limit or the dangers of passing cars on hills and curves. Once inside the safety of her apartment, she prowled back and forth like a restless captive.

A part of her said she had no right to react with such violence of feeling, that she had transgressed as much – more, in fact – than her father. She was the blackest sinner of the entire Grady family, and yet…and yet…she wanted to tear out her eyes to rid herself of the image of Curtis and the woman from next door. She kept hearing the seductive tones of the music. She saw flickering firelight, relived the cold night outside. The music. The touching. The cold.

If Curtis left Melba for Nancy Wright, wouldn't it mean he no longer loved his family? Wouldn't it mean he'd have no time or inclination to have a disturbed daughter in his life? And what if Melba found someone else, or worse yet, turned completely to Owen for support and affection? Owen could totally corrupt any tenderness she harbored for Shannon.

She went to the window, stared outside at the blackness of the cold night.

She was being selfish and cold. Just like Donna, caring only about her own wants. She shuddered. Anything, *anything* but being like Donna.

Now that she had seen the gaping hole in the only safe fabric she'd ever known in her life, she knew she would fall through it. Even now the tentacles of darkness reached for her, and she was slipping, slipping….

The telephone rang, piercing the fog and terror around her but unable to banish it. She clawed her way through the bad feelings.

"Yes?" she whispered into the receiver.

"Shannon? Honey, is that you?"

The familiar cadence of her mother's worried voice brought her to reality.

"I'm here."

"Are you all right?"

She wanted to scream, *No!*

"I'm here," she managed to say again. Scrambling through her broken thoughts, she wanted to spare her mother any pain. "Headache. Going to bed now."

"Honey, shall I come over—"

"I'm going to bed. Talk to you later."

She retained only the barest memory of hanging up the telephone or going to bed that night.

The thundering assault on her front door early the next morning dragged her into wakefulness. When she saw her father's chalky face, his eyes rimmed with fear, the whole sordid scene flared in her mind.

He scurried into the apartment and shut the door before she had opportunity to invite him inside or to shut him out.

"Did you bring those boxes to the lake house last night?"

She nodded once.

He tossed a wild look around, as if he expected the eyes and ears of his family, his town. and his church were on him.

"You saw?" he whispered.

Callously, to prolong his agony, she repeated, "Saw?"

"Did you see…anything?"

"You mean did I see you and Nancy Wright?"

His bloodless face turned even whiter. "Yes."

"A cozy little scene, Daddy, the two of you snuggled up like an old married couple."

"Oh, God." He collapsed into the nearest chair and buried his face in his hands. "Oh, God."

She wondered if he'd burst into tears like a child, or try to excuse his transgressions like a felon. Maybe he'd wheedle for understanding the way a kid begs for candy.

Last night's anger now lay in cold storage as she stood in the center of the room, arms folded, waiting.

SHANNON

"Are you going to leave Mom?" Shannon asked her father.

Curtis looked at her as if the question astonished him. "Of course not! Nancy and I are good friends. Nothing more."

She stared at him until he squirmed.

"You cheated on your wife of forty years with our trusted neighbor—in the same house where we've celebrated Christmas since I can remember—and yet you can sit there and tell me that you're 'nothing more than friends?' Excuse me, if I fail to grasp your logic."

Curtis squeezed his eyes shut. His face collapsed into a graph of intricate webs and lines. When he opened them, his eyes brimmed with anguish. Shannon fought a stab of guilt.

"I don't expect you to understand it. Your mom and I just…how do I say this? We haven't been…close…like a man and wife…or in any way, really, for a long time. It's been years since we've—"

Shannon raised her hand to stop him. "I don't want to hear it. Please."

She sank to the edge of the sofa and rubbed her forehead, trying to gather her wits.

"I don't blame you if you hate me, honey."

Those words broke her, the plea sounding so much like the yearning of her own heart. Tears pricked her eyelids.

"Oh, Daddy, I don't hate you. How could I hate you when I've done so much wrong and you still love me? I love you, but I just don't…I mean, it's you and Mommy, and I just never thought…."

"I know."

"Does Mommy know about this?"

He looked panicked. "No! And you won't tell her will you? It would kill her."

"I won't tell. But, if this has been going on for years, don't you think she may know, or at least suspect?"

He looked sicker than ever. "She's never let on. You don't think she knows, do you, honey?"

Shannon shrugged. "I don't know."

"I mean, it would probably never occur to her…would it?"

She knew he wanted reassurance, but she had no power to offer it.

"You won't tell her. Right?"

"No, Daddy."

"Or Owen or Donna or Julie. They must never know."

"Never in a million years."

Shannon kept her word, but for days after, the image of her father and Nancy Wright remained steadfast and crystal clear in her mind. No amount of tolerant understanding usurped the terror she felt when she thought of her father with another woman. If Curtis Grady, the town's wealthiest and most powerful man, an active and influential part of the Woodrow Worship Center, the strong cord that held the Grady family together, could betray his wife, was it possible that his righteous and kindly spouse, the quintessential Christian helpmate and mother, could also harbor malignant secrets? The notion would not leave her mind.

When she visited her parents, she watched them diligently. Every gesture, every sharp or careless word they shared drove unrest further into her thoughts. What would happen if their relationship ended? At Owen's and Donna's mercies, how would Shannon survive? Where would she find acceptance? Where would she find love? They would rail and criticize, belittle and degrade her until the darkness would consume her forever.

With the secure foundation of her childhood now fully warped, the mental pain that bore into her surpassed any relief she felt by cutting her flesh. Shannon tried to eradicate her terror by exercise, by hard work, by driving her car until the gas tank was empty. She watched television for hours. With anxiety dogging every step, every hour, she checked out stacks of books from the library but her mind could not stay focused long enough to digest what she read.

In early March, she'd reached the end of her endurance. She drove to Rex Jason's house. Rex Jason Litton was one of her schoolmates, one of the outsiders who'd spent his youth in foster homes or juvie. In and out of jail as an adult, he knew people and people who knew people. He could help Shannon.

"I need something. Anything."

He leered at her, ignoring the desperation in her voice. "I know exactly what you need. But you gotta pay me for it."

"Yes. I have money." She handed over every dollar she had. He counted it, took a few bills, let her keep the remainder.

He grinned as he stuffed the cash in his pocket. "I'll take the rest out in trade."

"Okay."

When she left a few hours later, she was worn out from Rex Jason's overactive libido but she had several Xanax in her purse. Mid-afternoon, a jogger found her in her car, in the park. She was unconscious and near death.

Curtis, Melba, and Owen stood in Shannon's small room in the hospital psych ward while the attending psychiatrist spoke to them. "It's clear this young woman is ill. Why did you wait so long to get her help?"

"We didn't realize she needed medical attention," Curtis said. "We just thought it was her way."

Annoyance spread across his face. "You thought mutilating herself was 'just her way'?" He lifted her arm and indicated the array of scars, some rosy and fresh, others old and healed. "You think overdosing is 'her way'?"

"Yes," Owen said loudly, firmly. "It's just one more of her ways to get attention." The doctor's frown deepened, and he started to respond, but Melba spoke first.

"We didn't know about that cutting." She wrung her hands like a fretful old woman. "We had no idea she hurt herself. We didn't raise her to be that way." Standing next to her, Owen rubbed Melba's back in small, gentle circles. She continued, "She has these spells."

"Spells," the doctor repeated. His gaze bore into her.

"Yes. Everything is fine, then she starts acting foolish, running after men, drinking, doing awful things. Before you know it, she gets to where she can't even get out of bed." Her voice turned shrill. "I don't know why she acts like that! I've told her and told her that sometimes I don't feel like getting out of bed, but I do it anyway."

Owen fixed his solemn gaze on his mother's face, gave her a brief, sad smile, pulled her to him protectively.

"It's interesting that you say you have times when you don't feel like functioning, either," the doctor said. "Did you know mental illness is genetic? Does anyone else in the family—"

"Of course not!" Owen snapped. "And Shannon isn't sick. She's just trying to get attention, like I told you already."

The doctor thinned his lips and for a moment or two he didn't speak. "Sometimes events can bring on episodes, but mostly it's a glitch in her brain chemistry. Cutting herself is a classic example of—"

"I don't believe that for a minute!" Owen said. "Everything from drunkenness to laziness is labeled as a sickness these days. 'Brain chemistry' is psycho-babble, an invented way of excusing wrong living. No matter what you call it, it's all sin, plain and simple. Read the Bible."

The doctor ran a speculative gaze over Owen, then he turned to Curtis and Melba.

"Bipolar disorder is a chemical imbalance in the brain which results in drastic mood swings. It can be inherited—and frequently is. It can no more be defined as sin than, say, cancer or diabetes—"

"You're wrong, wrong, wrong." Owen said, nearly shouting.

"Please lower your voice, sir. I am not wrong—"

"You probably believe we all came from monkeys, that the earth is millions of years old, and dinosaurs once walked around. We're not listening to this Satanic garbage." He turned to his parents. "Let's go."

The psychiatrist attempted to speak again, but Owen held up a hand to cut him off. "I said we're not listening to this."

The doctor shook his head, clearly bewildered, nearly angry.

"Let's go," Owen said again. Melba followed her son as far as the door then stopped to cast a brief, stricken look at Shannon, who was barely awake, hardly aware of their presence. Her thoughts really didn't function right then, even if she wanted to talk…which she did not.

"Come on, Dad," Owen ordered.

Curtis ignored him. "I hate to leave you, Shannon."

She smiled weakly. "Go on, Daddy. I'll be all right."

"But, honey—"

"Dad!" Owen's voice rang like a pistol shot. "Mom needs to rest."

"When it's time for you to leave this place, you're coming back home," Curtis told Shannon. "We'll take care of you as long as you need us."

"Thank you, Daddy," she managed to whisper just as she slipped into sleep.

The next day, Owen stole into her room like a bandit. Shannon, more awake and aware than she had been the day before, gazed at him in surprise.

"Listen," he said without preamble or pleasantries, "I heard Dad invite you to stay with them. Don't you go moving in with the folks. They got enough on their plates without having to nurse-maid you."

"I know that. But, Owen, I've lost my job. I don't think my landlord will extend me more credit on the rent. It'll only be for—"

"Then get a cheaper place to stay. Mom doesn't need to be looking after you. You're supposed to be grown up now, so stop trying to get everyone's attention. You need to straighten up and get right with the Lord. Then maybe you'll finally amount to something. In the meantime, don't go bothering the folks with your problems." He pinned her with a final glare then stalked out.

Shannon stared at the empty doorway. She gripped the edge of her sheet until her knuckles ached.

With Curtis's affair, her parents' marriage stood on an unsure foundation. If guilt ever broke her father's resolve and he spilled his heart to Melba, could the woman hold up under that betrayal, especially if Shannon's behavior weakened the two of them even more? And beyond that, Curtis and Melba were aging. The years showed in the deeper creases on their cheeks, in the slower, more measured ways they moved. The last thing two old people needed was to look after a crazy daughter.

She knew she'd never be able to hold down a good job, not with the way her mind was wired. The Grady name was not a guarantee of a decent job in Woodrow. In fact, sometimes it was a liability. The day she had applied for work at the Home Style Shop, for instance.

"You're Curtis Grady's daughter," the manager had said, giving her a critical look. "The wealthiest family in town, and yet you come in here, wanting to take work from someone who really needs it. If you need to feel useful, go volunteer at the Share Center or the library or something. Let folks who need jobs have gainful employment."

Shannon was humiliated and far too embarrassed to tell the woman her true circumstances. Even if she'd been hired, even at a job she'd love like interior decorating, she'd not be able to hold it down when the moods hit her.

The doctor at the hospital convinced Shannon that medication would help, but it had side effects. He explained no matter what she did, she would always have this illness. So after she got out of the hospital, she faithfully took her meds, saw her shrink every week, and filed for Social Security disability benefits. Denied initially, she sought the help of a seasoned attorney who touted his skill in television commercials. He met with success and took a full third of her back pay as his fee.

Shannon's inability to support herself meant she also qualified for government-subsidized housing, food stamps and energy assistance. With that measure of security provided, she ceased to worry about her own welfare, but innate shame of living on the dole reared its head every time she went to the grocery store. She saw the censuring glances from other shoppers in the check-out line, heard their murmurs. After a time, Shannon realized very few people shopped at nine o'clock at night, but she began to do just that.

One sunny spring morning the next year, Shannon opened all the windows and the front door of her apartment to air it out. Aunt Eunice told her fresh air and sunshine was the best housecleaner there was.

"Best of all, it's free," she had added with a smile. "And it sure beats all that air freshening spray folks pump out to damage the oolong layer."

"Ozone layer, Auntie," Shannon had corrected. "Oolong is a tea."

They had both laughed every day about the old woman's gaffe until Shannon went home.

When she stepped outside to shake dust from a small, braided rug, she noticed a young woman across the parking lot. Sitting on the stoop of the opposite apartment, a skinny dark-haired girl smoked steadily and watched

Shannon.

"Good morning!" Shannon called to her.

The other woman barely inclined her head.

"Beautiful day, isn't it?"

A shrug, a plume of smoke. "It's all right, I guess."

Shannon gave the rug one last vicious shake, placed it carefully across the wrought iron railing of her own stoop and walked across the parking lot. The unsmiling woman watched her approach; her aura was one of wariness and distance.

"You just move in?"

The woman nodded. "Yesterday."

"I'm Shannon Grady."

She looked at Shannon's outstretched hand for a moment, then put the cigarette between her lips to free her own hand.

"Evie Kendall," she said around the cigarette as they shook hands. "You lived here long?"

"A little over a year. It's a pretty nice place to be."

Evie shrugged. "I ain't seen anyone but old ladies."

"That's mostly who live here, but we have a couple of guys. Frankie Dale lives in the end apartment. He's legally blind, but he gets around all right with his dog Grace. And there's a single mom with a little boy in building number two. Most of the younger people, though, live in the apartments across town."

"Yeah, I tried to get into one of those, but they're full." She looked Shannon up and down, blew out a big curl of smoke. "So how come a young chick like you ain't across town?"

"It's quieter here."

Evie made a face. "Boring. Dull. Dead. Nearly dead."

"I do better when things aren't so lively," Shannon said then laughed because she didn't want to explain why. "Would you like to come over and have some coffee or iced tea?"

Evie crushed out the nub of her cigarette on the concrete step. "You got anything stronger?"

"Diet Coke."

Evie gave her a dour look. "I don't mean soda pop."

"Sorry."

Evie sighed and got to her feet. "Beggars can't be choosers, I guess." As they walked across the parking lot, she said, "I bet you don't let people smoke in your apartment, either, do you?"

One night in late summer a few years later, Curtis Grady collapsed in front of the television while the six o'clock news blared its ugly business. Shannon had dropped by her folks' home with a batch of brownies. She sat with them in the living room, nervously expecting her brother or sister to charge in and demand an explanation of her presence. They seemed to have radar to know she was there. They obviously believed she only visited Curtis and Melba when she wanted goods or money. The fact was, Shannon rarely asked her parents for anything. She needed to prove to Curtis and Melba, and especially herself, that she could survive without taking anything from them.

"Neither Owen nor Donna hardly ever drop in except when you're here," Melba had told her a few weeks earlier. "In fact, I have to make a special treat and invite them. I hope you know you're free to come over any time you want, Shannon."

She smiled at her mother. "I know. Thank you, Mama."

But that evening, her siblings' radar must have been unplugged. She sat with Curtis and Melba in the living room and watched the evening news.

"Have a brownie, Daddy," she said. "I put cashews in just for you."

He smiled, thanked her and took one. But he ate only a bite and laid it aside on the table next to his recliner.

"Don't you like it? Did I bake them too long? I think my oven gets too hot."

"Just not hungry tonight, honey."

"He didn't want his dinner, either," Melba said. "Tenderloin and baked potato, and he hardly touched it."

She held up the tiny scrap of lace she was tatting and examined it critically. Her recent attraction to the art of tatting replaced the time she used to spend knitting. "It's nearly a lost art," she always explained to anyone who asked. "I'm the only person in Woodrow who can tat." She once offered to teach her daughter, but Shannon took a single look at the fragile thread and tiny tatting shuttle and declined. Working on anything small and detailed set her nerves on edge and made her want to fly into a thousand pieces.

"I wish Owen could see this," Melba murmured, eyeing the lace, "but he hasn't been by since Sunday dinner."

"It's real pretty, Mama," Shannon said, but it was Curtis who had her attention right then. "Daddy, aren't you feeling well?"

"I'm not hungry," Curtis said again, but this time Shannon noticed a labored tone in his voice, as if he fought for breath. She gave him a sharper look. His face was grey and something in his eyes wasn't right.

"Daddy? What's wrong?"

He looked at her, his expression at first surprised then full of pain. A moment later he slumped sideways, his hands curled.

Melba gaped at him silently and continued to hold the tatting up like a banner.

"Daddy!" Shannon screamed. "Mama, call 9-1-1!"

Melba was frozen. Then the lace fell from her fingers and she jumped up.

"Is it his heart? Is it a stroke? Is he dead?" She alternately flapped and wrung her hands as she darted aimlessly around the room. "What'll we do? What'll we do?"

"Call 9-1-1!" Shannon yelled. She tugged her father's limp body from the recliner to the floor. "I'll start CPR."

But Melba was too panicked to listen. "I need to call Owen. I have to call Owen."

"Mama, call 9-1-1 now!"

Melba simply looked at her without comprehension and repeated "I have to call Owen" over and over.

With strength she didn't know she possessed, Shannon rushed to the telephone and punched in 9-1-1. Cradling the headset between her ear and shoulder, she continued the cycle of compressions and mouth-to-mouth breathing until the EMTs arrived. Melba seemed in an altered state as Shannon drove them to the hospital behind the ambulance.

"We have to call Owen," Melba said as they parked. "He'll help us. He'll know what to do."

Shannon wanted to scream, but one ranting woman was enough. She spoke quietly, hoping her composure would calm Melba.

"Mama, right now we just need to get Daddy taken care of. We'll call everybody soon." She guided the older woman into the emergency room waiting area and settled her into a chair. "I'll take care of everything. You just stay right here."

She paused long enough to look into her mother's stricken eyes. She patted the woman's clammy, shaking hand.

"I'll take care of everything," she repeated.

SHANNON

Shannon filled out the necessary paperwork, four pages of tedious questions secured by a clamp to a scarred, neon-pink clipboard. Dragging answers from Melba tested her patience.

"Mama, does Daddy have a living will or trust?"

Melba stared at her blankly. "I don't know. Ask Owen. He'll know all that. Have you called him?" She fumbled in her purse, brought out a cell phone. "Call him."

"Not yet, Mama," she said for the seventh or eighth time, "but I'll take care of it soon. When I get all these forms filled out, I'll call everyone."

Melba stared at her as if Shannon were a stranger. "You can't."

Shannon continued filling in the blanks and didn't look up. "Can't what?"

"Take care of things. You just don't...you can't." She shoved the phone at Shannon. "Call your brother."

Shannon was tired of being treated like an incompetent ninny, but right then she needed to focus on her father's welfare and that's exactly what she planned to do.

"Well, Mama, maybe I can't take care of things, but I have before, and I'm doing so now, so let me finish. You call him."

Melba looked fearful and shook her head. She sat back, but a moment later she got to her feet. She paced, wrung her hands, paused to pick up a three-year-old copy of *People* magazine. She stared briefly at the celebrity's overdone smile on the cover and threw the thing back on the table. By the time Shannon finished the paperwork and turned it in to the pinch-faced girl behind the desk, her mother had returned to some semblance of her usual self.

"Where is he?"

"He's in ICU right now. We can't see him yet, but—"

"I mean Owen. Where is Owen?"

Why did she have this absurd need for the man? What about him so inspired her confidence? Was it because he was her only son? Perhaps it was his rude, hounding ways. Could it be his ox-like stubbornness? Certainly it was not his extreme devotion because, other than placating his mother while mouthing platitudes at Sunday dinner, Owen rarely interacted with his parents. Curtis and Melba could be dead in their bed for days and Owen would know nothing about it until someone else told him. And yet he was Melba's golden boy who could do no wrong. What seemed duty to Owen was love and caring to Shannon.

That evening, she had done everything right. She had kept her father alive until the paramedics arrived and made the hospital administration happy completing their excessive paperwork. She curled her hands into tight fists and tamped down her anger. With effort, she remained calm. Calm as lake water in late summer.

"Why don't you sit down, Mama? Right over there in that nice chair. I'll bring you some coffee, then I'll call Owen. Okay?"

The promise worked, and Melba allowed Shannon to guide her to the upholstered maroon chair in the corner, away from the fretful toddler with a runny nose and a sullen teenager who cracked her gum and glared at the world.

"Here." Shannon offered her mother the least-battered copy of Good Housekeeping she saw. "I'll be right back."

Without waiting for a thank you or another order to find Owen, Shannon picked up her Melba's cell phone, walked toward the vending machines at the end of the corridor and called Owen.

He shot her with a barrage of questions ending with "Is he dying?"

"I don't know. He's stabilized, but they won't let us see him."

"Well, I'm in a church planning committee meeting right now."

"Aren't you coming to the hospital?"

"The Lord's work comes first, Shannon."

She wanted to call him an ass, a fool, a stupid, stupid man. "I don't see how building a church gymnasium is the Lord's work. He doesn't play basketball, does he?"

She heard Owen's sharp intake of breath.

"What do you know about the Lord's work?" he snapped and hung up.

Donna was not home. Shannon left a message on the machine. She dialed Owen's cell phone again.

"Do you have Julie's phone number?" she asked.

"Don't you?"

"Not with me."

There was a clatter on the other end as if he'd tossed his own phone on to the table. A bit later he rattled off the number.

"That's for her cell phone. It's the only number she's ever given me." He hung up.

Shannon's call didn't go through. She punched in the numbers at least five times before giving up and calling directory assistance. She got her older sister's landline number and punched in those digits.

The phone in California rang twice before someone picked up.

"Julie?"

"No, this is Gwen. Just a sec and I'll get Julie." A moment later, Shannon heard, "It's for you, baby. A girl with a sexy voice. Should I be jealous?"

A laugh and the reply: "Never, sweetheart." Then, into the phone, "Hello. This is Julie."

Shannon gulped and tried to speak, but the shock of discovery held her mute.

"Hello! Who is this?"

"Julie?" Her voice was a mere squeak.

"Who is this?" Spoken with an edge of suspicion and anger.

Shannon's astonishment kept her silent a moment longer, then she blurted, "It's me. Shannon. Daddy's had a heart attack."

"Oh, my God. Is he…?"

"He's stable. That's all I know…." Her voice broke.

"Do I need to come home?"

Shannon swallowed hard. "Don't you want to? He's our father; he might not live through the night."

"You just said he's stable."

"He is, but—"

"Hold on."

This time the conversation on the other end was muffled, as if she covered the mouthpiece.

"Okay, Shannon. Here's the thing. We're hosting a huge dinner party tomorrow night and unless Dad is…well, unless it's vital that I be there, I can't just up and leave. I want you to call me back as soon as you know anything else, or if he…you know. Gets worse or something."

"If he dies, Julie. Dies. Our daddy might die."

"Good God, Shannon. Don't go all hysterical."

"I'm not hysterical. And I'm handling everything just fine." Why did her family always assume the worst about her?

"How's Mom holding up?"

"She's upset. She wants Owen."

"Is he there? Let me talk to him."

"Owen says he has other things to do right now."

"Then let me talk to Donna."

"I can't get a hold of her, and I don't know where she is."

Julie heaved an enormous sigh. "Well, this couldn't have happened at a worse time."

Did her siblings care nothing about their father? Was she the only one who loved him enough to be here?

"Daddy did not plan to have a heart attack, Julie, just in case you haven't figured that out. I'll call you when I know something."

"Wait! Tell Owen to call me—"

Shannon punched the end button and cut off her sister's order.

Maybe I'm crazy but at least I'm not heartless.

She went to the nurses' station again, but they could tell her nothing more. The darkness in her mind tried to edge in, like a starving cat trying to gain entrance into a kitchen. Soon it would lay hold, sink its fangs into her days and nights, tear open and lay bare the grisly mess that was her soul. She refused to give way. She would fight to hang on, fend off the fear, battle the hopelessness that threatened to claw apart her strength.

Shannon glanced at her mother in the corner chair. The woman appeared old, small, and helpless as she steadfastly watched the door, anticipating Owen's arrival. Melba seemed to believe her son could make all things right, as if he were a healer of ills or, perhaps, a supernatural savior.

Shannon delayed rejoining her mother for a little longer.

She crossed to the large window overlooking a small park across the street. Streetlights thrust illumined fingers through the tree branches and into the darkness. A car drove past, headlamps revealing the road before it. Shannon envied the occupants, secure and content with no loved one languishing in the hospital.

But maybe they're as sad and lonely and worried as I am.

At last she turned, the weight of the secrets she held rubbing a raw place in her thoughts. What would any of the other Gradys do if they ever learned that Julie was gay? If they knew of Curtis's affair? Of Melba's own peculiar moods she hid from everyone but Shannon and her husband?

Should she call Nancy Wright and tell her what was going on? She pondered the complexities of doing so for a while. If Nancy were to arrive, what kind of situation would that create? Curtis did not need the stress, and Melba would probably collapse. No, she would not call her father's lover. The woman could find out when the general public did.

She glanced at Melba again, saw tears puddle in her mother's eyes and begin their rivers down her cheeks. Melba wrung her hands and kept watching a doorway that undoubtedly would remain empty for a while longer. Another surge of anger swept into Shannon.

If Owen won't come for Daddy, maybe he'll at least do it for Mama.

She called her brother for the third time that evening.

"You listen to me, Owen Grady. If you don't want to be a selfish pig your entire life, get down here to the hospital and comfort Mama. She needs you. And believe it or not, God can build his own playroom without your help."

Owen showed up in the waiting room less than fifteen minutes later. Melba threw her arms around him and sobbed.

"Thank God! Oh praise Jesus. Thank you, Lord, for bringing me my son."

She hung onto Owen as fiercely as a drowning woman.

Owen looked over their mother's head at Shannon. His expression seemed to accuse her of maltreatment. She turned from him, felt like crying from sheer frustration but refused to give him the satisfaction.

"Find out how your father is," Melba said, both hands on either side of Owen's face.

"Mama," Shannon said, "I just asked them a few minutes ago—"

"Hush, Shannon. Owen knows what to do. He'll make them tell us."

"If they don't know anything, how can Owen make them ... oh, never mind."

She said nothing more, metaphorically washed her hands of the episode and gave over the care of her mother to the one Melba trusted. She watched her brother approach the nurses' station, overheard them repeat what they'd just told her, grimly observed his powerlessness to change things.

"Mom," he said as he returned and sat in the chair next to Melba, "Dad's in ICU right now. He's stable, but they're keeping a close eye on him. They can't tell us more than that."

"Oh. All right, then." Melba took Owen's hands in both of hers and clung to them. At last, she seemed pacified.

If the situation hadn't been so bleak, Shannon might have laughed at the absurdity. As it was, she walked back to the window and stared again at the night. She prayed for her father and hoped her prayers were good enough for God.

When Donna made her appearance in a cloud of Dior fragrance and twinkling diamonds, Shannon stayed near the window. Only when a nurse approached the trio in the early morning hours did she join them.

Curtis would survive.

Shannon stayed near her father's ICU room while the others went to breakfast in a café down the street. She sat next to him for the allotted fifteen minutes each time the opportunity offered itself. His grey face, the tubes, and the wires frightened her. His fingers looked fragile, his hands waxy. She found that she could not take her eyes off the rise and fall of his chest except to glance at the beeping machines that surrounded him.

Owen took Melba home to rest after a quick stop at the hospital, then he returned to his office at Grady Wood Products. Sometimes Shannon believed he was more devoted to the family business than he was to God. Donna went straight home from the restaurant, but an expensive overdone arrangement of flowers arrived with her name scrawled on a card.

"Get well soon," Shannon read in silent scorn. She wanted to throw the whole mess into the street. Flowers weren't allowed in ICU rooms, anyway.

When Curtis rallied at last the next morning, it was Shannon's face he saw first. He weakly squeezed her fingers, asked about her mother, and drifted back into sleep.

About midday, Evie found her in the waiting room. Evie's breath smelled of alcohol and Listerine. She, too, had flowers for Curtis, a small cluster of red and white carnations in a jade-green vase.

"If you'd called me earlier, I would've been here earlier."

"I know, but I didn't want to bother you." Shannon refused to recount the dynamics of the last twelve hours and the seeming indifference of her siblings.

"I wish you had, anyway. You look like hell."

"I'm tired."

"I bet. Have you eaten?"

"I've been too upset."

"Yeah, but you know how you start to feel if you don't eat or get rest, Shannon. How about if I go get you a Big Mac or something?"

Shannon shuddered at the thought. "I'm not hungry."

"How's your dad?"

"He'll be OK, but he has to take it easy for a long time. Daddy is such a workaholic. It'll be tough for him."

Evie sat with her until Shannon was allowed to spend a few more minutes at Curtis's side. When the nurse gently told her time was up, Evie was still there, waiting.

"Where's the rest of 'em?"

Shannon sat in the chair next to her. "Not here."

Evie frowned. "Have they been here at all?"

"Some."

"At least you have a father," Evie said. "My old man left when I was two. Your mom ever beat the shit outta you?"

She shook her head. "My folks never raised a hand to me."

"My old lady walloped the hell outta me every day of my life. Every damned day." Evie looked lost in memories and said no more.

Shannon had heard this all before. Every time Evie drank to excess. Usually, Evie nursed her booze, kept her drunkenness low-key and her reactions to circumstances reasonable, but sometimes….

Shannon rested her fingertips on her friend's hand for a moment.

"Take care of yourself, Evie. Will you? Please?"

Evie shrugged then offered a crooked smile. "Don't I always?"

"No. Not always."

"You worry too much, girl. You need to take care of yourself instead of everyone else." She looked at her watch, an oversized piece she'd bought at a yard sale. "You coming home tonight?"

"I think I will. He seems to be doing so much better, and I'm beat."

Evie got up. "Stop at my place, and I'll fix you something to eat."

Shannon stood, gave her friend a quick, hard hug. "I'll do that. Thank you."

Evie smiled at her. "You bet."

In a few days, when Curtis was strong enough to be out of ICU and in a regular room, Owen brought Donna and his mother. It was the first time Donna had been there since the night of Curtis's heart attack. She stood apart from the others, near the door, as if she feared her father's condition was contagious. Melba stood weeping at the bedside.

"What will I do if you die, Curtis?" she sobbed, twisting her handkerchief. "How am I supposed to keep the household running? Where's the deed to the house? Have you signed those papers for Owen? He'll have to—"

"Mama, please." Shannon said.

"You're making yourself sick," Curtis said. "The doctors say I'm fine and will be fit as a fiddle in no time."

"You don't look fine."

Owen slipped his arm around her shoulders. "It'll be all right, Mom. I'm right here."

"That's right, Mel. Stop worrying about everything. Owen, take care of your mother. Take her to your house until I'm home." He turned to Shannon and smiled. He stretched out a hand and she put hers in it. "Shannon's been taking real good care of her old dad. She's hardly left my side."

"Well, I sent you flowers!" Donna said plaintively. "And I'm here now. Shannon didn't bring you any flowers, did she?"

"Thank you, honey." Curtis looked at his older daughter. "They're beautiful. And Julie sent a nice card." He dropped Shannon's hand, sagged back against the pillow, pulled the sheet closer to his chin and closed his eyes. "You all go home now. I'm going to be fine. Right now I just want to sleep."

Owen and Donna spent no time lingering, hustling Melba out of the room with them. But Shannon straightened his covers, made sure the little blue pitcher was full of fresh water. She rearranged the broad array of floral gifts that filled his room and fixed the cards so the pretty sides faced out.

"You need your rest, too," Curtis said. "You look all done in."

"I'm fine, Daddy. Just a bit tired. Is there anything I can get you before I leave?"

"No. These folks take real good care of me. I'm on the board, remember?"

They shared a chuckle.

"Daddy, can I tell you something?"

"Sure."

She smoothed one corner of his blanket, her gaze on her hands. "I never called Nancy Wright."

He said nothing, and she lifted her gaze. His face registered pain, and she wished she'd kept her mouth shut.

"I didn't mean to stress you—"

"You didn't." He drew in a deep breath and let it out slowly. "I'm just sorry you ever found out about that whole sordid state of affairs. And don't worry. After you saw us, we thought it best to break off our…relationship."

"Oh."

He smiled sadly and reached for her hand. She clasped both of his.

"All this time you've been worried over nothing. Forgive me for all that, Shannon. I was in a place in my life…well, I'm not going to make excuses."

"Daddy. It's okay. I forgave you a long time ago. And I understand why you did it. Let's just put it behind us."

He sagged even more into the bed. "Yes. Oh, yes. Let's do just that."

She sat beside his bed until he fell asleep. She watched him for a time, and feeling comforted at last, she finally went home.

SHANNON

A year later, Shannon met Teddy Stamp on a warm summer evening when the air smelled of sweet honeysuckle. That night stars glittered like blinding diamonds and voices of life screamed at her to live, live, live.

She'd faithfully taken her medication, but what did not make her yearn for sleep gave her jitters so badly she *couldn't* sleep. The overworked doctor at the clinic switched her to pills that fogged her thinking. Then he put her on other pills that made her feel completely disconnected from reality. Two months before Shannon met Teddy, she stopped taking all medication.

That night Teddy came into her life she felt driven and alive. It had been so long since she'd felt so vital and untroubled, and she feasted on the rush.

Men clustered around her and Evie in the bar that night, buying more drinks than Shannon had a taste for. Her friend, in her usual garb of worn-out jeans and T-shirt, didn't seem to mind that Shannon wore a short, tight red dress and was the focus of every male in the place. Evie's lover was in the shot glass.

Shannon noticed Teddy. He stood on the periphery with a glass of whiskey in his hand and never took his gaze off her. Tall, muscular and tattooed, he possessed a face with strong, masculine contours. Shannon's blood caught fire. She gave him the smile that hooked any man she chose reel in.

Without a word, he shoved past the other guys until he stood so close his body heat enveloped her.

"Well, hello," she said, letting her gaze leisurely travel his full length.

"Hello yourself." His voice was deep and warm, like his eyes.

"You want to sit down? Johnny, move." The fellow on the bar stool next to her grimaced and got up.

"Call me later, Shannon," he said as he left.

"Right, Johnny." Absently. She'd already forgotten him.

Her new conquest did not sit. He said, "I'd rather take you outside, away from all these clowns."

This was what she wanted; this was what her body craved. She went with him.

For two days, she and Teddy indulged in sex, alcohol, speed, and gambling. On the morning of the third day, they woke up in a rundown motel on the Oklahoma border, hung-over, strung-out and married.

"What the hell?" Shannon screamed, laughing and trembling from after-effects. "My family'll love you, baby. Especially my big brother. Oh, he'll love you, Teddy-boy!"

When Shannon proudly introduced her new husband to her family a few days later, he was warm, charming, the epitome of decent, responsible manhood. And yet he fooled no one. Stunned by this new addition to the Grady family, Curtis and Melba were courteous but visibly wary. The siblings neglected to conceal their contempt.

After a few awkward minutes in the living room where a frigid silence seemed unbreakable, Melba said, "We'll have a party for you, Shannon…and, er, Teddy, isn't it? A quiet family get-together, maybe a cook-out or we could—"

"No!" Owen said, looking at his mother as if she'd lost her mind.

"I hope you don't expect wedding gifts," Donna said.

"Oh, now, Donna, really—" her husband Craig began.

"No wedding, no gifts," Sarah Jean sang out cheerfully, as she fingered her blond coiffure.

"Exactly." Donna gave her plump, balding husband a look that gave no room for dispute. He glanced away and said nothing else.

Teddy looked at his new wife, at his fresh in-laws. He lost his charm.

"That's fine. We don't give a shit if we have a party or not."

Sensing he was working up to saying something coarse or insulting, Shannon laid her hand on his arm and laughed uneasily. She threw an apologetic smile all around.

"We understand how you feel. I mean, springing this on you has to be a shock…. Anyway, you'll get to know Teddy and everything will be fine! Just fine!"

Owen hawked deep in his throat, and Sarah Jean examined her manicure, her face pinched. Donna rolled her eyes and shook her head, while Craig smiled briefly and glanced away again. Curtis and Melba's smiles seemed forced.

A couple of days later a Howard's Furniture Truck pulled up to Shannon's door and two burly men unloaded a new tan suede sofa and matching chair. As they left, one of the delivery men handed her a sealed envelope. Inside was a card that read "Congratulations to our daughter and her new husband. Daddy and Mom."

She waved the card at Teddy. "See? They're coming around."

He read it, tossed it aside and flung himself on the sofa. "Bring me a beer."

Two weeks later, in the middle of the night, Shannon woke up with the dreaded and familiar darkness hovering. It was there to steal her joy and kill the good times. She curled her hands in to tight knots and squeezed shut her eyelids, shoving against the bad feeling. If she could stifle the depression this time….

Teddy rolled over in the morning and said, "How 'bout breakfast?"

Shannon tugged the blanket over her face and mumbled an apologetic, "You'll have to fix it yourself."

"You sick?"

When she did not reply, he prodded her side roughly with his elbow.

"Say! You sick?"

"A little."

He lay still for a minute or two then got out of their small bed.

"I'll make a run to Mickey-D's. Give me some money."

She said nothing.

"Shannon! Hear me?"

"I hear. I don't have any."

"C'mon, baby, you always got money."

She groaned. "Don't have any."

He stared at her, his eyes narrow, the muscles of his neck and shoulders flexing and relaxing.

"I mean it. Give me some cash."

"I don't have any, Teddy."

"Then give me your credit card. Sign me a check."

"I don't have those, either."

"Your folks have it."

It almost took more power than her body contained just to speak. "I don't want to take money from my family. You'll have to get a job."

He glared at her. "The fuck I will! Why should I? Your family's got money."

"We're not going to live off my folks."

"I ain't doing without when your family's got more than they know what to do with. I'm gonna get some of it."

"Don't, Teddy. No."

But he was gone, the door crashing shut behind him.

When he came home, she was still in bed, unbathed and in her pajamas. She shuffled out of the bedroom. He brought with him two cases of beer, two bottles of Jack Daniels, two of Jim Beam, four of Wild Turkey and a greasy bag of hamburgers and fries from the Dairy Diner.

"I see you got money."

"Told your old man we were out of food."

She stared at Teddy's plunder on the dining table. "I don't see any food except those hamburgers. How much?"

"How much what?"

"How much did Daddy give you?"

"Some."

Shannon felt her insides strain. "How much is some?"

"A few hundred, okay? Enough to see us through until your next check." He pulled a Baggie from his pocket, tossed it on the table beside her, and grinned. "Thought we'd party, baby."

She stared at it. "Crystal meth, Teddy?"

He lost his grin. "Whatsa matter? You like to party as good as anyone so don't go all holy on me."

She closed her eyes and turned her face away.

"Your dad told me you have a disease." She heard the distinct snap of a beer can being opened. He slurped then belched loudly. "Why didn't you tell me?"

She said nothing, listened to him slug down another swallow.

"Didn't you think I'd understand?"

"It's a mental thing…bipolar disorder…I have mood swings—"

"Yeah, so your old man told me. He said you're nuts."

She looked at him. "He didn't say that."

He finished off the beer, opened another. "Said you're crazier than a fuckin' bedbug. Goddammit! What have I got myself into? Fucking nutcase."

"I'll be all right in a few days." Every time she lived through the darkness, she feared she might live there forever.

"Fuckin' nutcase," he muttered again.

That night, drunk and high on meth, Teddy turned to her.

"Hey, bitch. Wake up!"

"I'm not asleep."

"Yeah, well, you been in that bed all the damned day. Get up and party with me."

"I don't want to, Teddy. Just leave me alone."

But he did not leave her alone. He ranted about the unfairness of his life and how he never got an even break.

"Lived in one foster home after another and never in one long enough to take a piss, let alone settle in. Teachers picked on me in school till I walked out my sophomore year. Bosses don't like me 'cause I do work my way and they get all pissed 'cause I can do their jobs better'n they do. Cops like to stop me 'cause they like to throw their weight around. Fuckin' jerks. Never met a woman worth a shit. Then I meet you, Miss Hot-Ass-With-Cash and I thought the world had done turned around for ol' Teddy Stamp. And what do I end up with? Damaged goods. A fuckin' nutcase! Ain't life just grand for ol' Teddy Stamp?"

His voice pounded her eardrums like the drill of a jackhammer. All day he swilled beer and whiskey; he smoked the meth and went out twice to buy more. Shannon watched through the fog of her depression. She wanted to stop him, to join him, to run from him, but her body seemed incapable of any motion other than observing his descent into chemical madness. She slipped further and further into her self-contained darkness.

He smashed the furniture and put his fist through the wall in the bedroom near her head when she wouldn't get up. Then he pulled her from her nest of blankets, railing at her for her mental illness and her needless poverty. He beat her with his fists until she lay bleeding and nearly unconscious on the bedroom floor. At some point, he slammed out of the apartment and did not return.

Evie found her the following morning and rushed her to the emergency room. Later, in the small recovery room curtained off from the rest of the ER, she asked, "I hope you gave as good as you got."

Shannon shook her head. "I couldn't."

"What do you mean you couldn't? Did you at least kick him in the nuts?"

"I didn't do anything."

"Good God, girl, why not? He could have killed you!"

"I know. But it never would've happened if I hadn't picked up a stranger in a bar and married him."

Evie looked as if she were about to scream. "So you're blaming yourself for this?"

Shannon shrugged. "Sure. It's my fault."

Evie's eyes got big and round, and her face went scarlet. She jumped up and paced the room like an angry caged tiger.

"I may not know much, Shannon, but I do know this: Teddy Stamp beating the shit out of you was not your fault."

Shannon wished she could believe that but she didn't.

"Is he gone?" she asked.

"He better fuckin' be," Evie muttered.

"Do you know where he went?"

"You planning to go after 'im? You want that asshole back in your life? I swear to God, Shannon, if you—"

"No. I just wondered if he was gone. I don't want to go home, if he's there."

"Well, he isn't, and he better not come back. He may be big and tough but if he tangles with me, he'll be singing soprano in hell's choir."

"I should have done something to defend myself. I just thought...." She lost herself in regret. "I really screwed up."

"You want me to call your folks, or anyone?"

Shannon looked at her in alarm. "God, no! They don't need to know anything about any of this."

But they found out just the same and showed up to take her home the next afternoon.

"Is she all right enough to be going home?" Curtis asked the nurse who helped Shannon into the wheelchair for her excursion to the outside world.

"We watched her closely yesterday and last night. She's banged up and bruised, but she's OK."

"Come back home where you'll be safe," her father said as he helped her into the backseat of his Lincoln.

Melba added, "Start attending church again where you'll meet the right kind of people. We have a good singles group. None of this would have happened if you'd been going to church all this time."

Shannon loved them and smiled at them, but she said nothing other than, "Please take me to my place. I'll be fine."

Evie, who sat next to her on that huge backseat, met Curtis's eyes in the rearview mirror. "I'll take real good care of her, don't you worry. Teddy Stamp won't have a snowball's chance against me."

Curtis hesitated then smiled. "I believe you."

Melba did not appear as convinced as her husband, but she said no more.

"You stay away from Mom and Dad," Owen told Shannon on the phone later that same day. "If that snake Teddy comes back, I don't want my folks in any danger."

"Well, for God's sake, Owen, I don't want that, either. I don't plan to move in with Daddy and Mom. Give me credit for a little sense, would you?"

"Ha! A little sense. That's rich. Just see to it that you—"

She hung up on him, swore at the telephone, then burst into tears.

The break-up of her only marriage scarred Shannon physically but not in her heart or mind. She yearned for a normal life where she knew from one day to the next that she'd feel all right.

"Evie, will I ever be free of it all?" she asked that evening. "When I think my whole life might be like this…." She stared down at her coffee cup, seeing not the dark liquid but the weeks and months and years of her life stretching in endless bundles of mania and darkness. "I don't know if I can do it."

Evie put down her beer, reached over and clutched Shannon's hand. "Sure you can. And stop talking like that. I got my problems, too. We need to be here for each other, Shannon." She squeezed Shannon's fingers painfully. "Look at me. We need to be here for each other. Right?"

Shannon smiled, just that much. "Right."

Exactly three and a half days after Teddy Stamp beat up Shannon and left town, Curtis had a second heart attack. That one killed him.

In the Macon-Thierry Funeral Home the night of the visitation, Shannon stared at the remains of the one man who had been her champion and support. In his charcoal gray suit, white shirt and burgundy silk tie, Curtis Grady looked as if he could open his eyes any moment, sit up and comfort his weeping youngest daughter and the wife who sat nearby, mute and motionless.

Owen, in his designer suit, hovered helplessly at his mother's side, beseeching her to look at him, to take comfort from the Bible, to listen to the Reverend Yeager's counsel, to admire the mass of flowers and potted plants engulfing Curtis's bronze casket. She sat silently and twisted a linen handkerchief she had trimmed with tatted lace.

Donna, in a black silk suit and pink blouse, sat on a padded seat, legs crossed at the ankles. She tapped the carpet with the toe of a black leather pump as she gazed around the room. She sighed, shifted slightly, and sighed again. The only time Donna moved was when one of her friends approached her, and it was obvious to anyone who cared to look that the second-born Grady daughter would rather be shopping or having lunch. Craig lingered on the periphery of the family, a part of it, but generally unseen and unheard. Shannon often thought she and Craig could have been friends, if Donna had allowed it. But, of course, she never did and never would.

Shannon overheard Owen tell the minister that his older sister would arrive in time for the funeral tomorrow, but she was leaving immediately afterward. "She's very busy, I suppose."

Shannon knew better. She knew Julie would rather be with her friends and her lover in California than have to bear her grief within the suffocating judgment of this family. Even so, it seemed selfish that she couldn't give more than a couple of hours to the woman who had raised her.

Shannon knelt beside her mother's chair and took Melba's chilly fingers in her own.

"Mama, are you okay? Can I do anything for you?"

Melba stirred, pulled her hand from Shannon's, and drew closer to Owen. She shivered.

"Leave her alone, Shannon." Owen braced his arm more firmly around his mother. "Haven't you caused enough pain?"

She ignored him for the moment.

"Your hands are like ice, Mama. Shall I run home and get you a wrap?"

Melba glanced at her and the expression in her eyes caused Shannon's stomach to clench.

"Leave me be." She turned away.

"Mommy!"

"Get away, Shannon. I'm tired of thinking about you, I'm fed up with your problems, I'm sick of the sight of you. Owen, make her go."

Owen patted his mother's shoulder and got to his feet. He smirked as he took Shannon's upper arm.

"Out."

"But Owen—"

He hustled her away from their mother, up the aisle and out the chapel door. Once outside his grip bit into bruised flesh as he shook her arm.

"How do you have the nerve even to show up here after what you've done?"

She stared at him while something dark rumbled awake deep inside her mind. His face, so near her own, terrified her unreasonably.

"Wh-what are you talking about? I haven't done…."

"You killed him! You killed our father as surely as if you'd pumped him full of bullets."

"I didn't! How can you say such a thing?"

"All your life you've been a handful, demanding this, wanting that, asking for the moon and expecting Mom and Dad to give it to you. And God knows they tried. Then, when you didn't get your way, you'd throw these fits where you'd either stay in bed for days or act like a drunken whore. How old are you now, twenty-five? Twenty-six? You still act like a stupid teenager. You made our folks old before their time. You gave Mom a nervous breakdown when you got pregnant, and she's never been the same."

"But I—" she began.

"You drag home that low-life dog and send him over to beg money from the folks," Owen continued, "then you let him beat you up. Look at you, Shannon. You have a black eye, a split lip and bruises all over your arms. What'd you expect Mom and Dad to do? Welcome him into the family? The stress was too much for Dad. You knew he was sick, but you just kept on being Shannon until you killed him. So now Mom's all alone, there's a big business that needs our father's leadership, a town that depends on him and a church that needs his help. You fixed it for everyone, Shannon. I hope you're happy. Go home, don't come to the funeral. Stay away from Mom and let the rest of us grieve for our father."

He gave her a little push toward the parking lot then stomped back into the funeral home. Shannon stood unmoving, bewildered, and silent.

SHANNON

Shannon stared at the closed door, unable to believe that she'd just been thrown out of the funeral home. It took a minute to gather her scattered wits, then she drew herself together and went back inside.

Owen saw her and came charging up the aisle.

"What did I just tell you? Go home and don't come back here."

Shannon pointed at the casket. "He's my father, too. I have a right to be here."

"You don't have a right to cause trouble."

"I haven't done anything! I'm—"

Donna struggled out of the cushioned seat where she sat. "Mom doesn't want you here. Can't you understand that?"

Both siblings stood in the aisle, blocking her view and blocking her way.

"But he was my daddy, too! He loved me; he'd want me to be here."

"More than likely, he's glad to be shed of you, Shannon."

The group of mourners around them grew silent, listening ears turned, curious eyes focused, somber and knowing expressions fixed. They shifted, parting for Melba who joined her children. Dried-eyed and pale, she faced her youngest daughter.

"Shannon, you may go up to the casket and say your final good-byes, and then I want you to leave. Don't come to the funeral tomorrow."

"Mama, you don't think I killed him, do you? You aren't blaming me for this, are you?"

Melba closed her eyes and breathed deeply, as if she were searching for patience. She opened her eyes and said, "If you have a smidgen of respect for me or your father, then for once in your life abide by my wishes."

Shannon froze in place for a few seconds, then turned to her brother and sister whose faces bore identical scorn.

"You two shoveled all this garbage into her head, didn't you? She would never turn me away from Daddy's funeral unless the two of you filled her with poison against me. If Daddy was alive, he'd not put up with it. He loved me, and you know it. He loved me, and you can't stand it because you two hate me so much!"

By that time the chapel was completely silent except for the soft, doleful dirges of canned organ music. Shannon stared at her siblings with such venom that Owen fidgeted and looked away. Donna blotted perspiration from her round face with a tissue.

Shannon shifted her attention to Melba and looked into eyes that seemed stony and unfamiliar. The older woman met her gaze steadily, then turned away.

"Get out of my way," Shannon said to Owen as she pushed past him and went to the front of the parlor.

Everything faded as she stood beside her father's coffin. Did his spirit linger, observing the cruelty of his family, the heartbreak and desperation of his youngest daughter? Did he believe what they said about her, or did he know the truth? If he believed them, did he forgive her?

"Oh, Daddy," she whispered. "I didn't mean to hurt you. You know that don't you? I didn't mean it."

She gazed at his beloved face, lingering on his eyes, praying to whatever power that guided the universe to bring him back to life.

Open your eyes, Daddy. Tell me you love me.

But Curtis Grady stayed silent, eyes shut. When she rested her trembling hand on top of his folded ones, the fingers beneath hers remained stiff and cold.

"Daddy! I'm sorry for everything. Please forgive me. Don't be dead. Please don't be dead." By degrees she slid to the floor and once there, on her knees, she sobbed into her hands like a lost child.

"That's enough." Owen spoke above her. "It's time for you to go."

But she ignored him and clung to her grief, sobbing anguish and desperation, calling for her father to return.

"Stop making a scene," Owen said. "You're embarrassing yourself and everyone else."

He reached down and tried to pull her to her feet. When she resisted, he dragged her away from her resting place like a bag of filthy laundry.

She kicked at him. "Leave me alone, you bastard!" she screamed at him. "Let me cry for my daddy."

He shook her, hard. "You're upsetting Mom to the point she's going to collapse. I want you to go now and stay away, or I'll call the police to haul you out of here."

His words penetrated her misery and grief, piercing a deeper level of remorse. She turned her tear-stained face to Melba.

"Do you mean it, Mommy? Do you really want me to go?"

The woman bent her head as though saying a prayer, then lifted her face. "I'm weary unto death, and I can't deal with you anymore, Shannon. I'm sorry, but I simply cannot do it."

Shannon hesitated, waiting, hoping against hope that Melba would take back the words. Instead, the woman turned to Owen with a look of pleading and desperation. Shannon swallowed down sobs that begged to be released and wiped both eyes with the flat of her hands. She got to her feet.

"Forgive me. I didn't mean to hurt you." Melba turned her face away. Shannon acknowledged the gesture for what it was. "I'm sorry."

She left the chapel. That was the last time she saw her mother alive.

When Melba passed away less than three months after her husband, Shannon slipped into the funeral service and sat near the back. Knowing full well how she'd be received if recognized, she refused to mar the dignity of her mother's funeral service. In a simple black pantsuit and her bright hair hidden beneath a dark scarf, she went unnoticed. She left before it ended.

That evening, she wept beside a bank of fresh flowers mounded over the new grave. Her father's burial site, still raw, had settled a little with summer rain and the passage of a few weeks. The floral arrangements that adorned his grave had long since moldered into the earth, leaving the sun-faded silk facsimiles.

She rested there, draped across the polished new headstone that bore her both her parents' names and the date of her father's earthly departure. The blank space after her mother's birth date would soon be etched in. Melba had died in her sleep, a gentle passing away. The coroner had scrawled "heart failure" on her death certificate. Shannon accepted responsibility for the deaths of Curtis and Melba Grady. How else could a couple in their mid-sixties die of heart problems unless it was brought about by severe stress? And who had dumped extreme anxiety and constant worry on them?

Shannon shivered in the twilight of that September evening. The depression that had gripped her soon after she married Teddy Stamp still laid hold of her without the benefit of even a day's release. Evie's support was too weak; her concern and her worry fell short. Subsequent events, guilt, and shame added layers of such weight that Shannon felt suffocated.

She yearned to be free of it all. She recalled stories from Sunday school and church, the stories in which God not only expected, but demanded blood sacrifices for the sins of his creations. Only with blood atonements could anything ever be made right again. She had to make reparation for the rotten waste of her life.

As the evening deepened into night and the moon rose, its light found the thin steel of Curtis's old-fashioned straight razor that Shannon had secreted from the house while everyone was at Melba's graveside.

Spilling her blood on her parents' grave seemed fitting and proper, the epitome of contrition. The moonlight flashed, pale flesh separated, crimson blood pumped free. Maybe it would be enough, at last.

SHANNON

Shannon woke slowly in a white, quiet place where sunlight poured through a window.

She had always heard that heaven was full of light, that it was pure and white. After everything she'd done, though, there was no way she was in heaven. Besides, if Owen and Donna eventually wound up there—and they firmly believed their heavenly rewards were guaranteed—she hoped to avoid the place.

The light hurt her eyes and she closed them. Something about where she was right then seemed too familiar. Something....

Gradually a memory leaked into her senses, and she knew. I've been here before.

She forced aching eyes open to observe, to focus. She saw a stiff-looking armchair in the corner, a small two-drawer chest near it, no pictures on the walls. A dark-haired woman looked out the sun-filled window.

Shannon gazed at her a moment, then smiled, felt her dry lips crack.

"Now I know this isn't heaven, not with the two of us here."

Evie whirled. She looked haggard and old, weary smudges cupped her eyes, worry lines etched into her face.

"You're awake!" Evie rushed to Shannon's bedside and gathered her friend in a smothering embrace. "Thank God."

She winced at the pain roused by Evie's strong clutch but she bore it and tried to return the hug.

"You've been hooked up to tubes and wires and a thing to breathe for you for four days. They said it was touch and go, touch and go, and no one would tell me if you'd be all right. I kept believing the best, and I prayed and…and…then they took out the tubes and wires this morning and said you'd be all right and…and…" Evie burst into tears, wetting Shannon's neck and shoulder.

She wept for a bit then pulled back and stared into Shannon's eyes. "How do you feel?"

Shannon felt as though she'd marched a thousand miles uphill. "Tired. Beyond tired."

"You lost a lot of blood, you know. You'd have lost it all if a couple of boys looking for ghosts in the cemetery hadn't found you. You scared the bejesus out of them."

Shannon's heavy eyelids refused to stay open. "I'm sorry. Are they okay?"

"Sure. But I bet they won't be ghost-hunting again any time soon." Evie paused. "I'm glad they found you when they did, Shannon. If they'd been a couple of minutes later…."

"Yeah, well." She sighed and forced her eyes open. "Guess it wasn't my time."

"Hell, no! What were you thinking, leaving me alone in the world? You're the best friend I've ever had so don't you go wasting yourself when I need you here."

She reached out, and Evie took her hand.

"It works both ways. Get on the wagon and stay there, Evie Kendall." Shannon's voice was raw and rough. "If I go down, who'll hang on to me? There's times I can't hang on to myself, when the pain just bears down and down and it seems there'll be no end. I'd do anything to get away from it, Evie. You hear me? Anything!"

She stopped talking and lay utterly exhausted.

Evie's hands trembled. "Shh. It's okay. I know, and I understand. You just want to stop feeling, and if there's anything to lessen the hurt, to make you forget, to let you escape, you want it. You need it, you have to have it."

Their eyes met in deep and total understanding.

"Shannon, you were the first person in Woodrow who treated me like I had worth. Those folks at the shelter, the ones at the housing office, people I saw in the stores and on the street, they treated me like I didn't matter, as if I wasn't here. That day you came over to introduce yourself,

I thought, 'Here comes some skinny blond chick to tell me I need to try to look like her.' But you didn't. And if I never told you before, I'm tellin' you right now, I appreciated that you invited me over, gave me some tea and a sandwich, laughed at my jokes and basically became a sister to me. Thank you for that."

"I needed a friend, too, and you have been that. What was it Anne of Green Gables called Diana? Oh, yes. Bosom friends. That's what we are. Bosom friends."

"Just leave my bosom alone, and we'll be friends forever."

They laughed together then Evie said, "I have a deal for you." She squeezed Shannon's fingers. "I won't leave you if you won't leave me." Her hand tightened. "Okay?"

Shannon's clasp was weak as water.

"I can't keep you away from the bottle if you won't keep yourself away from it. You have to help yourself."

"Yeah. I know. I know. I'll try my damnedest. And you come to me when you're losing your grip. Deal?"

"Deal."

"And another thing," Evie said roughly, "if that bastard Teddy Stamp comes strolling back into your life, don't you dare take him back."

"Dear God. Give me credit for learning the hard way."

Evie studied her face a bit. "All right, then. But I'm just saying…."

"Me, too."

Owen strode into the room and halted abruptly. Evie let go of Shannon's hand but didn't move from the bedside.

He sneered. "You a lesbian now, Shannon?" He glared at them both. "A dyke and nutcase locked up in the psych ward. What else are you going to do to ruin the family name?"

"Hey!" Evie yelled. "Shut up. She's been through a hard time."

"She put herself through a hard time," he snapped. "Shannon, do you realize this latest escapade of yours was in today's newspaper, on the front page? 'Daughter of Woodrow's leading family attempts suicide for the second time.' And the day after Mom's funeral. How are the rest of us supposed to defend ourselves to the community against your stupidity?"

"I don't know, Owen. Maybe you could look at it as practice for

Judgment Day."

He blinked, then narrowed his eyes to slits. "I won't have to defend myself on that day. I may not be perfect, but at least I'm trying. At least I don't try to kill myself. At least I didn't have a kid out of wedlock. At least I'm not a queer. At least I'm a Christian."

"Right." Evie's voice dripped sarcasm.

He glanced at her. "What do you know about it?"

Evie's eyes flashed. The expression that immediately filled Owen's face said he wished he'd kept his mouth shut.

"Oh, I don't know. Isn't a Christian someone who follows Jesus? Seems to me Jesus would be concerned for his sister, that he'd love her in spite of illness or bad choices or dumb mistakes. Seems to me Jesus wouldn't let others suffer by laying them off their jobs right before Christmas just so he'll be sure to have enough money for a Caribbean cruise or a new Mercedes or a new house or more diamonds for his wife. But maybe I'm wrong. Maybe a Christian is someone like you, someone so full of rules and regulations and self-righteousness that Christ gets completely left out. But I don't know, Owen. What do I know about any of it?"

He stared at her, his narrow face ruddy.

"Go away, Owen," Shannon said. "I need to rest now."

She closed her eyes, but when she realized he hadn't moved, she opened them again and added, "Don't make me call the police to throw you out of my hospital room. That wouldn't look good in tomorrow's paper."

His mouth opened and shut like a dying fish. Then, face pinched and spine stiff, he left.

Evie clapped her hands and laughed. "You shut him up, but good."

Shannon stared at the empty doorway, lost in memories. "When I was little, Owen liked me well enough. At least, I thought he did. He bought me little presents, took me to McDonald's, read me stories, things like that. Then, after a while, he got kinda mean, started bossing me around the way he does everyone else. Of course, I never did anything right, or good enough, or soon enough, and he'd tell me off."

"Yeah, I can see him being that way. He's an asshole."

Shannon continued. "When I got older, Mom always backed him. I'd feel stupid and incompetent."

"It's obvious your brother doesn't care about others."

"He only cares about appearances or what other people think of him…the right people, I mean. I guess what the lower-class thinks doesn't matter to him. Today is probably the third or fourth time in my whole life that I've told him off." She paused. "It kind of bothers me."

"Why? You needed to stand up to him."

"I know." She plucked at the sheet, thinking. "But it seems like maybe the other shoe is going to fall. Like something bad'll happen because I spoke up."

Evie frowned. "You're afraid of him?"

Shannon shrugged, still watching her fingers pleat and smooth the sheet. "Maybe. A little bit, I guess. I mean, he's my big brother. He's thirteen years older than me—he's always been an authority figure, so yeah, maybe I am afraid of him."

"You're afraid of him because he's a bully. Don't you know that when you stand up to a bully, he turns into a coward?"

Shannon thought about it and a slow smile dawned. "I believe you're right."

"I've been around bullies and dickheads all my life. Knock the shit out of them one time and they run home to mommy with their tails between their legs."

As Shannon pondered her friend's words, weariness crept so deeply into every cell that by then she felt herself drifting.

"What d'you know about that?" she murmured, eyes closing. "Owen's afraid of me."

On a warm morning in early June the following year, Shannon opened her mailbox to find a bright yellow envelope among the circulars and bills.

She extracted a stiff canary-colored card on which was written, "You are cordially invited to the Ten Year Reunion of the Woodrow High School Class of 1995. Family picnic to begin at 11 on Saturday morning, July 8. Formal dinner and dance for classmates and spouses, 8 o'clock Saturday evening at the Woodrow Country Club. RSVP."

"So are you going?" Evie asked later when Shannon showed her the invitation.

"I don't know. It would be nice to see everyone again, but I'm not sure any of my old friends would attend. I mean, none of us were the type for a family picnic or a formal dinner."

"After ten years, you don't know what they're like. I bet one of 'em is a preacher, another one is a cop and at least two of them sell insurance."

Shannon laughed. "More than likely one of them is in prison, another one steals car parts and at least two of them cook and sell meth."

"Think so?" Evie laughed with her, then added, "You won't know unless you go."

"Ah, well. I've seen a few classmates around town now and again, but I think most of them moved away long ago. The ones who stayed probably work for Owen, the poor shmucks."

Evie wrinkled her nose. "Probably. His company is the only game in town, unless you want to work at Walmart or one of the grocery stores."

They were quiet for a while, then Shannon said, "I'm having good days right now. The reunion is a few weeks away. If I'm still feeling okay, I might go."

"What do you mean 'if I'm still feeling okay.' Are you taking your meds, Shannon?"

"God, Evie! You sound like one of those two-dollar therapists at the clinic."

"Don't get mad. I'm just sayin'."

"I know." She shoved down her annoyance, reminded herself that Evie's concern was genuine. And any scolding she received was deserved. After all, for the last few years she'd played with her meds, taking them, not taking them, taking more than she should, or skipping doses.

She smiled at Evie. "Thanks for caring And I just meant that I don't trust feeling normal to last. It's been a while since I've had any bad mood swings, but still…."

"Trust the Copamin, girl. Trust it, okay?"

"Yeah. I do. But I still don't know if I want to go to the reunion."

Evie lit up a cigarette. She blew out a huge cloud. "Maybe you'll run into an old hook-up."

"No doubt."

"Party girl that you were."

"Yep." Then, "You think they'll still think of me that way?"

Evie shrugged. "You'll never know unless you go."

Shannon sighed. "Yeah. I guess it would be good for me to face down that part of my past."

Evie took another deep drag and stared at Shannon. "That's what I like about you. You got guts."

The reunion picnic was pretty much what Shannon expected, young children and infants wagged around like so much bounty to be admired.

Evie had been right, too. Most of the goths and the punks had metamorphosed into working-class married couples with current conservative hairstyles, blue jeans and T-shirts. They embraced Shannon carefully, as if she was fragile, asking, "How are you feeling these days" or "Things going better for you now?"

She needn't have worried about her reputation haunting her. No one seemed to care about that. They chatted about old times, the good times, agreed with each other that they'd lock their kids in the attic until they'd turned forty if any of them ever tried any of the shenanigans of their parents.

Eventually, though, conversation turned to child-rearing, homebuilding, fashion or sports, and by mid-afternoon, Shannon was thoroughly bored. She decided to go home, see if Evie wanted to have supper and watch a video.

As she walked toward her car a burly bear of a man approached her in the parking lot. Dark hair, neatly cut with a bit of a curl, blue jeans and plain, white Oxford-style shirt.

"Shannon."

She stopped and smiled at him.

"Hi," she said, hiding the fact she did not recognize him.

"Remember me?"

The hint of shyness in his coffee brown eyes triggered the barest of memory, but nothing solid.

"Uh…I think so…maybe…."

He grinned. "Nah, you don't know me. I've changed a little bit. I'm Dunn. Dunn Bradshaw."

She processed the name, recalled the boy, and felt her eyes pop.

"Dunn Bradshaw!" She looked him up and down. "You were…you used to be…."

He laughed. "I was the bashful beanpole you danced with at the Freshman/Sophomore Dance."

Shannon sorted through her recollections, the dances and parties, the boys she danced with, the boys she played with.

Dunn had been too tall for the out-of-style suit he had worn, the only boy in a suit that night, and painfully aware of his low rank. Knobby wrists, socks showing below his pants cuffs, scuffs on his loafers that shoe polish couldn't disguise. She'd flirted with him, danced with him, led him to a place beneath the bleachers. Like many boys his age, she'd been his first, and he had been eager, awkward, grateful. Beyond that she really had little memory of him.

"Well, how are you, Dunn? You've grown up…and filled out!" She looked him up and down and liked what she saw. He was neat and clean, fully male but not rough and tumble like a honky-tonk barfly.

He laughed again, shifted his feet as if he felt awkward.

"I'm doing good. Still live on the farm but got my own place, a little single-wide near my folks. It's nice out there, but I'm thinkin' of moving into town one of these days. Maybe get a job at the factory."

Grady Wood Products was the only factory in the area. She hoped Dunn didn't think she had any influence in getting him a job. In fact, she'd hate to see him go to work there. Since Curtis's death, Owen and Craig ran the place and, from what Shannon had heard, the business was not the same. Hours cut, benefits dropped, older employees let go too early.

"You think you'd like living in town?" she asked him. "I mean, you've lived on the farm all your life, haven't you?"

"A couple of years in the military after graduation then back to the cows. I'm ready for a change. Besides, there's not much money to be made farming these days. I'm tired of being dirt poor, and I'd like to help my folks."

"Well, that's great. That's great. I hope you make it."

"Are you…are you doing all right? I don't mean to pry or nothing, but I know you've been through some hard times. I, uh, I read about you in the paper…and, well, I'm sorry to hear about you losing both of your folks so close together that way. It must've been mighty hard on you and your family. I thought about calling you a couple of times, but oh, I dunno, I just thought maybe I shouldn't."

"Well, why not? I would have loved hearing from you."

His face lit up. "Really?"

"Yes. Really."

Theirs was the first genuine conversation she'd had all day. She felt his warmth, and tears stung her eyes. She touched his arm.

"Thank you, Dunn, for caring. I really appreciate it."

He smiled, ran the fingers of one hand through a mop of curly dark hair.

"You always were nice to me. You never made fun of me or my family, and…well, I always thought you were the sweetest girl in school."

"Why, Dunn!"

He gave her a lopsided smile she instantly recognized. It was that smile which called to memory the gangly boy who always seemed on the outside edge of every school group and function, his patched jeans and faded shirts too short, his hair either too long or skinned too short by a cheap barber. She remembered the popular crowd calling him "Dung."

"I knew things weren't easy for you back then, even if you came from money and your family owned the town. But you always smiled at me in the hall. That time that we…you know…it was just that once but, well, it meant a lot that you liked a poor boy from the sticks enough to…."

She felt her face burn, wishing she recalled more of their single encounter that had meant so much to him. As it was, the best she could remember was the lovable, tongue-tied boy he had been.

"You were a special guy."

"I appreciate you saying so, but I was just me. A kid who didn't know anything."

She laughed. "You knew enough." His face reddened and to take away the awkward moment, she said, "Are you leaving or just now getting here?"

"Just got here. We had some trouble at home with a broken fence line and some of the heifers got out." He glanced toward the park.

"I was just leaving, actually," she said.

His gaze came back to her. "Oh yeah? Not having a good time?"

"I just don't feel comfortable here," she said.

"I know what you mean. The main reason I came was just to see what changes ten years had brought. None of 'em will remember me."

On the fringe of the gathering, Shannon and Dunn studied their old classmates.

A singular high-pitched trilling laugh came from a group near the drinking fountain. Babie Winton, who'd been the cute, petite head cheerleader, hadn't modified her laugh in the past decade.

"Babie Winton bleached her hair," he said. "And Donny Fox doesn't look the same at all since he got Lasik eye surgery. Remember his glasses?"

"Oh, lord, yes. A different pair every week, seemed like."

"In all colors and shapes. He wanted to be like Elton John. I hear he plays the piano at the First Baptist Church in Green Springs, Kansas."

"'Amazing Grace' probably has a brand-new sound."

"Hey." He lowered his voice and nudged her, dipped his head toward a willowy, dark-haired beauty. "Take a look at Maddie Hickman."

She followed his gaze and stared. "Really? That can't be her. She used to be so mousy and bookish. She graduated at the head of the class, but I don't think she's been back since." She squinted hard. "You sure that's her?"

"I swear it."

She scoffed. "Now, Dunn. If Maddie isn't a doctor or professor in some big city somewhere then she's probably a nun. She loved church."

He looked at Shannon, his eyes dancing with laughter. "I'm telling you, that's her. Underneath those baggy clothes she used to wear was a smokin' hot body."

"How do you know?"

He guffawed. "Take my word for it. Now, look at her real close."

He was grinning, watching the young woman flirt with a couple of buttoned-up business types and a balding jock who had gone soft around the middle.

"I hear she dances," he said.

"Oh? As in ballet, or as in exotic?"

He laughed. "As in Midnight at Spanky's over in Champion."

She gawked at him. "I don't believe it. Besides, I never heard a word about it until this minute."

"I swear it's true." He raised his right hand.

She gave him a teasing grin, felt a bit of her old flirting self resurface. "You wouldn't know that from personal experience or anything?"

"Who me? When do I ever have time to get off the farm?"

They chuckled together, then sobered and gazed steadily at each other. Shannon found herself completely drawn to him, wanted to be with him more than she'd wanted a man in a long time. But beyond the sexual attraction that thrummed through her blood, lay something deeper and more solid. In all her life, the men she'd known, with the exception of her father, had been users, abusers, takers and bastards. Dunn Bradshaw was like none of them. Why hadn't she paid him more attention when they were in school?

"No kiddin', Shannon," he said, breaking into her thoughts, "you always treated me real decent, like I was somebody, like I didn't smell like the barn or something."

"I was a wild child, I admit, but I tried to be nice to people."

He met and held her gaze. "You were great."

Shannon did not want to stray into anything that was more personal than what they'd already discussed. A relationship with a guy right now? She wasn't ready; didn't know if she ever would be. But a new friendship would be good.

"How committed are you to staying at this reunion?" she asked.

"I'm not. Like I said, I just wanted to see what some of these clowns looked like ten years later."

"Well, we got 'em beat."

"You bet."

"And I say, let's get out of here and go see Evie."

"Can't say as I know anybody named Evie, but if you're going, I'm willing."

"You'll like her, I think. And we'd have a lot more fun."

He grinned. "Let's go. Your car or my truck? On second thought, I had my pickup out in the pasture earlier today. It's still got cow shit on it."

"Then let's take my car."

"If you'll stop at Melvin's Package Store, I'll get us some beer," he said as they walked toward her car several yards away.

"Maybe just some Dr. Pepper or something," she said.

"You a tee-totaler these days?"

"Not exactly, but let's leave alcohol out tonight. Okay?"

SHANNON

"Did we go to school with this Evie chick?" Dunn asked as he settled into Shannon's Corolla, now six years old and its blue paint a little faded. "I don't remember anyone named Evie."

"She moved here from Chicago a few years ago."

"Why?"

Shannon shrugged. "Said she wanted to try small town living." She did not tell him that Evie had done time in prison. "She's the best friend I've ever had."

Dunn smiled. "We all need friends. I don't have a lot of them, but I've been blessed—I guess that's the right word for it—with a great family. Great-Grandpa still lives with us but he's gettin' feeble. Mom cries when she thinks about putting him in a nursing home someday. She says she hopes he just dies in his sleep while he's still among the living. I got three nieces and a nephew and another nephew on the way, if the doctor knows what he's talking about."

"That's great, Dunn," Shannon said and heard the wistfulness in her own voice. She hadn't seen her nieces and nephews since Curtis died, and then it had been at a distance at the funeral home.

The drive to her apartment complex was short and they pulled into the parking lot less than five minutes later. She turned off the ignition and said, "Funny I haven't seen you since we graduated. Woodrow is a pretty small place."

"I've seen you around a few times."

"You have! When and where?"

"Here 'n there. Mostly out at the Share Center."

"You should've said something."

He shrugged and looked embarrassed.

"I volunteer at the Share Center sometimes when I'm not ... that is, when...." She stopped. No sympathy from anyone tonight, thank you very much. She was feeling normal and cheerful and planned to stay that way. "I like helping, and they're always willing to let me." She smiled brightly, grabbed her purse and the door handle. "That's my place." She pointed to the stoop with potted geraniums in the window box and a dried wreath of sunflowers and daisies on the front door. Hers was the only apartment with any kind of adornment. It always looked cozy and welcoming.

"Nice," Dunn said. "You got it fixed real pretty."

"Thanks. I love home decorating. I used to think I might study interior decorating but then I didn't."

"Maybe you will someday," he said.

"Maybe." There was an awkward silence for a bit. She was glad Dunn was too nice to pursue the subject. "Evie lives across the way," she said. "I'll throw some eats together and we'll go over there. It's her turn to play hostess. Come on in." She unlocked the front door and they went inside. "Evie won't be surprised I came home this quick. She predicted how the reunion would turn out."

She smiled at Dunn as he stood in the center of the room and gave his surroundings an openly appreciative scrutiny.

"But I bet she didn't expect you to bring home an old friend," he said. "Sure you don't want me to run to the package store for Bud or Jack? We're having a party, aren't we?"

She lost her smile. "I'm sure."

"Okay, then. Want me to help you with the food?"

"Sure. I've got some guacamole in the fridge, and I'll throw together a fruit salad, a veggie plate, and some sandwiches. Would you get out the bread and cold cuts? Evie will have all kinds of chips and cookies. She loves junk food."

"Hey, I like her already."

A short time later, they loaded up a laundry basket with food, and Dunn carried it across the parking lot. Evie stood in the doorway, smoking, watching Dunn without the hint of a smile.

"Who're you?" she said around the cigarette as she held open the door for them.

Shannon scowled at her. "Evie! For God's sake. You're acting like a security guard. This is an old friend from high school. Dunn Bradshaw."

Evie raked a long study up and down him then back up to his face.

"You can set the food on the table there." She shifted her gaze to Shannon and spoke volumes with her expression.

"Stop looking at me like that, Evie. Dunn and I have known each other since forever. We went through all twelve grades right here in the good ol' Woodrow Public School system."

"Uh huh."

"He's not another Teddy Stamp, if that's what you're thinking."

"That's exactly what I'm thinking," Evie replied. "Nice of you to read my mind."

Dunn stood next to the table and glowered at the women. His own features were none too friendly right then. "I resent being compared to that shithead."

"You know Teddy?" Both women said in surprise.

"Hell, yeah. Biggest loser in the county. You did right to kick him out, Shannon."

Her mouth wagged a couple of times. "How'd you know about me and Teddy."

"Woodrow is a small-ass town. Nothin' stays a secret very long."

How many secrets did he—or anyone else, for that matter—know when she never spoke of them aloud? The rest of her family hid their own mysteries and bits of shame behind white-washed façades. How did Dunn know she'd kicked out Teddy when she didn't remember kicking him out; she remembered very little about the night he left.

"I'm just glad he's gone," she said lamely.

"Me, too." Dunn and Evie in unison.

"And I ain't nothin' like him." Dunn fixed an angry look on Evie.

"Of course you aren't," Shannon agreed. "Evie's too much a mother hen sometimes. She didn't mean anything by that. Did you, Evie?"

The other woman shrugged as if she had no interest in the conversation. The three of them stood in an awkward silence, then Shannon blurted, "I forgot the gherkins!" and dashed out of the apartment.

By the time she returned with her friend's favorite pickles, a jar of black olives, and a block of pepper jack cheese, Evie and Dunn were sitting on the sofa, laughing together. Shannon sighed in deep relief…until she saw cans of Budweiser in their hands.

"I thought no drinking tonight." She looked at Evie uneasily.

"I'm sorry," Dunn said. "I thought you didn't want me to go buy a case of booze, so when Evie offered…."

"It's a party. I'll take it easy, I promise." Evie smiled, set the can on her scarred coffee table and tapped the top of it with her index finger. "Still half-full." When Shannon said nothing, Evie grinned at Dunn and jerked her head toward their friend. "Now who's being Mother Hen?"

He looked from one woman to the other then set his can aside and said nothing.

"So you two friends now?"

"We're working on it," Evie said.

"We both want what's best for you," he said, "and that seems a pretty good starting point."

"And guess what? Dunn says he heard Teddy is in jail out in Washington state. Ain't that great?"

"Really? It's the best place for him. Dunn, for someone who doesn't get off the farm, you sure know a lot of gossip."

He laughed, a rich, ripe, deep sound that brought a smile to her heart. "My sister Tammy is a hairdresser at Wanda's Styles. They hear everything in that place."

By dark, friends filled the small apartment. Most of those friends drove old cars, wore second-hand clothes, had been married at least twice, and had kids living with someone else. Everyone but Shannon smoked, and they turned the air opaque. They liked country music, and they liked it loud. Most had toted in beer, whiskey, wine, or vodka. They dove into the food with voracious appetites, teasing Shannon about the fruit and vegetables, lauding Evie for the chips and sweets.

At ten-thirty someone knocked on the front door. Shannon stood close enough to hear it over the noise. She opened the door and light spilled over the wizened little woman from next apartment over.

"Can you keep the racket down? I can't sleep."

"I'm sorry, Mrs. Dixon. I'll tell them to be quieter."

"There's rules here about this sort of thing, you know."

"I'll take care of it."

The old woman glared at her, stretched sideways to see into the apartment. "I'll call the cops."

"You don't have to do that. I'll take care of it, Mrs. Dixon."

"I know your type. I'll call the cops if I have to."

Shannon did not know what else to say to smooth the old lady's ruffled feathers. She smiled, nodded, and closed the door.

"Guys!" she yelled. "Hey, you guys!"

Dunn saw what she was trying to do, and his piercing whistle hushed everyone at once.

"We have elderly neighbors here, and they need their rest," Shannon said. "Keep the noise down, will you?"

The volume dropped briefly, raucous laughter turning to chuckles and snickers. Someone turned off the music. As the food supply dwindled, the flow of booze increased.

The noise level elevated again, and before long, Evie forgot her promise to Shannon.

SHANNON

Shannon had seen her friend stumbling drunk before. Dazed, incoherent, loud, funny, mouthy, angry, foolish. "I don't give a shit what they think," she'd slurred more than once about a random person she'd insulted. "They can get outta my way."

But since the night Shannon had nearly ended her life on her parents' graves, Evie's drinking had been minimal, a quiet nursing of beer or whiskey, as if the drink was an aid to conversation or a mere social prop while she watched out for Shannon.

That night, Evie knocked back drinks with enthusiasm. Shannon emptied ashtrays, picked up bottles and cans, plied the partiers with what little food remained, and constantly admonished everyone to keep the noise down. She also kept a wary eye on Evie.

"How about a Dr. Pepper?" she said when Evie grabbed another can of Budweiser.

"Nah. I'm all righ'."

"She's a big girl," Dunn murmured to her a little later. "Why are you trying to stop her from having fun?"

"Because she's an alcoholic."

"I didn't know that."

"She's done really well for quite some time." Shannon felt like crying. "I hate to see her fall off the wagon like this."

Dunn eyed the woman who staggered toward the refrigerator. She knocked into the table and scattered its contents, then laughed uproariously with two men in cowboy hats when one of the grabbed her.

"Hands off my ass, Rex Jason!" she yelled, striking at him playfully.

The next time someone came to the door, the knock was the thunder of threat and demand.

"Woodrow Police Department. Open the door!"

On the sofa between her current boyfriend and a girl who'd passed out an hour ago, Toni shrieked, "The cops?" She doubled over with laughter. "Are we a bunch of criminals? Evie, you crook!"

"Lemme go, Rex Jason," Evie shouted, slapping his hands away for real this time. She stumbled to the door and flung it open before Shannon could get there.

"Wha…?" She squinted at the uniformed man on her doorstep. "Why you here? We ain't doin' nothin'."

"We're getting complaints from your neighbors. You need to—"

Evie flung out a hand in a broad beckoning gesture.

"Tell 'em to join the party. We got food." She lolled her head back and looked blearily at Shannon. "We got food, ain't we?"

"Listen," the officer said, "just keep the racket down. We don't want to have to come back here."

"Yeah, yeah, yeah." She slammed the door in his face and turned to her guests. "You guys shut up 'cause I don't want no cops at my party." She slapped Dunn on the shoulder. "Dunndee, gimme another beer, wouldja?"

As before, the chatter and raucous laughter diminished a little, but in less than ten minutes, the noise level climbed. Glass shattered, and Evie's smoke-filled apartment became more like a neighborhood joint than a place to call home. She was beyond reason by then, railing at the world one minute and blubbering on someone's shoulder the next. Shannon watched helplessly.

"Evie, let's take a walk, you and me and Dunn?" She gave him a pleading look, and he nodded. "Let's get some fresh air and—"

"And leave my guests? Absolutely nope. No way, Jose. Nuttin' doin', Charley. You got him tonight." She pointed with the hand that snuggled the brown neck of a beer bottle. "He's a big boy; he can take care o' you. Tonight," she leaned forward into Shannon's personal space, "you ain't gonna cut open your wrists 'cause my new friend ol' Dunndee is here to watch over you and ol' Evie can relax."

Before Shannon could speak, someone yelled from the kitchen.

"Hey, Evie! Ain't you got any clean glasses in this dump?"

"Ah, go fuck yourself, you four-eyed greaser!"

"What'd you call me, you stringy-haired old twat?"

"Don't talk to her like that!" Rex Jason shouted.

"You wan' stop me, li'l man?"

Rex Jason, red-haired and wiry and always itching for a fight, leaped off his chair and climbed over the coffee table, shoving Toni and anyone else in his path out of his way. In a blur of blue jeans, T-shirts and ball caps the room burst into chaos. Curses and shouts rose above the laughter until no sound seemed to exist but rage and destruction. Shannon ducked a punch by mere millimeters.

"Get down and stay out of their way," Dunn yelled in her ear. He pushed her down.

Over and over Evie screamed, "Get outta my house, you motherfuckers, I'll kill you all."

The front door burst open and three blue uniforms scattered into the group like birdshot to break up the fights.

"This party is over!" one of the cops yelled.

"Outta here, motherfuckers!" Evie screamed again. She waved her arms wildly and seemed to be everywhere at once.

"Stand back," an officer cautioned her.

She charged and he raised his stick.

Shannon grabbed his arm. "Don't hit her! She doesn't know what she's—hey! Let go of me!" She struggled but he had her in a grip so tight pain raged through her arms and hands. He jerked her arms behind her and slapped cuffs on her wrists.

"Hey," Dunn yelled. "What're you doing? She's done nothing wrong."

"Assaulting a police officer is a felony. She's going to jail."

"C'mon, man. She didn't assault anyone. She's been trying to keep everything under control here."

"Well, she didn't do a very good job, did she?"

He shoved Shannon out the front door and toward the patrol car with its striating lights.

"I didn't assault you!" she protested.

"Ma'am, you put your hands on me in a threatening manner."

"I did not. I was trying to stop you from hitting Evie with that stick."

"And now you admit to impeding a police officer in his duty. You got any guns, knives, needles, or weapons of any kind on you?"

"Of course not. But—"

As he patted her, searching for God knows what, Shannon used a tactic she long ago had sworn never to use.

"Do you know who I am?"

"No. Why don't you tell me?"

His snotty voice grated on her. "I'm Shannon Grady. My father was Curtis Grady and my brother is Owen Grady."

The officer froze. Then, "You got something to prove that?"

"You can ask anyone in that apartment. Or we can go to my place right over there, and I'll get my driver's license."

He glanced across the parking lot toward her place. "You telling me that one of the Gradys live in low-income housing?"

"That's what I'm saying."

He sneered. "Yeah. And I'm Bill Gates. I just work for the Woodrow PD for kicks. Now, listen to this: I'm placing you under arrest for assaulting a police officer and for interfering with the lawful duties of a police officer. You have the right to remain silent…"

"Ask anyone here who I am. You want to see my driver's license? It's in my apartment—"

He shoved her toward the cruiser, ignoring her pleas. His voice went on, a litany of familiar terms she'd heard only on television, but he put her in the backseat and Shannon no longer heard him. The mere fact that cops were hauling her to jail blotted out her senses.

The Woodrow City Jail was a small brick building, old and smelly, cluttered and dirty. Shannon sat on a metal chair in the holding room and waited to be booked. She'd been there for a while, and she ached all over.

"Can't you take these handcuffs off of me?" she asked the old man behind the desk.

"Nope." He didn't look up from whatever paper he was reading.

"Please. My shoulders hurt. My hands feel numb."

"Shoulda thought of that before you hit a police officer."

"I didn't hit anyone!"

He said nothing.

"What about my phone call?"

"Later."

She glanced at the clock. "That's what you told me two hours ago."

No response.

"I have to use the bathroom."

"Hold it."

"Please. This isn't right."

He looked up. "Boo hoo. Be quiet, willya, or we'll put you in a cell instead of in here. And this here is a lot nicer than the holding cell."

Shannon slouched down in her chair. No one was going to help, obviously.

The officer who arrested her walked past. He stopped at the desk, scribbled something on a clipboard then looked over his shoulder at her.

"You still here?"

"No. I went home."

"Smart ass."

"Will you please do something? This waiting is ridiculous."

"You aren't the only one in place and we're shorthanded." He turned to her. "What'd you say your name was again? Oprah Winfrey?"

"Shannon Grady."

He turned to the old man.

"She look like a Grady to you?"

"A Grady?" The old man gave her a once over. "Nope. And neither did that Black boy who claimed to be a Grady last month."

"Look, call Vernon Fletcher," Shannon said. "He knows me."

The officer got that frozen look again. "The chief knows you?"

"I just said."

She hadn't wanted to say it at all. Owen and Vernon were close friends, and it seemed likely that if Vernon got involved she might go to McPherson, or worse. If it was up to Owen, he'd send her to the lock-up for life. On the other hand, maybe Vernon would help get her out, or at least speed up this farce of booking.

"I'll be back," the officer said, going down a darkened hallway.

Shannon tipped her head back and rested it against the wall. She stretched her legs straight out and arched her spine. Nothing helped her discomfort. She closed her eyes.

"Sit up straight there. You're creatin' a hazard."

She popped open one eyelid then the other. She glanced around. "There's not a soul in this godforsaken place but you and me. You gonna get off that chair and walk over here in front of me?"

"Sit up."

She struggled upright. "God."

The ancient round clock on the wall opposite read 3:18.

"I have been here forever. And I have to pee."

"And I got bunions. Cry me a river."

The arresting officer came back. "Come with me."

He grabbed her arm and escorted her down the hall. He opened a door to a small dingy office and pointed to another metal chair.

"Sit there."

He left and shut the door behind him. The room, with its peeling pea-green walls, was lighted by a single bare bulb hanging from the ceiling, and smelled of stale sweat and cigarette smoke. The desk was piled with folders, loose papers, three coffee cups, a small pizza box, a pint fruit jar holding an assortment of pens, an open face-down paperback book, and a full ashtray.

Shannon closed her eyes and tried to imagine she lounged in a fresh clean room with cream colored walls and white overstuffed furniture. She pretended a vase of fragrant red roses perfumed the air and soft music surrounded her. She had almost reached the place in her mind when the door burst open.

She opened her eyes and saw the heavily-jowled face of Vernon Fletcher, Woodrow's chief of police. Without his uniform and gun, he looked like any other tubby, middle-aged man.

"Well, well," he said as he closed the door. "What do we have here at four o'clock in the morning?"

"Tell them you know me, Vernon," she said. "Tell them to take these damned cuffs off me and let me go to the bathroom."

"So, Miss Shannon Grady." He did not take his eyes off her as he rounded his desk and lowered himself in the worn-out brown swivel chair behind it. "What have you got yourself into this time?"

"I didn't do anything!"

"That's not what I hear."

"Come on. I saw that officer raise his stick to my friend and all I did was grab his arm. I didn't hit him, I didn't do anything else. I just did not want him to hurt my friend."

Vernon leaned back, peaked his fingers, and looked at her over them as he tapped the tips against his mouth.

"Owen isn't going to like this," he said.

"I know that."

"All his life, you've caused your brother all kinds of trouble."

"So he says."

"So does everyone else, because it's the truth."

"Okay, then. Whatever. Just take these cuffs off me, please."

"Don't you want to go home?"

"Of course I do, but that's not going to happen, is it?"

He leaned forward. The chair squeaked.

"I wouldn't be so sure. You see, Owen's a good friend. To me, to this town. I hate to see anything mess that up for him. Having a sister in the lock-up isn't exactly conducive to good PR. Is it?"

She felt a stirring of hope. "Are you going to let me go home?"

He got up, pulled a set of keys out of his pocket.

"Stand up."

She did.

"Turn around."

She turned. A moment later the cuffs let go.

"Thank you." She rubbed her wrists. "May I use the bathroom?"

He opened his door and pointed to next room on the left.

"Right there. You got someone to pick you up?"

She shook her head. "You mean you didn't call Owen?"

"No, and I'm not going to. I see no reason to bother him with this."

"Thank you, Vernon. I don't want to have to listen to him harp at me."

"I didn't do it for you, Muffin Cakes. I did it for Owen. Who do you want to take you home?"

She couldn't ask Evie, even if Evie had a car.

"Dunn Bradshaw," she said.

"I'll call 'im for you." He started to walk away then paused. "And Shannon. Don't ever do something like this again. I can only bend the law so much."

Thirty minutes passed before Dunn arrived, looking somewhat disheveled and more than a little concerned.

"God, Shannon, I tried to get you out of here earlier but of course I couldn't, the law bein' what it is. I wish now that I'd stayed, even if I'd stayed out in the parking lot all this time. Are you all right?"

He walked her to his pickup, his hand protectively around her arm.

"Yeah," she said, but she wasn't. Something had happened in that old building and she needed to process it.

As Dunn drove her back to the apartment, she stared unseeing out the window. A blackness, creeping from the gutter of her mind, reminding her, reminding her....

"He called me Muffin Cakes."

SHANNON

"Who called you Muffin Cakes?"

"Vernon Fletcher."

"Why would he call you that?"

She shook her head, studied the dark sky outside the window. A thin line of lighter gray shone in the east.

"I don't know. I hardly know him. I mean, 'Muffin Cakes' is something you'd call a baby…or a sweetheart…." She shuddered. "But it's not sweet. I know that much. It's not a sweet name."

She was shrinking inside herself, bit by bit. She tried to shake off the feeling. Hadn't she resolved to stay on top of these moods, analyze and control them before they took over? Wasn't she taking her medication faithfully? Look how calmly she'd coped at the reunion. At the party last night she did not go crazy with the need to indulge. Even during those awful hours at the police station, she'd kept the darkness away.

"Thank you for coming back into town and picking me up, Dunn. I didn't know who else to call. I sure didn't want to get anyone else from the party down there. No telling what would have happened."

"I was glad to do it. That's what friends are for…and I hope we're gonna be good friends."

She smiled at him. "I hope so, too. You can't have too many good friends."

"Evie's sleeping it off, I bet," Dunn said a minute later as he pulled his pickup into a parking place near Shannon's apartment.

"I'm sure she is." Shannon stared out the window, seeing nothing in the darkness but her own worry. "She won't remember last night, you know."

"She blacks out?"

She nodded. "She's not done it in a long time, but when she drinks like that, she gets surly and picks fights, sometimes with complete strangers."

"Does she pick fights with you?"

"No. She's always good to me, maybe because I'm the first person who's ever treated her right."

She paused, gave him a small smile. "We try to take care of each other, Evie and me. Like last night, we both fail miserably at times, but we keep trying."

"I'll help in any way I can, Shannon. Call me when you need to. All right?"

"Thanks, Dunn. I will." She reached across the seat and hugged him. "And thanks again for bringing me home. I owe you one." She paused. "Would you like to come in for some coffee?"

He looked at the clock on the dashboard. The pale light from the instrument panel and the pickup's headlights painted his face golden and shone in his eyes.

"Thanks, but I gotta get home and start the milking. Cows wait for no man." He reached across her and opened the passenger door. As he started to straighten, he paused, looked into her eyes. For a moment, Shannon thought he meant to kiss her. Which might have felt nice but also would have been awkward. She didn't want him to think she was ready for that sort of thing with him or anyone else.

She gave him another smile and slid out the door.

"I'll bake you a pie."

He grinned. "Apple is my favorite. With a big ol' slice of cheddar on top while it's hot."

"I'll remember." She slammed the door, winced at the sound it made in the early morning air and watched him drive away.

Mid-afternoon, Evie gave her customary three raps on the door and opened it without waiting for an invitation. Puffy-faced and red-eyed, she looked as if she'd slept on the shoulder of a busy highway.

"Hey," she mumbled as she sat at the table.

"Good afternoon. How you feeling?"

"Like shit."

"Um hm" Shannon eyed her sharply. "And you look like shit, too."

"I don't care. I just got up. You got coffee?"

"I will in a sec. How about some toast?"

"Coffee."

Evie said nothing and did not move while Shannon made fresh coffee. She set a steaming mug in front of her friend then sat down across from her.

"Some party, huh?" Evie said after she'd sipped half the cup in silence.

"You could say that, yes."

"I don't remember much past Toni showing up with her latest." She frowned. "Was Rex Jason there or is he still in the clink?"

"He was there."

"We have enough food?"

"No."

Evie took a long drink. "Dammit. Every time I have a party the bastards eat me out of house and home." She finished off the coffee. "Next time, your turn."

Shannon got up and refilled her cup.

"Evie," she said quietly, "there can't be alcohol at the next party."

Evie rubbed her temples. "You going all holy on me?"

Shannon wondered if her friend understood what had happened.

"I went to jail last night."

Evie had the cup halfway to her lips but set it down with a hard clunk.

"You what?"

"Jail. Me. I was arrested."

"What'd you do?"

Shannon jumped up, paced a few steps, tried to shake off the anger she felt toward her best friend.

"You came at a cop, claws bared, he raised his stick, I grabbed his arm, he cuffed me and hauled me away."

Evie stared at her. "Just tell me you're lyin'."

"I'm telling you the truth."

"Then why are you here instead of jail?"

"Because they let me go."

"Well, then. But still…you. In jail." She gingerly shook her head. "Nah. I don't believe it."

Shannon did not reply, just curled her hands into fists to keep from screaming.

"Girl, I'm sorry," Evie said. "I am so sorry." She stared off at nothing then, "You went to jail because I'm a shit."

"You are not a shit."

"Then because I acted like a shit."

"I'll give you that. Evie, I don't ever, in my life, ever want to go to the Woodrow City Jail again. Ever. Do you understand me?"

"I understand. The lock-up is a bad place."

"Vernon Fletcher thought Owen didn't deserve to have a sister in jail, so he didn't file any charges against me. If he had, who knows what Owen might have had him do to 'teach me a lesson'? My brother has power in this town, Evie, and it's not a good thing. He could have told the chief to keep me behind bars for years, and the man would have done it."

Evie looked down. "I'm sorry, Shannon. I don't know what to say. I don't know what to do."

"Well, I do. Get yourself some help. The mental health clinic here is for the birds, but maybe you can find a good AA group."

Evie lifted her gaze. Shannon had fully expected defiance or refusal, but the woman had tears in her eyes.

"You're the best friend I've ever had and I'm sorry I caused you more trouble." She reached over and grabbed Shannon's hands. "Help me locate a group and I'll go. It's gonna be hard, and I ain't kiddin', but I'll do my best to stay sober."

SHANNON

With Evie's resolve and faithful attendance to AA meetings, Shannon reaffirmed her own promise to stay on the Copamin, no skipping doses and no quitting. As much as she hated it, she went to therapy with dogged regularity every week.

The sessions consisted mainly of recounting her activities of the past seven days, promising to stay on her medications, and giving a wellness rating on the one to ten scale. This practice remained every time she had a new counselor, which happened every few weeks. The clinic, state-funded and state-run for low-income mental health patients, seemed to have a rotating door for professionals. She no sooner adjusted to one therapist when she'd step into the room and find someone new.

With each new counselor, she had to recount her history, go over her medication regime, her diet, her vices. She rarely divulged too much about herself. Why should she? All they wanted was for her to take her medication and cause no problems for the clinic. Often Shannon told herself if it wasn't for Evie, she'd blow off the whole mental health field and their so-called.

She longed for her manic days, with their boundless energy and extreme highs. But she did not miss the weeks of suffocating darkness and despair. She couldn't have one without the other. So, every morning she swallowed her meds and every week she stepped into the shabby clinic.

Shannon went through the next four years in a flurry of boredom.

One July morning the year Shannon turned thirty-four, she and Evie came home from the Share Center to see a shiny new Mercedes in front of her apartment. With a sinking heart, she parked her Corolla in the space next to it and said, "It's my brother. Must be time for the annual Fire and Brimstone Revival at the Woodrow Worship Center."

Evie grimaced. "Want me to stay?"

"No, it's okay. I can handle Owen."

They got out of the car. "Call me if you need me," Evie said. "I'll be watching out my front window." Shannon nodded, then paused at her stoop while Owen and another man got out of the car. Owen gave her smile. She couldn't remember the last time he'd smiled at her.

"Hello," she said warily.

The other man, tall and razor-faced in a well-tailored suit, came around the front of the car. Her impression of him was one of paleness—pale cream-colored suit, pale skin, pale blue eyes. It gave her the creeps.

Owen said, "This is Doctor Leon Pressman."

Was her brother there to get her evaluated and institutionalized? She took a step back and curled her hands.

"Doctor? Owen, I'm just fine—"

"A doctor of divinity," the man said in a voice as smooth as well-aged bourbon. "I have no license to hold a stethoscope or scalpel." He and Owen chuckled. "No, indeed." He stretched out one thin hand and when Shannon shook it, she found it cool and bony, the silky hand of a man who rarely indulged in manual labor.

She glanced from one face to the other, waiting for the inevitable invitation that had brought Owen to her apartment—a well-rehearsed summons for her presence in church, a sheet of paper printed with time, place, and service topics thrust at her, a sharp look of expectancy on his face before leaving. She knew those empty requests merely shored up his self-righteous dignity and conceit.

"It's certainly warm today," Pressman said with a smile. "May we come inside for some iced tea, or maybe a cool glass of water?"

Neither man looked the least bit hot. Riding around in Owen's air-conditioned luxury car had to be comfortable, but she gave them the benefit of the doubt and invited them inside.

Her apartment was cool and dim after the bright, hot sunshine. Both men blinked a few times then delivered an appraising, none-too-covert examination of her apartment. If they found any fault, it would have to be something other than lack of cleanliness. Shannon loved her home to look, feel and smell as clean and fresh as line-dried laundry.

"Please sit down." She gestured toward the threadbare sofa she kept covered with an inexpensive, colorful quilt. "I'll fix you some iced tea."

The men murmured to each other as she poured their tea over ice and brought it to them in sparkling glass tumblers.

Owen said nothing when she handed him a glass, but eyed it critically, as if expecting to see cracks or lipstick marks on the rim. He held it rather than raising it to his lips.

"Thank you kindly," Pressman said as he took the cold glass from her slightly trembling hand. He swilled half the contents in one gulp. "Ah, that hits the spot. Delicious!"

"Would you like more?"

He held out the glass. "Indeed I would, thank you. Shannon, you have a lovely home here."

As if the man's comments sanctified the immaculate apartment and the tea's purity and taste, Owen finally took a sip.

"Very nice," he said. "And your place looks nice, too."

Shannon forced a slight smile. He was there for a purpose, and that purpose was not to visit, placate, or flatter, or in any way uplift her. No doubt he was about to expose the mess of her life to the well-tailored man beside him and launch into a catalogue of her faults.

She preferred to keep the encounter polite and impersonal, but she perched on the edge of the armchair and waited, ready to do battle, if necessary.

Owen cleared his throat and set his glass on the small end table. His gaze rested briefly on the stack of library books she'd checked out the day before. Would he rail at her for reading the latest Stephen King and Nora Roberts novels instead of something by Tim LaHaye or one of his cronies?

He cleared his throat again and glanced at Pressman who gave him a slight nod and smile.

"Hmm. Umm. Shannon. Well." He cleared his throat again.

"Just say it and get it over with," she said.

He took a deep breath. "Yes. Well. Here's the thing. God spoke to me last night."

"Oh, God," she groaned. She rubbed her forehead, gathered her grit, and met his eyes. "I really don't want to be preached at, Owen. I've heard it all a thousand times, the Bible verses, the come-to-Jesus invitations, the threats of eternity in hell for someone like me." She turned her gaze to the other man. "Forgive me, Mr. Pressman—"

"Doctor Pressman," he corrected, smiling brightly.

"Doctor Pressman. But I know my faults and my failings. I don't want to be rude, but I prefer not hearing what a terrible and unworthy person I am again."

He held up one thin, well-manicured hand. "You misunderstand, Shannon. Your brother has not come to 'preach at you,' nor have I. I am here as a support for this dear man as he bares his soul to you. Please listen to him with an open and forgiving heart."

She blinked in surprise. Her brother baring his soul, to *her*? Meeting his sister's eyes clearly disturbed him. A shred of memory fluttered into her mind and out again, like the shadow of a passing butterfly.

Pressman laid one hand on Owen's shoulder, probably as support for whatever was coming.

"The Lord spoke to me last night. He revealed that I could have been a better brother to you, and convicted me of not caring enough. I want you to forgive me for that."

The words were clipped then abruptly halted. She half-expected for him to stand, dust his hands together and announce, "There! That's done."

"You see, Shannon," Pressman spoke up, filling the silence that followed, "your dear brother wants to mend fences, so to speak. This rift you've created is displeasing to the Lord."

"The rift *I've* created? I hope you aren't saying I'm responsible for Owen treating me as if I'm diseased."

The evangelist passed a glance back and forth between the siblings. Owen squirmed, but Shannon held steady.

Pressman gave that bright smile again. "Well, what does it matter who created it? The fact is Owen wants to make amends."

Shannon found the preacher's pronouncement highly suspect. Impossible to believe, in fact.

"Do you mean this, Owen?" Shannon said. "Or is it some kind of religious fever you've caught but will be gone a week or two after the revival services have ended?"

He blinked at her as if his mind was blank, and he looked to his companion.

"Oh, I believe his resolve is strong and true," Pressman assured her. "And now it's up to you as to whether or not you'll forgive him."

She got up, walked to the window and looked out. Evie sat on her stoop across the parking lot, smoking, her gaze fixed on Shannon's apartment. She raised one hand, as if to say, "I'm here for you."

Shannon lifted a hand in acknowledgment and turned back to the two men in her living room.

"I'm not sure what you know or what you've heard, sir, but let me assure you that I loved my parents. I'm truly sorry I disappointed them and caused them so much pain. I never wanted to hurt them. I never want to hurt *anyone*. It broke my heart when they died. Being banned from my father's funeral was horrendous. I wasn't even allowed to attend the visitation before Mom's funeral, and I was kept away from her service, as well."

At this, the visiting preacher turned a startled look on Owen.

"What's this?" he said.

Owen's face turned bright crimson and he shot a brief, murderous glare at his sister. "I…I…." His Adam's apple bobbed as he gulped. "I thought it was best … for the rest of us … she seemed out of control and my other sisters …." His voice trailed and he looked down. "I guess I should have let her attend."

"Indeed so!" Pressman said. "Very much indeed so."

Shannon plowed on. "I don't know what you told Mama to turn her against me, Owen, but it sure did the trick. The way she looked at me the last time I saw her will haunt me the rest of my life. She must have gone to her grave believing the very worst."

Owen's face shone scarlet above his white collar. Sweat covered his forehead, and he mopped it with a monogrammed handkerchief.

"You did not tell me these things, Brother Grady," the preacher said.

Owen blotted his neck, and he ran the handkerchief across his brow again.

"Well…it's…that is…I confessed it to the Lord last night. I

…uh…didn't think it was necessary to…ah…tell *you* everything." The evangelist waited for more, and Owen spluttered. "It's enough that I asked the Lord for forgiveness…." He glanced nervously at Shannon. "And my sister."

Shannon allowed herself the luxury of silence for a couple of heartbeats. Then, "You admit you were wrong to exclude me?"

He swallowed hard and nodded.

"And what about everything else?"

His face paled as he stared at her, eyes wide like a trapped creature. "Yes, yes. All of it. I'm sorry."

There was so much to forgive: threats, lies, accusations, harsh words, undeserved ill will, estrangement. She studied him as his hands clenched and unclenched, plucking at his trousers as if he saw dirt embedded in their fabric.

"I don't know if I can forgive you, Owen," she said. "That's a lot to ask."

Pressman cleared his throat to draw her attention. "Shannon, as difficult as this was for me to hear, I invite you to think how doubly difficult it was for your brother to confess—"

"And for me to live through," she told him grimly. "Think about that part of it, if you will."

He reached out, placed one soft, cool hand on top of hers.

"Yes, Shannon." She frowned and pulled her hand free. "It must have been rough for you. But now you can be a part of the healing of this fractured relationship. Your brother has done the hard part; he has come to you with a broken and contrite heart, begging pardon, hoping that once more you can truly be a family." He paused. "Don't you want that to happen?"

Dead silence fell. After all these years, did she even want this?

"There have been a lot of years of this division," she said. "I'm not the same as you and Donna, but that doesn't mean I'm a bad person."

Owen said nothing.

"You know I'll never forget what you did to me, don't you?'

His hands shook as he nodded silently, still avoiding her gaze.

"I'll think about it," she said.

Another silence fell, then Pressman said, "We trust the Lord will lead you into the right decision."

Shannon said nothing.

"Now!" said Pressman, as if he was about to get down to business. "Another reason we're here. Owen, would you like to…?"

At this Owen straightened his spine and lifted his head. In a matter of seconds he was back to being Owen Grady again.

"This summer's revival meetings have been powerful. Dr. Pressman knows his Bible, and he delivers a strong sermon."

"He must be good if he got you to take an honest look at yourself," she said.

His face reddened again. "Yes. Well. When the Lord spoke to me and convicted me of my…my indifference toward you, he also told me he still cares about your soul. He told me to compel you to come to the revival."

"Compel me?"

"As the Bible says, 'Go out into the highways and byways, and compel them to come in, that my house may be filled.'"

"Aha."

"You see, Shannon," Pressman said, "in this context, the word 'compel' doesn't mean to force you to attend, but to bid you to come, to invite you. You'll be blessed, I promise."

She thought of those days when she attended church with her parents every Sunday. She had loved the singing and the warm fellowship. Sunday school picnics and vacation Bible school. Lock-ins and Christmas parties. Concerts and youth trips. Potluck dinners and church camp. But after she grew up and the moods continued to grip her, she stayed away, convinced the members of the Woodrow Worship Center despised her as much as Owen and Donna did. Was it possible to mend and rebuild a relationship with her past? Did she even want that?

"Will the people want me to come back?"

"Of course!" Pressman said with enthusiasm. "We're all part of God's family. You'll be welcomed with open arms, or I've missed my guess about the good folks at Woodrow Worship Center."

Maybe she should go, just once, and test the waters. Maybe it would be a big step to creating the closeness she craved with her family.

"What time does the service start tonight?"

At her words, Pressman beamed; Owen looked startled.

"Seven o'clock every night. Will you be there?"

"I'll think about it," she said again.

SHANNON

"Have you lost your mind?" Evie yelped a short time later. "Church? You want *me* to go to church with you?"

"Just this once. Tonight."

"But…but…. Are you crazy?" She crushed out her cigarette on a broken saucer in the kitchen. "Church? You and me? I think I'm gonna have a broken leg, a bad cold, a migraine, something. Anything."

Shannon laughed then she sighed a little. "I know it seems all out of whack to you—"

"Yeah. Completely. Good God, Shannon, how'd you let that brother of yours get to you?" She narrowed her eyes. "You stop takin' your meds?"

"No. Every morning, as directed." She scowled briefly. "Dr. Kendall."

Evie made a face. "I just don't want that bozo yanking you around is all."

"He isn't. I'm just testing the waters."

Evie picked up a glass of iced tea in which most of the ice had melted. She met Shannon's eyes over the rim. "Church waters."

"And maybe family. You don't have to make that awful face. I'm only asking you to go with me tonight, just for a little moral support."

Evie guffawed. "Moral support. Me, in church, for moral support. You're too much, Shannon. You know I have no morals."

"Of course you don't."

The two laughed again, then Shannon sobered and said, "So will you? Go with me tonight? Please?"

Evie heaved a big breath, gave her a long look that held some softness and quite a bit of amusement.

"You know I will. But if they try to baptize me, I'm outta there."

Shannon and Evie slipped into the brightly-lit, half-occupied sanctuary of the Woodrow Worship Center just as the service began and sat on the back pew.

Near the front, Owen reared up his head on his long neck like a snake and searched the room. When his gaze landed on Shannon, he gave her an abbreviated nod, fixed a startled glance on Evie, then turned around. He spoke to Sarah Jean on his right who seemed oblivious to him. He leaned toward Donna on his left and whispered to her. She shot a quick look at the back pew, wrinkled her nose then faced forward.

Shannon seriously doubted her sister would apologize, ever. At least Owen had once been a good brother, playing with her or reading to her, but Donna had always seemed to hate her.

Evie snickered. "Your sister looked like she smelled shit on somebody's shoes."

Evie shifted on the pew, folded her arms across her chest and slouched down,. eyes bright and probing. The woman would miss nothing; that air of indifference was merely a mask of self-protection. Evie had been belittled and scorned too often in her life to trust any organization that smacked of religion.

"Is this one of them churches where folks talk in tongues and roll around in the floor and stuff?" she asked under her breath.

"No."

"Well, shit. I was hoping for some entertainment, at least."

"Evie, be quiet!"

Evie held her silence until the collection plate was passed. Shannon reached into her purse and took out one of the four dollars she had left.

"You gotta pay for this?" Evie said aloud. Several heads turned.

"No," Shannon whispered.

"Well, I ain't got a dime."

"That's all right."

Dr. Pressman approached the pulpit, a thick black Bible in one thin hand. Under the bright spotlight, his pale skin seemed to glow with a supernatural sheen. Rather than the cream-colored suit he had worn to her apartment earlier in the day, the suit he wore was a somber dark gray, almost black. He presented a haunting image.

He placed the Bible on the pulpit, then stood with both hands resting on either side. For a long silence, only his eyes moved, taking in every person the congregation. Shannon read nothing in that dispassionate gaze. For all she knew, the man could have been counting heads or thinking about tomorrow's breakfast. His gaze landed on her for a moment, moved to Evie, then he opened his Bible. His lapel microphone caught the soft rustling as he found his text. He lifted his head, smiled.

"Good evening. It has been a blessed and glorious day! I'm so happy to see you fine people in the Lord's house on a beautiful evening when so many others are chasing after more temporal pursuits."

People smiled at each other, settled more comfortably in the pews now that their presence had his notice and his blessing.

"To those of you who are visiting, may the Lord richly bless you. I'm sure I speak for Pastor Yeager when I say we extend an invitation for you to return tomorrow night. Come back, too, on Sunday morning. Our final service will be Sunday night. We hope you will join us, and I promise, you will be blessed." He paused. "Good people, this world is a complex and dangerous dwelling place. Crime runs rampant through our cities and towns. Just last week, I read where murder has increased eight percent since this time last year, rape ten point three percent, robbery twelve percent. With the help of the Internet, child abuse flourishes. White collar crime continues to rise. Our beloved senior citizens are having their very livelihood threatened by indifferent politicians in Washington. Alcoholism and drug abuse has quadrupled over the last twenty years. Poverty and homelessness abounds, and the effects of all these deplorable conditions are far-reaching."

Evie leaned into Shannon and whispered, "He ain't sayin' nothin' I don't already know."

"Last night," Pressman continued, "you heard me speak of hypocrisy in today's church. I mentioned the responsibility of God-fearing men and women to take a stand for the Lord and be firm in their resolve. We cannot win lost souls if we do not honor our own vows."

He ran his gaze across the congregation and rested on Owen for a moment.

"We were blessed when one of our dear brothers came forward last evening and confessed all to Jesus at this altar of prayer." He gestured gracefully to the two long mourner's benches just below the pulpit on either side. "And I was privileged to go with him today and watch as he made good on the promise he'd given to his Lord and Savior last night." He smiled then sobered. "That's what we need, folks!" he said so suddenly and loudly that both Evie and Shannon jumped. "Dedicated servants of the Lord who take seriously their mission to go out, spread the Gospel, and bring in the unsaved."

Shannon glanced at her brother who nearly preened beneath the praise of the evangelist. Sarah Jean smiled at him proudly.

"Open your Bibles to my text for this evening. Second Chronicles 7:14." He waited a few seconds while pages turned, then in a richly resonant voice, he read, "'If my people, which are called by my name, shall humble themselves, and pray, and seek my face, and turn from their wicked ways; then will I hear from heaven, and will forgive their sin, and will heal their land.'"

With his Bible open in one hand, its leather cover falling like soft wings on either sides of his palm, he looked out over the congregation.

"This is what we need, people. To humble ourselves, pray, seek his face. For those precious lost souls out there without the hope of salvation or heaven's glory, we have to seek the face of God. We must pray, we must fast, we must turn from our selfish pursuits, and show our Lord that we're serious about him! Look around you, dear ones. Look at all the empty pews which, on Sunday morning, will be full of pew-sitters, friends and neighbors who are content to warm the benches but make no effort to study God's word or come to services or spread the good news of salvation to a lost and dying generation. This is what revival is all about, brothers and sisters! We need an awakening, a renewed call to service. Revive us again! Soften our hearts! Create in us a new heart! Open our eyes to the lost and our ears to their cries!"

With each admonition, his voice rang out and he struck his fist against the pulpit.

"A great and terrible day is coming when it will be too late. On that day our unsaved friends and neighbors will stand before the judgment seat of Christ. They will call out for salvation, but all hope will be lost. In anguish, they will point an accusing finger at you and cry, 'I'm going to hell because you never told me about Jesus. Why didn't you tell me about him? Why didn't you tell me about hell? Why didn't you lead me to the path of salvation?' What are you going to say to him, my dear friends, on that day when we all stand before Our Judge and you failed to win souls for the kingdom?"

"Is he serious?" Evie hissed in Shannon's ears.

"Yes."

Evie sat forward for a minute, listened while the evangelists continued his dire warnings. She grabbed Shannon's arm.

"He makes me want a drink. I gotta get out of here."

Something in Evie's eyes convinced Shannon that she meant what she said. "Okay. Let's go."

They slipped out of the sanctuary as silently as they had entered.

SHANNON

"Never again," Evie said as Shannon drove them back to the apartment. "All that pounding and hollering and talking about sending people to hell gave me the creeps. Reminds me of my mother."

"Your mother was a preacher?"

Evie gave her a dark look. "No. And you know what I meant."

Shannon laughed. "Dr. Pressman isn't as bad as some I've heard, but I understand if you don't want to go again. Now that I've been there once, I can go again by myself."

"You're not going back?" Evie's tone said she didn't believe it.

"I'll go Sunday morning. If I don't, they'll show up on my doorstep again."

"If they do that, call the cops on 'em. Say it's harassment."

Shannon shook her head. "I just want to be left alone. Going to the service will appease them, and then it'll be over."

Evie took a long draw on a cigarette, then peered at her through the smoke. "Why don't you ask Dunn to go with you?"

"Ha. I'm not dragging Dunn to that."

"But you'd drag me. Thanks a heap."

Sunday morning revival sermons at Woodrow Worship Center were typically evangelical in content and dogged in execution. She'd heard it all before. Wretched sinner, a filthy rag, unworthy of heaven and bound for hell but still precious in God's sight.

At that moment, the entire concept—as old and hackneyed as it was—made no sense to her. How could you be a filthy rag and precious at the same time?

And yet, at the end of the service as the choir began to sing "Softly and Tenderly Jesus is Calling," something trembled inside her.

The congregation was asked to stand, with every head bowed, every eye closed. The quiet music washed over her.

"Come home, come home," the choir sang in hushed tones. "Ye who are weary, come home."

Memories swept through her, memories of her parents and their goodness in spite of their flaws. Their love, their support. The protective harbor she had always found with them. She yearned for her parents with a young child's extreme longing.

"Come home, come home."

With an intensity she had not felt in years, Shannon ached to go home to that place of shelter and love and acceptance. A touch on her arm startled her.

"Don't you want to come home, Shannon?" Pressman stood next to her and spoke in a low voice. "Don't you want to come forward, kneel at an altar of prayer, confess it all to the Lord, and have a fresh start?" She looked into his pale blue eyes, into a warmth and a tender regard. His touch on her arm applied gentle pressure. He spoke again. "Give it up, Shannon. Give up the anger and the hatred, the uncontrollable carnal desires that rule your life. Leave behind your need to wallow in the cesspool of depression when life gets tough. Abandon all greed for things that aren't yours. Follow your brother's example—renew your heart to God's holy purpose."

His words wormed through the aching loneliness for her parents and her home. She realized what he was saying. Her anger and hatred? She was rarely mad at anyone, and never without provocation. She had never hated a person in her life. As for uncontrollable desires? Those were a symptom of her illness, not the product of an evil heart. And greed? She craved only a simple life filled with love. She had no need to "wallow" in depression. It had always sought her out, pounced and swallowed her before she knew it was there.

"You believe my illness is a sin, don't you?" she asked the man.

"All sickness is from Satan. He cannot lay hold of a pure and Godly heart."

Shannon stared into those ice blue eyes and knew the man actually believed what he said.

"The Bible says, 'Behold: Now is the accepted time. Behold: Now is the day of salvation.' We know not when our soul will be required of us. We are not guaranteed even the rest of this day. Don't let this opportunity pass you by. Come forward. I'll walk with you."

"And if I do this, will I become like Owen?"

Pressman gave her a gentle smile. "Your brother sets a fine example for you to follow."

A high-pitched hum needled through her brain. She shook her head to clear the hum and to clear the man's words.

"Then I won't do it," she said.

An expression flickered across his face then. He dropped his hand from her arm, turned away, and walked back toward the front of the church.

By that time, few heads were still lowered, and hardly any eyes were closed. Most of them were looking at her. She picked up her purse and left the church before the evangelist had returned to the platform.

When she got home, she called Dunn, then she called Evie.

"Dunn and I are going to the lake. Come with us."

"You taking food?"

"You bet. Tuna sandwiches. Dunn's bringing pop. You bring chips. Be ready in ten minutes."

"How was church?" Evie asked as they drove toward the lake.

"Long. Boring." She wanted to shove the service, the sermon, the preacher and his probing gaze out of her mind. And she did not want to talk about it. Evie would just say "Told ya so."

"You gonna get baptized, or something?"

"The only water I'm going to get on me is up at the lake."

When she returned to her apartment that evening, tired, sunburned and grimy, she found a small business card with Pressman's name in her door. A note was scrawled on the other side.

"We're praying for you," she read aloud.

She fully expected Owen to show up the next day, reading to pounce.

SHANNON

Around noon on Tuesday, Shannon scraped the last of the mayonnaise from the jar and spread it on a rather dry heel of bread. Maybe Evie had some bread left, but by the end of the month everyone's refrigerator and cabinets were nearly as bare as Mother Hubbard's. She folded the bread in half and took the first bite of her meager lunch. Thank God she still had some cornflakes and a little milk. She'd have to ration it, but she wouldn't starve until her disability check came Thursday.

She'd just put the last bite into her mouth when someone knocked on her door, three firm raps. Owen hadn't shown up yesterday to chew her out, as she'd expected.

She took in a deep breath, gathered her grit, and opened the door. A dark-haired young man stood on her stoop. His eyes were as clear and blue as any she'd ever seen, and he'd fixed them on her as if he wanted to bore into her brain. Something about the boy, the shape of his eyes, the way he held his head, the contours of his lips, all seemed startling familiar, yet she was sure she'd never seen him before.

"Hello," she said through the screen of the storm door.

He fidgeted a little at the sound of her voice then gulped and said in a voice that echoed a Deep South drawl, "Excuse me, ma'am, but are you…" He broke off, cleared his throat and met her eyes. "Are you Shannon Grady?"

"Yes. Who are you?"

He leaned closer to the door, and his gaze traveled every contour of her face. When he straightened, he gave her a hesitant smile.

"Do you know me?" he asked.

She studied his face again, then shook her head. "I don't think so…oh, wait. Are you one of the high school kids who used to come into the Dairy

Diner when I worked there?"

"No, ma'am. I'm Garrett. Garrett Overstreet."

"It's nice to meet you, but who are you?"

He cleared his throat, held his head straight and looked into her eyes. "I'm your son."

The world swam around her, and she grabbed the door frame. "My…my son?"

"Yes, ma'am. When I turned eighteen, I told my folks I was goin' to find you, and I usually do what I set out to do."

"My son. Oh my God." She closed her eyes and sagged against the door.

"Are you all right, ma'am? I didn't mean to scare you. I'm sorry. Maybe I should come back another—"

"No!" She roused herself, fumbled with the latch and finally flung open the door. "Get in here!"

When he stepped over the threshold, she threw her arms around him and hung on. "Oh, my God, oh my God."

His hold on her was just as tight, just as intense. He laughed softly near her ear. A sound so longed for that it was like music.

"I guess maybe you're glad to see me?" he asked, his voice choked.

"Oh yes! Oh, my God, yes, yes, yes!"

She pulled back and looked at him, the eyes that were hers, the wide-open smile that she used, the strong nose and chin, the muscular arms and shoulders that promised to mature into brawny manhood.

"Your name is Garrett? That's a great name." She cupped his face in one hand and turned his head to the right then to the left. "A handsome name for such a handsome fellow. Oh, my God. My son!" She embraced him again.

"And you're even more beautiful that I imagined you'd be." When she let go, he tilted his head to one side and gave her a crooked smile. "You're so young. I sorta thought you'd be…well, *not* so young."

"I was barely fifteen when you were born. A little girl, really."

They stared at each other for another stretch of time before Shannon finally said, "Please have a seat, Garrett. Can I get you some iced tea?"

"Yes, ma'am. That'd be real nice."

When she brought it to him, he said, "Thank you, ma'am."

"You have very good manners," she said. "Your parents raised you well."

"Thank you, ma'am. Yes, they did." He took a drink. "This is good tea."

She studied him, the dark hair which showed red tones in the light, his strong profile, the muscular column of his neck, his broad hands with short clean nails. The neatly pressed jeans and crisp white cotton shirt. No holey, slouchy pants or grubby T-shirts. His sneakers were so clean they looked as if he'd bought them an hour ago. Her heart swelled that this young man was her son.

"I look like you," he said.

"Yes, you do."

His gaze traveled over her blonde hair caught up in its careless ponytail.

"But I have dark hair."

She nodded.

"Guess I got that from my father," he added.

Shannon didn't want to talk about that yet and felt a stab of remorse for disappointing him. Once she revealed the truth, he might turn away.

"Tell me about yourself," she said.

He smiled, shrugged, and fidgeted a little. "I'm not too interesting. I live in Macon, Georgia, have a brother and a sister. Trevor and Bobbi. They're natural born to my folks. Mom and Dad had been trying for ten years to have a baby before they got me. Right after I was adopted, Mom got pregnant, like maybe two months later. And right after Trevor was born, like maybe four months, she got pregnant again."

She smiled. "I hear that happens a lot."

"Yes, ma'am."

All these years she had hoped with all her heart that her son had been given to warm, loving parents. She'd prayed that his family showered him with the affection she'd been prevented from bestowing.

"Would you tell me about your family?"

He nodded. "Dad teaches high school math and Mom teaches fourth grade. Dad's lookin' forward to retirement, but Mom says she wants to teach for another thirty years. They're great. I mean, they're a pain in the butt sometimes, but I guess that's because they're parents." He smiled. "I was raised kinda strict, but it's all good."

"They sound like wonderful people."

"Yes, ma'am. They are."

She hesitated, then asked, "How'd they feel about you looking for me?"

He studied the ice in the glass as if searching for the right words. "They weren't against it, exactly. I mean, they didn't try to stop me or anything, but they didn't encourage me, either." He looked up. "I think they thought you might not want to meet me."

"Well, they were certainly wrong about that."

They smiled at each other, then he sobered and looked away for moment before adding, "I think they were afraid I'd want to stay with you, or something. They wouldn't tell me your name until after I turned eighteen. I've been wantin' to find you since I was twelve. That's when I found out I was adopted."

"How'd you find out?"

"They just sat me down and told me. I was real surprised. Mom's got dark brown hair, and Dad has blue eyes. I mean, I don't look so different from them or my other relatives."

She touched his hand lightly, briefly, wondering how that hand had looked when he was tiny. Had he sucked his thumb or chewed on his fingers? What toy had he first reached for?

"Did it bother you…knowing that you were adopted?"

He shrugged. "Maybe a little, right at first. I mean, it sorta makes you feel like the world isn't what you thought, but I didn't hold it against them. I'd seen kids in school whose folks didn't care about them at all, who left them home alone, sometimes, or beat them. Or worse. And then there were the foster kids who looked lost or worn down or whatever. My folks loved me, and I knew it, and that was enough." He met her eyes straight on. "I didn't come here looking to get away from them. I came here because you and I are blood, and I wanted to know my blood. Mom will always be my mom, and Dad is my dad, and that'll never change."

She smiled at him, feeling something inside her break open and flow with joy.

"I'm so happy for you, Garrett. So, so happy." Tears stung her eyes, but she blinked them back. "Tell me about Trevor and Bobbi."

"Oh, them." He grinned. "Trevor, he's tall, like six foot two, and he'd rather play the violin than basketball. Can you believe that? He wants to be in a symphony orchestra one of these days. And Bobbi can be a brat, but she's sweet and really funny. She plans to go to California and be an actress. Maybe a stand-up comedian, something like that. I bet she does it, too, because she is hilarious and doesn't mind making a fool out of herself."

"You're close to your brother and sister?"

"Oh, yeah. I can't imagine not having Trevor and Bobbi around. Guess I'll have to, someday, but I hope we'll always be close in our hearts."

Something inside Shannon let go, a fear, maybe, that her son would be rejected or reviled by his siblings the way she'd been. At that moment, she ceased to regret losing him all those years ago. Had she kept him, her own family might have transferred their antipathy for her to Garrett.

"I want you to know that I didn't want to give you away," she said. "Even though I longed for you every day of my life, I realized my father was right when he said I wouldn't be able to take care of you. I was far too young…and I was ill. But now I'm so very glad I let you go because you've had such a good family to grow up with."

He blinked hard, but not before she saw a sheen in his eyes. "Thank you for doing what was best," he said. "I always wondered if you ever thought of me. I'd hoped you did."

"I did. I thought of you every day, wondered about you, hoped good things for you."

They shared a smile, then she glanced at his empty glass.

"Let me freshen that iced tea," she said. From the kitchen she said, "You've told me about your folks, but I really want to know about you." She brought his tea and handed it to him. "Tell me everything."

He grinned. "I start college in a few weeks at Emory University in Atlanta. I got a full scholarship."

"Wow! You must be pretty smart."

His face reddened. "I guess. A little bit, anyway."

"So are you going to follow the family tradition and be a teacher?"

"I want to go into medicine."

She sat down with a plunk. "Really? As in a doctor?"

He nodded. "I think I'd like to work in geriatrics."

"That's interesting. You like old people?"

His eyes lit up. "Yes, ma'am. They're so cool. And they know so much. I mean, my friends think old people are a waste of space, you know, boring with their stories about they've done in their lives, but I just think they are way cool." He took a big quick drink. "I don't have any grandparents. I mean, I did, but they're all dead now. Do I have grandparents here in Woodrow?"

He looked so eager, his eyes brimming with hope.

"Oh, honey, how I wish you did, but my father and mother both passed away seven years ago."

"Oh, geez. I'm sorry for the both of us. What were they like?"

"Well, my father was Curtis Grady, and he ran Grady Wood Products. That's a company my grandfather started with a sawmill. Daddy was a decent, gentle man. Generous and kind. He was patient, and ready to believe the best in most people. My mother's name was Melba. She was a good woman, but she could get testy sometimes, especially as she got older. I think she loved being wife and mother, taking care of the house and raising us kids. She absolutely doted on my brother."

"I have an uncle?" he asked eagerly.

"And two aunts and five cousins."

"Awesome! Do they live around here?"

"Owen and Donna, my brother and sister, live here in Woodrow with their families, and my other sister Julie lives in California. They are all older than me."

"Does Julie have a family, too?"

She hesitated, thinking of Gwen whom she'd never met and whom Julie had never mentioned. "Yes. But they don't have kids."

"May I meet them? Owen and Donna and their families? Back home, I have one unmarried uncle and one widowed aunt. Neither of them has kids so we never got to play with cousins. Holidays are quiet in my family."

Shannon gazed at him, this exceptional young man with his handsome, clean appearance, his open and friendly demeanor, his high intelligence and compassionate ambitions. Any family would be happy to have him as a part of it, and yet she wanted to protect him from Owen's hard, narrow world view and from Donna's vicious materialism. But maybe Owen's recent awakening had softened him, taken out the need to be right and righteous. Maybe he could persuade Donna to become more sensitive and selfless. Maybe meeting Garrett and witnessing his admirable character would mean something to all of them.

"I want them to meet you," Shannon said.

SHANNON

The afternoon wore down to a nub as Shannon and Garrett talked and laughed and devoured the carry-out pizza Garrett bought.

"May we go meet my uncle and aunt now?" he asked eagerly.

Her stomach tightened but she said, "Sure. Let me freshen up and we'll go."

The sun's final rays caught Garrett's dark hair and burnished every strand like bronze as they stepped outside a short time later. Shannon glanced across the parking lot.

"My friend Evie lives over there. I can't wait for her to meet you. She never comes over when I have company unless it's Dunn, and now she's at her meeting, but she'll be home by the time we get back. You guys can meet then."

"From what you told me about her I bet she's great."

"She is. And so is Dunn. You'll like him. He's got a new girlfriend who's a real looker." She gave him a teasing glance. "You'll like her, too, or I'll miss my guess."

He grinned. "Is she hot?"

"I've heard her described that way."

Toni Feeney was not classically beautiful, but she kept herself dolled up and never set foot outside the door until she was powdered, perfumed and pretty. For someone who did her shopping at the Share Center, Toni looked as if she belonged on the pages of Elle. She was twenty-five years old, and it didn't take a genius to see why Dunn went out with her, though it seemed to Shannon that his heart wasn't really involved.

Shannon and Garrett got into her Corolla. His shiny red SUV was parked next to it.

"Nice ride," she said.

"Thanks." As he shut the passenger door, he said, "I can't wait to meet my new family! You think they'll like me?"

Shannon smiled, started the car and backed out. Her stomach clenched again, but she said lightly, "How could they not?"

As they rode toward Owen's house, Garrett said, "What should I call you?"

"What do you want to call me?"

"Well, no offense, but not 'Mom.' That wouldn't feel right."

"I understand. So, what would you call me if we were just friends?"

"Miss Shannon," he said immediately.

"Then that's it. I'm happy to be Miss Shannon."

A few minutes later, as she turned onto the wide avenue leading into Fairborn Estates, Garrett leaned forward and gazed around them in awe.

"Dude! Look at these houses. Does Uncle Owen live here?"

"He does."

"He must be rollin' in dough!"

"That's one way to put it. Actually, the Gradys are pretty influential around here. We're fourth generation Woodrowians. Or would that be Woodrowites? Grady Wood Products is the town's lifeblood. Daddy ran it until he passed away, and now Owen and his brother-in-law Craig have taken over."

"That's pretty cool."

Shannon kept silent about how the lack of a decent wage seemed to be draining that lifeblood from Woodrow, that lay-offs happened more and more, and hiring was at a stand-still. She didn't mention the grumbling she'd heard from her brother's employees about how he and Craig continued to drive new luxury cars every year while living in homes most people would see only on the television or the movie screen. Shannon wanted her son to believe the best of his blood kin and never realize some branches of the family tree were thorny and brittle. Not for her sake, not for Owen's or Donna's, either, but for his. She did not want Garrett ever to be ashamed.

"That's Owen's place there."

"Look at it!"

A mansion by anyone's standards, the house with its leaded windows and imposing chimney had been built of imported stone. It more closely resembled an English manor house than the home of a small-town business owner. A long curving driveway, lined with young oak trees, led to the courtyard, complete with fountain and English garden. Owen and Sarah Jean employed a full-time gardener to keep the grounds meticulous.

Shannon had been in her brother's home exactly once. Curtis and Melba had bid her to accompany them to the housewarming even though she had not been invited. Sarah Jean or Donna had taken turns keeping her in their lines of vision as if fearful she would steal something. When she used the small pink and white marble powder room near the foot of the stairs, Sarah Jean was outside the door when she came out. The woman slipped inside with a can of Lysol and did not bother to hide the sight of her spraying every fixture in the tiny room.

"Do you think I'm dirty?" Shannon had asked.

Sarah Jean's smile dripped with pride. "I just like to keep everything germ-free."

Shannon had sought out her father and stayed by his side until he took her home. She wished he were with her right then. Had she done the wrong thing, bringing Garrett here? Too late now. She'd fake her way through it for his sake. She parked the car, gave her son an encouraging smile as they walked to the massive oak door. She rang the bell.

When Owen opened the door, he blinked, as if surprised. Garrett might as well have been invisible for all the attention Owen gave him.

"Well." He gave Shannon a narrow look. "We've been wondering what happened to you since you ran out of church Sunday morning and failed to return that night as you'd promised."

"I didn't run out of church—"

"And Dr. Pressman said you refused to return to the Lord. He was very disheartened when he left us Sunday night."

She refused to respond to that. "I have someone here who wants to meet you."

Owen held her gaze for a bit longer, then turned to look to Garrett. "We're not currently hiring," he said and started to shut the door.

"Owen! He's not here to ask for a job. Good grief. May we come inside?"

He frowned, raking his gaze over them both as if expecting to find dung on their clothes. "I suppose so. For a minute." He stepped back, still frowning. "Come in."

They entered an Italian marble foyer large enough to comfortably hold a couple dozen guests or more. Garrett looked up at the high ceiling, gaped wordlessly at the angels fresco painted there until Owen gruffly cleared his throat.

Garrett dragged his gaze away and looked at the man.

"Owen, this is Garrett Overstreet."

Garrett showed his beautiful smile and extended his hand. Owen shook it, his face serious, openly suspicious.

"Garrett is my son."

Owen froze. Garrett grinned, reached out and embraced him. "Hi, Uncle Owen."

The older man stiffened and drew himself inward as if afraid of contact. Garrett lost his smile, stepped back, sending a confused look to Shannon.

"Your…son?"

"Yes."

Sarah Jean's high heels clicked against the polished floor as she entered the room. "What's going on? Shannon, why are you here? We're just about to have dinner. And you know your friends are not welcome in our home."

"What…?" Garrett stared at the thin, well-dressed couple. "What'd you just say?"

Owen ignored the boy and looked at his wife. "Do you remember when Shannon had to go stay with Aunt Eunice?"

He lifted his eyebrows, pursed his lips, and tilted his head just that much toward Garrett. Sarah Jean's eyes widened, and she lay her left hand against her upper chest. A huge diamond and ruby ring caught the light from the chandelier above them.

"Oh, my. What's he doing here?"

Garrett turned to Shannon. He was ashen-faced, stunned into silence.

"Are you kidding?" Shannon managed to sputter. "Garrett is my son. He's a part of our family."

"He is not a part of this family," Owen said.

"Just because you gave birth to him," Sarah Jean said, "does not mean he's part of our family."

"That's right. He's your shame and our embarrassment."

Shannon's vision misted over with red, and the sound of her blood pumping drowned the rasping strangle as she tried to breathe. She trembled violently from a place deep the very center of her being.

"I can't….oh, my God," Garrett sputtered. "Are you serious?"

Owen and Sarah Jean stood in their opulent entrance hall, stony and silent.

"Garrett is good and sweet and kind," Shannon said in a strangled voice. "He's been raised by good parents—"

"So you've been in touch with him all this time?"

"No. He sought me out—"

"When?"

"When what?"

"When did he seek you out?"

"Today! We have visited all afternoon. He was so excited to know he has an uncle, aunts, and cousins—"

"So you really don't know him, do you, Shannon?"

"This is so typical of you," Sarah Jean put in. "A handsome face, a pretty smile, and that's all you need. Any man can delude you into believing anything." She gestured toward Garrett. "This boy is probably not the child you gave birth to at all, just someone wanting to cash in on the Grady money."

"Now, wait a minute!" Garrett's blue eyes looked like points of fire in his flushed face. "I don't know anything about Grady money, and I don't care about Grady money. All I wanted was to meet my birth mom and any other family I might have."

Owen's cold gaze bore into the boy. "Young man, I recommend that you hightail it back to wherever you came from. You'll not get anything from the Grady estate, now or in the future. Even if you are my sister's illegitimate son, the trust funds have all been set up for the *real* grandchildren. There will be no changing that."

When Owen Grady was in his self-righteous mode, he never stammered or seemed at a loss for words.

Shannon stared at her brother, angrier at him than she'd ever been in her life. "You listen to me, Owen. You and your wife have said and done some despicable things, but I believe you have topped yourself today. I thought you wanted to mend fences. Wasn't that how Dr. Pressman phrased it? I hoped that maybe, by some remote and nearly impossible chance, you had actually had a change of heart. And crazy ol' me, I actually believed—at least for a little while—that you wanted to be a brother to me instead of the rotten, self-righteous prig that you are. I'm embarrassed that the same blood runs in our veins. Daddy and Mama are probably rolling in their graves at your nasty behavior."

Owen's face flushed so deeply that it was nearly purple. Shannon didn't care. She turned to her sister-in-law. "Yes, Sarah Jean, you are absolutely right. I allowed myself to be deluded by another man once again. Only this time, the man who deceived me was my own brother. I should have known better." She took a step back, her hand protectively on Garrett's arm. "Garrett and I are leaving now, and neither one of us will ever bother you again." She looked back and forth between them. There was so much more she wanted to say, but knew it would go unheeded. "You are both blind, raving fools."

She shook so hard in her vented rage she could hardly walk. She held onto Garrett as they started to step outside. She turned back to see Owen and Sarah Jean rooted in the same spot.

"One last thing you should know. I've been thinking about how to live a better life, maybe reconnect with church and renew a relationship with God. But if you two are an example of God's nature and how he expects people to behave, then I want no part of him." She narrowed her eyes. "I wonder how many others have turned from God because of you, Owen Grady. You need to think about that. And if it's too hard for you to understand, maybe Dr. Pressman can help you digest it."

SHANNON

Shannon drove to the intersection of Fairborn Estates and the highway before all strength left her extremities. She pulled the car to the side of the road and stopped to rest her head against the steering wheel.

Garrett, who had remained silent since he spoke to Owen, moved restlessly. "No one has ever talked to me that way in my whole life—as if I'm some kind of cheat or black-hearted liar. Uncle or not, I wanted to punch his lights out for what he said to you, the shithead. Who does he think he is?"

"I shouldn't have taken you there," she said, lifting her head. "I'm so, so sorry."

He reached over and rubbed her shoulder. "Hey, it's not your fault, Miss Shannon. That man back there? He's an asshole, forgive my language, but he is. I don't understand why…."

"I don't, either. He told me he'd changed, that he was going to make an effort….It was all a lie." She glanced at him. "I wanted to spare you the gritty details about my family, but I will tell you all, if you want to know."

"Yes, ma'am. I think I should know about my blood."

"Then let's get out of this ritzy neighborhood and go back to the real world."

Back in her apartment, Shannon told him about Owen, Donna, and Julie. She underscored the goodness of her parents; she mentioned their flaws, as well. She even told him about Teddy Stamp. Lastly, she talked about her disorder, how it controlled her life.

"Have you had any problems with depression or feeling out of control?"

"No, ma'am. Sometimes I'm a little happier than other times, but I'm never really sad unless somethin' has happened to make me sad, like every time one of my grandparents died. I'm sure sorry you've had to go through all that yourself."

She smiled a little grimly. "Well, as long as I take my meds and play nice, I'm okay."

He squeezed her hand. "Then always take your medicine, Miss Shannon. I just found you and I don't want to lose you anytime soon. Of course, you'll understand if I never want to have a thing to do with those others. Nasty people."

"I completely understand. And now, let's go over to Evie's. This will be a totally different experience, I promise."

Garrett immediately won over Evie, Dunn, and Toni. He took them all out to dinner the next evening.

"I can't get over how much he looks like you," Dunn said, his gaze passing back and forth between mother and son.

"It's the eyes," Toni said.

He nodded. Evie's odd smile alleged she knew something no one else did, but she merely said, "There's a lot of resemblance all over the place." To which everyone laughed, and the rest of that night was taken up with a lot of chatter, jokes, and several hands of Crazy Eights.

Garrett stayed five more days with his mother. The night before he left, they sat at her small dining table and munched on apples and cheese.

"You and I have talked about almost everything there is, I guess," he said.

She smiled, picked up a small cube of bright yellow cheddar. "That we have. I've nearly lost my voice from talking so much."

He laughed but sobered quickly. "There's one more thing, though. I haven't mentioned because I've been waiting for you to tell me."

She looked down at the teeth marks in the cheese she just bit in half. She knew without asking what it was going to say.

"You've not told me about my father."

It took every ounce of her strength to meet his eyes and say, "I can't tell you."

He frowned. "But don't I deserve to meet my father as much as I deserved to meet you?"

"Of course you do."

"Then please tell me about him—who he is and where he is. Do you think he'd be interested in knowing me?"

"Any man worth his human flesh would be proud to know you."

She got to her feet and busied herself with pulling out a box of saltines from the cupboard and arranging a handful on a small plate. She brought them to the table, then sat down again. She looked into her son's eyes.

"I wasn't a good girl. What I mean is, I wasn't chaste."

"Obviously not. I've never heard of a second virgin birth."

She smiled slightly at that. "Boys liked me."

He nodded. "You're pretty and funny and sweet. They thought you were hot."

"Well, I was. I liked boys. I liked them *a lot*." He said nothing, and she continued. "A lot of boys, Garrett. Not just one."

"Right." Still he waited for more information. "Your father is…could be…any one of a number of guys."

"I see," he said slowly. He looked away from her, stared blindly at a place on the wall. His face twitched as his mind absorbed these details.

She felt sick, but she had to say it and hoped he'd not reject her. "I was promiscuous. There's no other way to say it. But that was not, and is not, the real me. I think if I was not bipolar, I would have been a good girl. I really do. But I just felt…driven. I had to do things. Had to or I would've exploded."

Eventually his gaze came back to her.

"I believe you, Miss Shannon." He searched her face. "And it's okay, really it is. I know you, and it's enough."

When he was ready to return to Georgia, she held and wept. "Come again, please."

"I will, Miss Shannon. Just as often as I can. And remember you promised you'd come to visit me."

"But only if it's all right with your folks. I don't want them to feel uncomfortable or threatened by me in any way."

"They won't. I'll have two copies printed of that really cute photo that I took of us at the lake, and I'll send you one."

"I'm going to frame mine and display it right there on that little table. When anyone asks, 'Who's that?' I'll proudly say, 'He's my son.'"

Tears slid down his cheeks and he wiped them with the back of his hand.

"I'm gonna miss you, Miss Shannon."

"And I'm gonna miss you, my son. I wish things had been different, in so many ways, but…."

"But we have each other now, and it's okay. Right?"

His wide smile was so like hers when she was happy, but his crooked smile held a wistfulness that she'd seen elsewhere—a smile that seemed to hold a longing that would never been satisfied.

Through her tears and with trembling lips, Shannon returned his smile, cupped his face with gentle fingers and kissed both cheeks tenderly.

"Come back soon," she repeated.

He nodded, got into his car, and she stood in the parking lot long after he drove away.

SHANNON

Parting from her son for the second time opened a new wound in Shannon, and in spite of her meds, depression strode into her mind like an arrogant soldier. This time, because now there was someone else to fight for, to live for, she fought back.

She grimly approached the Woodrow County Behavioral Health Clinic, knowing the questions, the suggestions, the interventions—or lack thereof—that would be set before her. Up to that point, her attendance at therapy sessions had been as regular as healthy bowels because rules for her to maintain a disability pension demanded it. Now she went because of her son.

In the waiting room, she sat on an old green vinyl chair, its arms dark and grubby, slightly greasy. The other chairs were worse. The dull gray tile floor needed to be swept, mopped, waxed and polished. Just the sight of it gave Shannon the urge to cry. Country music piping from the speakers in the office leaked into the waiting room like sludge moving through rusty plumbing. How were patients expected to listen to songs about love gone bad, whiskey-cured ills, or dying children, then leave the behavioral health clinic with cheer and optimism? Shannon would rather listen to dripping water.

"Shannon Grady?"

She looked up at the strange voice, a silent groan in her throat. Another new therapist.

The woman who'd called her name wore a fitted navy suit, complete with white shirt and a red scarf knotted at the throat. She wore her jet-black hair in a tight chignon and stood at least six feet tall. Her long knobby fingers held Shannon's chart. She was the fifth therapist to see Shannon that year.

"This way," she said, as if Shannon had not trod that hallway several dozen times. The woman indicated the room three doors down on the right. "Please sit down. I'm Joanna."

She quietly closed the door behind them, and Shannon glanced around the office.

"You've hung some pictures," she said. "And put in some different furniture." She looked down. "And a blue and green rug."

"You like the changes?"

"It sure beats bare beige walls and worn-out stinky old chairs. You ought to put some new rugs on the floor in the waiting room, brighten the place up a little."

The woman smiled slightly.

"Would you like a bottle of water? Some juice?"

"No, thank you. I thought you weren't supposed to give us anything."

The woman waved her large, unadorned hand dismissively and laughed.

"We aren't. But I never follow strictly by the rules."

"As in 'Rules are made to be broken.'?"

The therapist folded her long frame into a chair and crossed her legs. Her feet, in their black flats, looked like gunboats. She examined Shannon through slitted eyelids then wrote something in a yellow legal pad.

"So…." She scanned the contents of the medical chart. "Are you still cutting yourself?"

"Not in years."

The woman chewed on the inside of her lips then said, "Let me see your arms."

Shannon sighed, pushed back the sleeves of her dark red sweater.

"Old scars, nothing new. See those right there? Those are where I tried to kill myself. And before you ask, no I do not have any thoughts of hurting myself or anyone else today."

Joanna gazed at the scars that showed almost purple on Shannon's fair arms then she glanced at the chart again.

"How long since you wanted to cut yourself?"

"A long time. Since before I started taking Copamin."

"You take it once a day?"

"Faithfully."

"Do you skip or double up doses?"

"No."

The woman looked up. "But you used to."

"Not the Copamin."

"But the other?"

"Yes."

"Why?"

"Because I didn't like the way it made me feel."

"How was that?"

Shannon sighed. It was all written down, right there in that chart the woman held. Why couldn't she read it for herself?

"Different meds made me feel different ways."

"Tell me about that." The pen was poised over the legal pad.

"Do we have to go through all this? I mean, good God, I tell you people the same thing every time someone new sits in that chair. Don't you have anything different to ask?"

Joanna sucked in her cheeks. "Are you always hostile?"

"I'm not hostile. But I just wish…oh, never mind." Her energy began to drain.

"'No, finish what you were going to say. 'I just wish…'"

Shannon didn't respond for a moment, then she said, "Do you really want to know, or are you just asking so you can fill the hour and bill the state?"

Something flickered across Joanna's face. She twitched in her seat and straightened her shoulders, then placed the legal pad and pen on her desk. With her fingers laced together loosely in her lap, she seemed friendlier somehow.

"Is that what you think we do here? Fill in hours just for money?"

"That's what it seems like to me."

Joanna leaned forward a little. "Tell me why you think that."

Their eyes met. This was the first time Shannon felt like a therapist was actually interested in what she had to say.

"Because of what I just said. Same questions every time I'm here. It's like none of you bother to read the charts and or even care to remember anything about your patient. Even when I see the same person for a month or two, it's still 'Are you taking your meds? Have you cut yourself? Have you skipped or doubled doses? Have you been drinking alcohol or using any narcotics? Rate your feelings right now, one to ten.' And then they talk about bipolar disorder again and the different medications used to treat it as if they're trying to teach a class. I know all about my illness. I probably know as much as you do, so I don't need any more education on it. This whole therapy business is a colossal waste of my time, and yours."

"So you think no one at this clinic cares about you."

"Or about any of the clients here. I only come because I have to."

"To get your disability check, you mean?"

She nodded. "And to get the meds I need but can't afford. I know how that sounds, believe me. I wish I could work," she said fervently. "I really would like to be a normal person and have a normal life and support myself."

"Have you tried to work?"

"Oh, God, yes. Ma's Pizza, the Dairy Diner, the Smoke Shop, Kidz Clothes, Max 'n Mabel's Market…you want me to go on?"

"No, that's fine. But even with the Copamin, you still feel you can't function at work?"

"I'm terrified I'll screw it up and get fired and by then I'll have lost the disability pension and have no way to survive."

"You harbor a lot of fear." Joann picked up her legal pad and started writing.

"I know."

"But you'd like to support yourself."

"I'd love to. Maybe my family wouldn't be so ashamed of me then."

Joanna's chin came up, just that much. "You think your family is ashamed of you?"

"Oh, I don't think it. I *know* it."

"Tell me about that."

For the next forty-four minutes, Shannon told Joanna about Owen and Donna. She mentioned Julie and the female lover she kept a secret from her family. A small timer rang on the desk to signal the end of her hour, startling her. Time had never gone so fast. No counselor had ever encouraged her to talk so much. When she walked out of the clinic, Shannon felt weak all over. She went home and slept for two hours.

Over the next few weeks, she spilled her family's secrets, her dead hopes and dreams.

"I've always liked interior design and decorating," she said with a smile. "I'd like to do that."

"Anything else?"

She thought about it. "I'm pretty organized. I might be good as an events planner."

"Okay. What else?"

"I really would have loved to be a wife and mother."

Joanna scribbled a while, then said, "You like traditional female roles."

"I never thought about it that way, but you're right. Home, hearth, family." She paused, then went on, "Come to think of it, interior decorating and events organizing and planning…wives and moms do that sort of thing all the time."

Joanna smiled slightly. "Yes. They do."

She talked about Garrett and the cold reception Owen offered him. "You should have been there, Joanna. They were just awful."

"But you told them how you felt?"

"I did."

"And if your brother were to walk in here right now and ask you to give him another chance, what would you say?"

"I'd say, 'You've had enough chances. Prove you've changed, and maybe we'll talk about it.'"

"So you'd still let him back into your life."

"I didn't say that. But a decent person extends grace."

Joanna gave her a long steady look, wrote on her pad and set it aside.

"I'm not sure I agree with you, but I reserve the right to be wrong. Your time's up. I'll see you next week."

"You've come a long way." Joanna told her at the end of a session one cold, rainy day in early November.

Shannon smiled. "You're able to draw a lot of things out of me. I've not even told my best friend some of the things I've shared with you."

Joanna handed her a tissue, and as Shannon wiped away tears, the woman said, "That's because once you finally let down your defenses with me you realized I care. Clients hold back so much for such a long time that sometimes I despair of them ever getting any better. But you were ready. You just needed to meet the right counselor."

"Yes. And I thank you."

Joanna smiled. "It's my job." Her smile slid away. "But you may not thank me for what I'm about to say."

Sharon's heart sank. "You're going to leave, aren't you? You therapists are like shifting sand."

"I'm not leaving. But there's something more."

"More what?"

"More going on in your life."

Shannon frowned. "I don't know what you mean. I live as quietly and simply as I possibly can. Nothing's going on."

Joanna studied her, then shook her head. "No. Something has happened to you, and you've never mentioned it."

"I've spilled my guts to you, Joanna." She shifted in her chair, irritated by the woman's words.

"Not completely."

"Yes. I have."

Joanna just sat there and looked at her without speaking. Waiting, Shannon supposed, for her to come clean with some sordid detail she'd deliberately hidden away.

"There's *nothing*," she said again.

But Joanna waited, and while she waited Shannon searched her mind for what she'd never mentioned.

"There are those times that I don't remember," she said at last.

Joanna blinked. "What?"

"But that was a long time ago. When I was little. By the time I was in junior high, I stopped having those memory gaps."

"Memory gaps."

"Yes."

"You blacked out?"

"Oh, I don't know as you'd say that. I just don't remember certain things, like the Christmas when I was five. Or that time I went camping in the backyard with Owen and Vernon Fletcher when they were trying out their camping equipment. I mean, I remember that those things happened, but I just don't remember them happening. Does that make sense?"

Joanna scribbled on her legal pad so fast her hand seemed to blur. Finally, she stopped writing.

"Have you ever had snippets of memories connected to those events?"

"No."

"Not even a tiny little memory of anything?"

Shannon shook her head, then stopped. "Wait a minute. Maybe."

"Go on," Joanna prodded.

"Sometimes…sometimes there's a…." She broke off, remembering all at once that shadow which used to come out of the dark night, that memory which hovered, just out of reach, dim but malevolent, creeping in….

"No!" she said suddenly, snapping up her head and meeting Joanna's eyes. "I can't. I won't."

"Shannon," she said so quietly it was almost a whisper, "whatever it is holds the key to your life. If you want to get better, you have to remember and face down whatever it is you're afraid of."

It was like her heart stopped beating. "No."

"You'll have to."

"But if I do…if I remember…."   She struggled to catch her breath.

"What, Shannon? If you remember, what will happen?"

She stared at the other woman, tried to moisten her dry mouth and could not.

"Something bad," she whispered.

"What is it?" Joanna's voice was soft, encouraging.

Shannon said no more.

They sat in a heavy silence until Joanna said softly, "Our time is almost up today."

"I know."

"When you come in next week, we're going to start tapping into that dark memory."

Shannon stiffened, feeling cold to the middle of her body. "I don't think I can," she managed to say. "I'm afraid."

"I understand, but I'll be right there. I'll help you."

Shannon stared at her, looking for something, anything, that she could use as an excuse not to comply. She glanced at one of the framed certificates on the wall, the one that showed Joanna was a trained, certified hypnotherapist. "Are you going to do something weird, like try to hypnotize me?"

"Not exactly, but we'll discuss it next week."

She swallowed hard and clenched her hands in her lap. "What if I go over the edge completely? What if I lose my mind altogether?"

The therapist broke the "no touching" rule and took both Shannon's trembling hands in hers.

"You won't. Nothing bad will happen, I promise."

Shannon looked into the eyes of a woman she'd grown to admire and respect. Joanna had listened to her, understood her, helped Shannon to make sense of feelings that had confounded her for years. She shook to the very center of her being.

"Remember why you are here." Joanna squeezed Shannon's fingers. "Will you trust me?"

Her voice weak, she said, "I'll try."

SHANNON

Joanna's dimly-lit office was pleasantly warm but not stifling. The light tones of New Age music played so softly, Shannon barely heard it. A thick, cream-colored pillar candle burned on stand, scenting the space with sandalwood.

"I thought you said you weren't going to try to hypnotize me," she said as she removed her coat.

"I'm not. This," she gestured with one hand, "is just staging to help you relax. No bright lights, no chilly air, no loud music."

"No country music. Joanna, why does the office staff play that god-awful country music so loud the rest of us have to hear it. I don't mind a good Garth Brooks song from time to time, but…."

"Does the music bother you?"

"Yes! It's depressing. Listen to it sometime."

"I will. Now, please sit on the sofa, or lie down on it. I want you to get as comfortable as possible."

At least Joanna's furniture was clean. She told Shannon once that she had paid for it herself because she couldn't stand to see her patients sit on the other.

"Who knows what germs lurked in years of dirt on that stuff?" she'd said.

Shannon sat on the dark green chenille covered sofa. She wasn't sure she could get comfortable, not when she faced remembering something she knew instinctively was better left forgotten. She settled onto the sofa, pulled a plump throw pillow to her and clutched it like a child with a teddy bear.

For a while she sat cuddling the pillow as Joanna busied herself with something at her desk. Bit by bit, Shannon began to relax. A downy, sage green throw lay folded on the far end of the sofa. She reached, pulled it over her and snuggled beneath its comforting softness. In a moment, she tucked both legs on the sofa and rested her head against the back.

"I don't think I've ever sat on a nicer couch," she told Joanna.

The woman looked up from the papers on her desk and smiled. "Comfortable, isn't it? Wish I had one like it at home."

"Me, too. In my home, I mean."

Joanna went back to her paperwork. After a bit, without looking up, she said, "Are you still nervous?"

"No. I'm too warm and snuggly."

"Good. I won't be much longer, so just close your eyes and listen to the music. Doesn't that candle smell nice?"

She closed her eyes. "Hmm. Sandalwood's my favorite." She listened to the gentle rise and fall of the flute, the quiet tones of piano, the accompaniment of the ocean surf. Or maybe it was the gentle rumble of a faraway storm. Shannon felt herself slide away into the embrace of velvety twilight and imagined she stood at the water's shore while on the distant horizon, clouds shimmered with faint lightning. She did not know she had slept until the timer bell rang.

She sat up and looked around. Joanna was still at the desk, but her gaze was focused on Shannon rather than the paperwork.

"How do you feel?"

Shannon did a brief internal assessment. "Rested. Relaxed but not sluggish."

In her chair, with her long hands folded together like a pair of elegant gloves and the candlelight touching a glow to her shining dark hair, Joanna smiled. Shannon read behind that expression. She threw off the chenille afghan.

"You hypnotized me! You promised you wouldn't."

"I did not hypnotize you. I provided you a means of releasing everything around you so you could go deep inside yourself."

Shannon gave her a look of measured skepticism and moved the pillow off her lap.

"So deep I went to sleep."

Joanna's knowing smile remained as she swiveled her chair and took something from her desk drawer. She turned back to Shannon.

"Take these things home with you." One by one, she handed Shannon a thick spiral notebook and two pens, a sandalwood pillar candle and candle warmer, and a music CD by Carlos Angelica. "You have a CD player?"

Shannon nodded as she eyed the offering. "Yeah. It's practically an antique."

Joanna laughed. "So's the CD, but it's what I have."

"You aren't supposed to give gifts to your patients. I know that rule."

"These are not gifts. These are part of your therapy intervention."

Shannon said nothing but she lifted the candle to her nose and inhaled.

"I have an assignment for you."

"Homework?"

"Something like that. Now listen. Each night when you go to bed, I want you to turn on the candle warmer. It will help the candle exude fragrance without burning. Slide the CD into your player and go to bed. Turn out all the lights and get warm and comfy. Don't think about anything, just let yourself relax."

"Oh, come on, Joanna! There's no such thing."

"No such thing as what?"

"As not thinking about anything."

"Oh?"

"Yeah. I mean, try it and you'll see…." But even as she spoke, she realized how easily she'd slipped into a quiet place where thoughts left her. "Okay. Well, maybe I'm wrong then."

"In the morning, before you get up, take that notebook and one of those pens and start writing. I want you to start writing down everything you remember, and I want you to begin with your earliest memory."

"For how long?"

"How long what?" Joanna had the most irritating habit of answering a question with another question.

"How long do I have to do this 'homework?'"

"For as long as it takes. And before you ask me how long it will take, I have to tell you, I don't know. It depends on how deeply buried those lost memories are and how determined your mind is to suppress them."

Shannon gave her a sharp look. "Is this regression therapy?"

"No. I'm not putting any suggestions into your mind at all. You can be sure your memories are accurate and nothing I've said to create false ones."

"Seems to me hypnotism would be easier."

Joanna smiled. "Yes. But this is more reliable. And you have made it perfectly clear that don't want to be hypnotized."

Shannon sat on the wondrously cozy sofa for a moment longer, looking at the items she held. Finally, she lifted her head.

"If this will help me, then I'll do it."

Shannon followed this new regimen faithfully. In fact, she became so devoted to it that, for the first time in their friendship, she withdrew a bit from Evie. Being the kind of woman she was, Evie gave Shannon plenty of space without resentment or unprovoked questioning, but she called daily. The concern in her voice roused Shannon's sense of guilt but she did not talk about this new treatment tool, fearing she'd spill her memories to Evie rather than record them on paper. She wanted them in black and white, where she could return to them if she needed to. Shannon spent the better part of most days filling the lines of that notebook. When it was full, she bought two more.

Then came the early hours of a cold January when she jumped awake in terror. The stalking black shadow had finally crept out of the darkness and into the light where she saw it all and the shades that accompanied it.

YOUNG SHANNON

The summer Shannon was three years old, her parents went to a church retreat and left her in the care of Owen and Donna. Julie, who usually took care of Shannon when their mother was gone, had graduated from high school and moved to California. Shannon missed her older sister, especially when Donna refused to play with her, which was always.

"Leave me alone," Donna said the morning after Curtis and Melba left. She was in the kitchen, rummaging through the cupboards. "I'm not playing with you, I'm not reading to you, I'm not watching cartoons with you. Go bother Owen."

She found her brother lounging near the swimming pool. He lay facing the sun, his eyes closed.

"Whatcha doin'?"

He jumped and opened his eyes.

"Don't go sneaking up on people like that. It's rude."

"I'm sorry I sneaked up. Whatcha doin'?"

"I'm getting some sun." He closed his eyes again and said nothing more.

"Me, too." She stretched out on the grass near the tiled deck of the pool.

Owen turned his head and opened one eye to look at her.

"No. You'll sunburn."

"Why will the sun burn me?"

"Because you have fair skin. Go play in the shade."

"What's fair skin?" she asked.

"It means you get sunburned easy."

She puckered her face into a frown. "But I—"

"Listen." He sat up, his face and chest pink. "Run inside and tell Donna to play dolls with you."

"She said for me to bother you."

"Why me? What's she doing?"

"She's in the kitchen."

He slumped and sighed. She went to him. When she laid her hand on his shoulder, his skin was all hot and sweaty.

"I think the sun wants to burn you too, Owen. Do you have fair skin?"

"Yeah. A little." He sighed again. "Go get a book and I'll read you a story. And tell Donna to bring me some lemonade." Shannon had almost reached the back door when he called, "And tell her to make lunch. For all of us, not just her."

Donna got mad and swatted her bottom when Shannon delivered the message.

"I'm not fixing lemonade," she snapped. "And I'm not making lunch for everybody. Make your own."

Later, with Shannon on his lap, Owen stopped reading in the middle of the story. He looked toward the house and said, "I wish Donna would hurry up with that lemonade. I'm hot and thirsty."

"She said she ain't making it."

"Say what?"

"She said you make your own lunch."

He frowned. "She told you that?"

"Umm hmm. And she spanked me, too."

"Spanked you?"

She nodded, clambered down, turned her back to him and pulled down her pink shorts. "Right there on my bottom." She pointed to her buttocks.

Owen was silent and she looked over her shoulder at him. "It hurted."

He blinked and said, 'Pull up your shorts, Shannon, for Pete's sake! You don't go around showing your rear end to people."

"I was just showing you where she hitted me." As she tugged up the shorts, she said, "I'm hungry, Owen. You gonna make me lunch now?"

He was looking far away. She followed his gaze, saw nothing different than usual.

"After lunch are you gonna finish that story?"

"I don't know." He got up and stalked into the house but did not stop in the kitchen. Instead he went upstairs to his bedroom and shut the door. Shannon trotted after him and knocked on his door. "Aren't you gonna make me somethin' to eat?"

"Go away."

She waited for a long time, but he did not come out. Pretty soon the smell of something baking in the kitchen drew her there.

"Whatcha doin', Donna?"

"I'm baking me some brownies. You want another spanking?"

"No."

"Then leave me alone."

"I'm hungry."

"I don't care. Get out of here."

"Can I have some brownies?"

"No."

"Why?"

"'Cause they're for me. Now go away."

"I'm hungry!"

Donna glared at her. "Ever since you were born I'm the one who has to take care of you, and I'm sick to death of your whining all the time. Go away."

Shannon wondered why Donna was mad. If Julie was still here, Julie would fix her lunch and play with her and read her books and everything. Donna never wanted to do anything with Shannon.

She went back outside and looked at the book Owen had been reading to her. She lay down on the chair where he'd been getting some sun and tried to get the sun to burn her. If the sun burned her, maybe Donna would feel sorry for her and give her some lunch. But soon Shannon got too hot and sweaty and moved to the shade beneath the big tree far away from the pool. Even though she was hungry, she went to sleep on the grass. When she woke up, the sunlight wasn't very bright anymore, and the shade of the house covered the whole backyard. Her stomach was so hungry she felt sick.

Inside the kitchen, Donna was stuffing a hamburger in her mouth.

"I'm still hungry," Shannon told her. "You forgot to give me lunch."

Donna rolled her eyes, her cheeks all fat and lumpy from the food in her mouth.

"Can I have a hamburger, too?"

"No." Donna crammed a fistful of potato chips between her lips.

"But I'm hungry." She began to cry.

"Shut your whining mouth." Still munching on her hamburger, Donna went to a cabinet, pulled out an unopened bag of potato chips, a box of Goldfish crackers, a package of Oreos, then threw them on the table. From the refrigerator she got out a bottle of Pepsi, a carton of French onion dip, yesterday's left-over peach cobbler, and a package of sliced salami. She grabbed a carton of ice cream out of the freezer and plunked it down next to the salami.

"There. Shut up and leave me alone. Stupid, spoiled brat."

Shannon stared at the array of treats on the kitchen table. Mommy never let her have treats for lunch or dinner, only as a small snack once a day. Donna sneaked treats all day long, but Mommy never saw her to do it. Shannon got a spoon from the drawer, climbed up on a chair and ate until she couldn't hold another bite. When her tummy began to feel funny, she went to her room and curled up on the bed.

It was dark when she woke up again. Her tummy hurt so bad. When she sat up, everything she had eaten for dinner came out. It was all over her bed, and her pajamas and her skin. She began to cry but no one came to help her. She crawled through the nasty on her bed and went out into the hall. The light was on under Donna's door across the hall and under Owen's door on the far end. The rest of the house was dark. She went to Donna's door and opened it.

Her sister sat in the bed, reading a paperback romance novel Mommy had forbidden her to bring into the house. She had a bag of Fritos on her lap.

"I throwed up," Shannon announced.

Startled, Donna looked over the top of the book.

"Haven't you ever heard of knocking?"

"I throwed up and my tummy hurts."

"So?"

"I'm all dirty. I got throw-up all over me and my bed."

"Oh, for the love of…." Donna slammed down her book. She looked

Shannon up and down. Her face got puckery, as if she were going to throw up, too. "I'm not cleaning up your mess. Owen!" she yelled. "Owen!"

His door opened and a few seconds later he stood in her doorway. He wore pajama bottoms with a drawstring around the middle and no shirt. His chest and face still looked pink.

"What?"

She pointed at Shannon.

He looked down then took a step back. "What happened?"

"My tummy hurt and I throwed up. It's on my bed, too."

"I am not cleaning up her nasty mess." Donna folded her arms defiantly.

"You think I want to?"

"No, but someone has to, and I'm not doing it."

Owen took a deep breath and blew it out loudly between his lips. "Shannon, go take a bath and I'll clean your bed."

She blinked up at him. "I'm not supposed to touch the hot water knobs. Mommy said."

"I'll start your bath water."

She followed him into her bathroom and watched as he started the water. "Mommy puts in Mr. Bubble." She pointed to the box on the shelf near the tub.

Owen poured it into the water then looked at her. "I'll take your pajamas to the laundry room. Can you wash yourself?"

She nodded as she stripped off the smelly clothes. "Sometimes Mommy lets me wash myself, but she always dries me off."

He stayed in the bathroom until she was in the tub and the bubbles were all around her. Without a word he handed her a pink washcloth, a bar of soap and the bottle of baby shampoo. "Wash your hair, too. I'll bring you some clean pajamas and put clean sheets on your bed."

Shannon smiled at him. "You're the best brother in the whole world!"

He smiled at her and tousled her hair. "Yeah. I know."

Later, he carried in a pair of blue pajamas with white lambs on them. "Here. Put these on when you're through."

She stood up, the suds sliding in soft piles down her skin. "I'm done. I never washed my own hair before. Is it clean?"

"It doesn't have puke in it anymore."

"OK." She held out one hand. "Mommy always helps me get out so I don't fall."

Owen held her hand as she straddled the wide edge of the tub then stood dripping on the pink mat.

"That towel." She pointed to a pink one on the towel rack.

He handed it to her.

"I can't dry my own self," she said.

"Yes, you can. You're a big girl."

She stuck out her lower lip. "Mommy always does it cause she says I don't never do it right."

For a moment, Owen looked as if he'd throw the towel at her. He shook out the folds and said, "Come here."

"Don't tangle me," she said as he began to rub her head.

He blotted her long hair carefully then dried her face. "Don't forget my ears. Mommy says if I get water in my ears, I'll get the earache."

Owen swabbed out her ears with the corner of the towel, then ran the towel quickly over the rest of her body. She didn't feel dry.

"I'm still wet," she said as he started to hang up the towel. She lifted her arms and he dried her. She pointed to her belly button and he blotted it. She hoisted out her bottom.

"Mommy says I have to have all my down-here real dry so I don't get the itchies."

He hesitated, then knelt and began to dry off her bottom and private area. He turned her back to him, wiped off her plump little cheeks, then spread them apart and ran a bit of the towel slowly between them. He moved the towel forward and up into that place. He did it longer than Mommy ever did. Then he dropped the towel and she felt his fingers rubbing back and forth, touching her, making her feel funny.

"Mommy never does that," she said, "but I like it."

Owen jumped up, threw the towel over the tub. "Don't you tell Mommy."

"Why?"

"Because she won't want to dry you like that."

"Why?"

"Because it's too much trouble and she's too busy."

"Oh."

"You don't want to cause Mommy any trouble, do you?"

"No."

"Then you mind me and don't tell her or Donna or Daddy or anyone. You understand?"

"Cause they'd want to be dried like that and it's trouble?"

"Yes."

"Okay, Owen."

"It's our secret forever?"

"Yup."

She went back to bed and crept between the clean sheets.

"Owen is the best brother in the world," she whispered to the friendly night around her, "to get me bath water and Mr. Bubble and clean jammies, and to dry me. He doesn't call me a brat like Donna does."

She was almost asleep when her door opened. Slowly, quietly, just wide enough for someone to come into her room and shut the door silently. The room was dark, and Shannon could not see her visitor.

Maybe Mommy had come home early and was going to kiss Shannon good night.

"Mommy?"

"Shh! Mommy's not here."

"Owen?" she whispered.

"Yes."

He stood, a dark shadow in a dark room. She could not make out his face or even the shape of his body. He peeled back the covers.

"Scoot over," he said.

Owen came into her room late at night a lot after that. He told her that someone watched through her window after dark. He said if she ever mentioned what happened between them to anyone, even God, the boogeyman that hid outside the windows and in the dark, shadowy corners of her room would come and get her the middle of night and she'd never see Daddy and Mommy again. She never mentioned any of it to anyone, even when Mommy or Daddy asked her why she was so quiet these days.

When Shannon was five, Curtis and Melba went to St. Louis for a wood-products show and seminar.

At the supper table Melba said, "No company while we're gone, neither one of you. Not even for pizza or a game of ping-pong. You'll have to take care of your little sister, Donna. You know she's not been feeling well lately."

Donna pooched out her lower lip. "I'm spending the night with Karen. She's having a slumber party. If you ever listened to me when I talk, you'd know that, Mother."

"Then I guess your brother will have to watch her."

Owen looked up from his dinner plate and shrugged. "Yeah. I can take care of her."

Donna sneered at him. "You're such a goody-goody."

He pointed his fork at her and gave her a threatening look.

"As long as I don't have to look after the brat," she told him.

"Donna, you're about to be grounded," Melba warned. "And you'd do yourself a favor if you'd try to be more like your big brother."

She looked at her mother, her eyes defiant. "I'm fifteen and too old to be grounded."

"You are never too old to be grounded. Now go clean the kitchen."

Donna shoved back her chair and got up. "You always treat me like hired help!"

Her glance fell on Shannon, and her eyes filled with venom. "Just you wait," she said. "Someday you won't be little and cute, and the world won't fall at your feet the way it does now."

Confused, Shannon looked her mother, who seemed lost in thought, then at Owen.

He shrugged, gave her smile, and said, "She means you always get what you want, Shannon. I'll take you out and buy you an ice cream. Okay?"

She grinned. "You're the best brother in the whole world."

"Yeah. I know."

The night Owen babysat Shannon, he took her to McDonald's. He bought her a Happy Meal and afterwards a sundae. They went to Walmart where he bought her a pair of fuzzy slippers that looked like Winnie the

Pooh. They looked at the toys and he bought her two story books, a giant coloring book and huge box of crayons, a Barbie doll and assortment of doll clothes. There were no Happy Baby dolls like the one that died at Christmas. The company did not make them anymore.

Back home, he played Candy Land with her until the doorbell rang.

"Hey, guys!" he said when he opened the door.

Two boys from Owen's senior class at school came into the living room. Shannon waved at them and went back to playing with colorful little pieces of her game.

"Thought as long as you're stuck here taking care of her, I'd bring a video," said the boy named Vernon Fletcher.

"What'd you bring?"

The two boys nudged each other and snickered.

"You'll like it," J.J. Forbes said. "We've nearly worn it out."

"'Bout melted the VCR." They snickered again.

Vernon dipped his head toward Shannon. "Will she stay here, you think?"

All three looked at her.

"Oh, yeah. She's a good girl. Aren't you, Shannon?"

She nodded vigorously. "I do everything I'm told."

"And you won't tell Dad and Mom that Vernon and J.J. came by tonight, will you?"

He gave her a look that made her feel creepy inside, and she knew the boogeyman might get her.

"Okay, Owen."

"Let's go. This thing's burning my hands."

They left the room, but Owen stopped in the doorway and said, "We're going down to the rec room to watch videos. You stay here until I tell you otherwise." He gave her another one of those looks.

"Okay. Can I play with my new Barbie you bought me?"

"Sure. Just stay out of the basement."

She played for a long time, changing the doll's clothes and pretending to go to town, to church, to visit friends, but after a while the room got chilly, and she got bored and lonely. Maybe Owen forgot her. She crept quietly down the carpeted steps to the rec room with its Foosball game and ping-pong table. The big television sat on the far side of the room near the fireplace.

The television was on. There was a naked little girl on the screen. A grown man touched her in the way Owen touched Shannon. She had on makeup and she smiled, but Shannon could see that the television girl was scared.

"Why is she scared, Owen?" she called out.

All three boys jumped.

"Get upstairs!" her brother roared at her. "I told you to stay upstairs, didn't I? What're you doing, sneaking down here like that?"

She fled up the steps and back into the living room, shaking hard, terrified by the anger in his voice. She sat on the couch and hugged one of the throw pillows. After a while Owen came into the room. She looked at him through wide eyes.

"You gonna hit me? Are the boogies in the corners gonna get me?"

"Only if you don't do what I tell you. Come with me."

She slid off the couch and followed him downstairs. The other two boys watched her, and she did not like the looks in their eyes.

"Vernon and J.J. want you to make them feel good the way you make me feel good."

She took Owen's hand, held it tightly and hid behind him. "I don't want to."

"But I want you to. Didn't I take you to McDonald's and buy you Pooh slippers and a doll? Didn't I play a dozen games of Candy Land with you? Aren't I the best brother in the world?"

She blinked up at him, terrified.

"You have to do what I say, Shannon."

Owen wasn't the best brother in the world, after all.

PART

THREE

OWEN

Owen Grady unfastened the top button of his shirt and loosened his tie. His leather chair creaked as he leaned back and closed his eyes. He wished he could get her out of his mind once and for all. They were wrong, these thoughts. Satan was doing his utmost to corrupt Owen's soul by constantly filling his head with her. Ever since Randall Yeager came to serve as minister to the Woodrow Worship Center last year, Owen had battled the urge to dwell on the image of the preacher's wife, Patty. Her shining light brown hair, her hazel eyes, her full lips—

He leaped out of the chair and strode across his second-floor office to look outside. The view of the parking lot did little to cool his heated notions and turn his mind to nobler themes. Not that he would ever indulge in anything as base as sleeping with the wife of his pastor, but now that she was the church secretary, Owen saw her several times a week. It wasn't easy for him to control his wandering eyes and straying thoughts.

There were times in the church office when Patty lifted her gaze from her work to meet Owen's eyes, and he wanted to sweep her into his arms, kiss those full lips, bury his fingers in her hair, fondle her breasts. Sometimes, when Pastor Yeager was absent and Owen found himself alone in the office with Patty, he stood so close to her that her warmth and perfume filled his senses. For days after he was sure her scent lingered in the air around him. He gave wide berth to his wife during those times.

He knew Patty wanted him, knew she fought the same urges he did. Yesterday, when he bent close, pretending to read the computer screen as she retrieved information for him from the Internet, she had looked up at him as he gazed down at her, his heart thundered as her lips parted and her sweet breath came warm and fast near his. He leaned in, ready to toss aside caution and kiss her with all the pent-up passion he had stored.

"Owen!" she'd gasped, as if shocked, and rolled her chair back. She stared at him wide-eyed.

He'd murmured some sort of foolishness, backed out of the room, and left the church. By the time he reached home, he was convinced that he never would have kissed her, not really. He told himself he'd never made the move if she hadn't looked at him so provocatively, had not been so close, had not smelled so sweet. It was her fault, the whole scenario, because he never would've presumed to make a move without her tempting him.

Now he looked down at the array of older model cars owned by his employees in the Grady Wood Products parking lot and forced his mind to other problems. Trouble brewed and covering his tracks was going to prove tricky, if not impossible.

Not that tapping into the company's discretionary fund was illegal. After all, he owned the place. But now, every cent was gone without a receipt to show for it, and the year-end audit was next week. The Lexus Sarah Jean just had to have, his Rolex, the imported Louis the XIV desk.... Owen didn't have the cash in his private account for these things, and he couldn't replace the money.

Lack of funds was why he'd borrowed the money in the first place, trusting the Lord would heal the economy and send more business his way. He'd always prided himself on having the very best of everything, from designer clothing and luxury cars to private schools for his children. Over his father's protests, Owen had built the manor house to prove to the people of Woodrow, Arkansas, how very grand he was and how much God favored him.

What he chose not to share with anyone else in the family was that the place tapped him dry. Even with cutting back worker hours, the layoffs and canceling employee health insurance benefits, company finances were still too short. He would have to lay off more old-timers and hire younger ones who were willing to work part-time for minimum wage and no benefits.

Right this very minute Sarah Jean and Donna were in Memphis on a shopping spree, and Christmas was barely a month gone. His wife was greedy, and that was the honest truth.

Oh, the whole thing looked bad. It made him look bad. He could not let anyone find out anything just yet. And how he would manage that with the audit next week....

Where was the Lord when you needed him the most? For all the good Owen had done for his church and his town, he deserved a miracle, and he deserved it *now*. In the meantime, he needed to cover his tracks.

He turned from the window to see his secretary Cindy at his desk, rifling through papers.

"Cindy!" he shouted, startling her so bad she dropped the folder she had been holding.

"Gracious, Mr. Grady, you scared me out of twenty years growth."

He strode to his desk, crowding her out of the way.

"I'll take care of this." He gathered the scattered papers and shoved them into a folder.

"You know that odd purchase-order paperwork from Keene & Company we were talking about last week?" she said. "The paperwork purchasing sent up here for your approval? Keene & Company are the ones who pulled their order—"

"I know who they are!" he snapped.

"I got a letter from the bankruptcy court today and they—"

His head shot up. "Don't tell me they've gone under."

She nodded. "So I need all the paperwork we have connected with them."

"I'll take care of it," he choked out. His head felt ready to burst.

"Oh, but—"

"Go home, Cindy."

"But it's only three—"

"Don't argue with me. Go home." He pulled himself as straight as possible, refastened his shirt button and tightened his tie. Slipping his arms into his jacket, he added, "I'm going home early myself."

Cindy looked at him wide-eyed. "Do you want me to schedule a doctor's appointment for you? Shall I run and get you some medicine?"

He wanted to smack her upside the head. "I want to go home. I'll give you a full day's wages if you just leave right now and stop bothering me."

"Well, then." Her face registered confusion but she was a brown-noser if there ever was one, and she'd leave, if only to please him. She reached for the jumbled folder in which he'd stuffed all paperwork from his desk. "I'll just take those papers with me and look through them at home for that—'"

He snatched it back. "I'll do it myself! Leave. You're making my head pound."

"Yes, sir. All right." She went to the door, gave him a curious appraisal. "Are you sure you don't want me to…?" He pinned her with a murderous look, and she responded with a bright smile that held fear in it. "All righty then. I hope you get to feeling better. See you tomorrow, Mr. Grady."

At home, he shoved the paperwork into his safe. Right then, all he wanted to do was think, figure out how to save himself from humiliation and gossip. He sat in his favorite chair in the study and opened his Bible. He read a chapter or two of Lamentations, which did not make him feel any better. He read the final chapter of the Book of Revelation, which did. He read several of the Psalms and finally found himself calm enough to have a bite of supper.

He had just built a thick sandwich and had a bite in his mouth when his phone rang. He swallowed hard and fast, felt the food hit his esophagus in a hard lump.

"Owen Grady here," he barked into the phone.

"Owen!"

The voice on the other side seemed familiar but unidentifiable in its hoarse, strangled tones.

"Who—"

"You are a nasty, filthy pig of a man. You almost got away with it, you wretched barnacle."

His ears rang from the attack.

"Who is this?" he managed to gasp.

"This is Shannon! Your baby sister. The one you turned your back on, the one you ignore, the one you asked to forgive you and promised to treat better. Maybe I could have forgiven you someday, but now I never will. I remember it, Owen. I remember all of it."

He gulped, terrified to the marrow of his bones by the rage in her voice.

"Now, s-see here, Sh-Shannon. Why…what…why are you so m-mad?"

His eardrum vibrated from her scream. "Are you kidding me? You know what you did, you filthy dog. You know, you know, you know!"

"If you m-mean that boy you brought over l-last summer…you know I couldn't l-let him parade around as a G-Grady. He…he's illegitimate."

"You fool, Owen. You fool, you…you whited sepulcher! Full of righteousness on the outside but full of rot on the inside. You make me sick. But that's not what I'm talking about, and you know it!"

"I didn't know about the missing money, I swear it! And it's all Sarah Jean's fault, anyway."

There was the briefest of pauses from her end, then she shouted, "What in the hell are you talking about. Missing money? I don't give a flying fuck about missing money. I'm talking about what you did to me as a little girl. You and Vernon Fletcher and J.J. Forbes."

"Y … you're crazy …." he croaked. All strength left his legs. His sandwich hit the travertine tile with a splat. He followed the food and lay in a heap, certain his heart had stopped completely, that his breath would never return. He kicked, hands clawing the floor as he struggled to hold on. Far away her voice kept coming through the receiver, railing and ranting.

Owen passed out as efficiently as a Victorian lady in a tight corset. Out of a fuzzy gray fog, he found his way back to the solid world of his kitchen—the Dacor stainless steel range, the black granite countertop, the cherry cabinets.

He hoped he wasn't going to have a heart attack like his father did.

"Jesus, help me," he whimpered. He couldn't die until that money was accounted for, somehow.

Weak as he was, Owen sat up. His vision swam briefly then cleared. The remains of the chicken salad splotched his shirt. His gaze fell on the telephone on the floor nearby and his blood froze.

Maybe it hadn't been a dream, after all. He stared at the phone, reached for it, turned it off so she couldn't call him again. How long had he been out? Minutes, hours?

It would be just like his youngest sister to break in, hide someplace inside his house then attack him in the middle of the night. Just like her to do it! Maybe even enlist some of her vile cohorts to help her. He struggled to his feet. His legs shook, but he was all right.

Wishing he had a couple of Rottweilers standing guard, Owen set the security alarm. He checked every door and window upstairs and down, then checked them again. He closed blinds; he pulled draperies. He searched his home, under every bed, inside every closet, behind every door.

Shannon always did such stupid things. Teddy Stamp for instance. A lowlife if there ever was one and she had dragged him right into their lives with no thought for anyone but her own self. And look at the way she had shown up on his doorstep last summer with that boy, shamelessly proud of him. The kid gave Owen the creeps, the way he'd been so friendly. He'd been after the Grady fortune, no doubt about it. One other thing was sure: Shannon would never get another penny from the fortune their father had worked so hard to build. And neither would her bastard son nor any of her disgusting friends.

Owen stood in the middle of the great room. Its soaring ceiling, the huge fireplace, the resplendent antique furnishings Sarah Jean had chosen…none of it offered him an iota of comfort and safety right then. If Shannon went around telling people about when she was little….

The house phone on a table near the fireplace rang and he jumped a foot. He let it ring until the answering machine caught it.

"Pick up the phone, you coward," came Shannon's voice, "unless you want me to come over there right now—"

"Don't come over here!" he squeaked from a place of safety behind a large chair.

Her voice continued to rail at him. "I want you to tell me why you raped me when I was a little girl. I want to know if you've molested your own girls. Did you touch Donna's kids? I'm gonna talk to her, you know, tell her—"

He picked up the receiver and screamed at her, "You liked it, Shannon. You always said it made you feel good. You made me do it. You made me, and you know it!" He shook so hard his voice trembled, made him sound like he was on the verge of tears.

"You nasty, filthy liar. I was a little girl. What about that time in the basement? You and your friends watching kiddie porn and then you let your friends molest me."

His mouth worked before words finally came out. "It's n-not true. You're, you're c-crazy, and you're m-making it up."

"I am not making it up." How could she, the troublemaker of their family, sound so in control when the world was crashing? Why was this happening?

"Yes, you are. If you aren't lying then why'd you wait until now to say anything? Because you're m-making it all up. Everybody knows you're crazier than a loon. No one will believe a word you say."

"I'm not making up anything," she said in a measured tone. "And I haven't said anything before now because I didn't remember it until now. My God, no wonder I've been so sick all my life, you and your perverted—"

"You can't prove anything," he shrieked. "You just w-want to ruin me and my f-family. That's all you've ever wanted, Shannon. To take our money and to ruin us."

"Have you touched your own kids, Owen? What about the kids at church? If you think I'm going to let this slide, you can think again. I'm going to the authorities first thing in the morning and I'm going to the newspaper. I'm going to let your preacher know, too."

Panic laid hold of him in ways he'd never known. He lost his ability to think, to speak. He yanked out the phone cord from the wall, cutting off her voice. Drowning in fear, Owen watched his life flash before his eyes, just as the old cliché promised. He sank to his knees on the polished cypress floor. Terror filled every cell. He had to save himself, save the Grady name and the family fortune, but his mind seemed unable to function. For hours, he knelt, frozen in place. All he could do was rock back and forth, awaiting divine intervention that never occurred.

Echoes of Shannon's threats sounded in his head until he grasped either side of his skull and squeezed. Her voice would not stop. Images of her as a tiny girl, her blue eyes turned trustingly to him, her bright smile shining on him, then her small round body as bare as the day she was born stirring up his lust, her willingness to touch and be touched. It was all her fault! Now she was going to ruin him because it was in style these days to cry abuse or molestation by popular and powerful public figures.

"I can't let her do that," he whispered. In his mind's eye, Owen saw a way to stop her.

Coldness reached the marrow of his bones.

OWEN

The pistol had belonged to his grandfather, an old .38 Special that Curtis had kept in his lower desk drawer at work.

"I never want to use the thing," he'd told Owen once, "but I'd rather take down a violent threat than let someone hurt me or some of my workers. I have it here, just in case."

The revolver was part of the Grady legacy, and Owen had kept it, but he hated the sight of it. There had been a time when he liked guns as well as the next man, but these days, with workplace violence so often on the news, any instrument of hostility frightened him. He kept the gun in a metal lockbox in the far corner of his basement.

At two o'clock in the morning, while the night sky hung onto frigid stars and the moon hid behind a cloud, he took the revolver out of its hiding place, filled the chamber and stashed it beneath the front seat of his Mercedes. On the seat next to him was a thick throw pillow from the vast array Sarah Jean had stored in the basement for whatever fool reason the woman had to collect pillows.

He drove toward Shannon's apartment. Every light was off in the complex, but streetlights were his enemies. He pulled into a construction site five blocks away and parked behind a huge Dumpster. Gingerly, Owen slid the pistol from beneath the seat. He gazed at it for a moment, shuddered, and got out of the car. He tucked the gun into his waistband, stuffed the pillow under his large sweatshirt and pulled his coat snugly about him.

Keeping to the far limits of the light, he moved through the frigid air like a skittish stray cat until he reached the corner of her building. From that point and until he got inside the apartment, there would be no hiding in the shadows. He eyed Evie Kendall's apartment across the way.

That ol' gal better be sound asleep. The other apartment dwellers were older than dirt and slept the sleep of the dead. He figured most of them were deaf and half-blind, anyway.

Sucking in a deep breath, he walked quickly to Shannon's door, never looking right or left, wanting to appear as normal as if this were broad daylight. Shannon likely had men coming and going at all hours of the day and night, anyway. One more would rouse no suspicion, and the pillow in his shirt disguised the build of his body.

The storm door was unlocked, a lucky thing since he had forgotten about it. Storm doors generally had locks only on the inside. He raised his left hand, pretended to knock, his fingers missing the door panel by a millimeter.

Blocking anyone's view with his body, he slid his credit card between the lock and the frame and gained easy access. It was a trick he'd learned years ago when he forgot his key and didn't want to face Sarah Jean's wrath. That had been in the old house, though. In the manor house, two keys and a computerized key press combination opened the doors.

Owen closed the doors as silently as he had opened them and stood in total darkness. He paused, waiting for his eyes to adjust, and tried to remember the layout of the apartment. He had only been in it once or twice, the last time in the summer with Dr. Pressman.

What a bust that endeavor had been, feeling the need to apologize for his detachment, her broken promise to try to live right and attend church, then her getting so angry just because he and Sarah Jean would not accept that boy. At the revival meeting when he'd gone forward to pray, he honestly believed God was leading him to seek his sister's forgiveness, but now he saw it was just a ploy by Satan, something to confound his life and distract him from right living. If Dr. Pressman were here right now, Owen knew the man would agree, but he doubted the evangelist would sanction this current undertaking.

Not that it mattered now. The important thing was to preserve the family and all it stood for. Shannon had been a thorn for too long. If she were allowed to continue, nothing good would remain for his children. Or his children's children.

He made out dim shapes in the darkness—the dining table between the kitchen and living room, her shabby old chair, the sofa along one wall. The bedroom door was on the other side of the room. He moved toward it, bumped into a small end table and sent the lamp teetering. Heart pounding in his throat, he caught the lamp by its shade just before it crashed to the floor.

He paused. Listened. Heard nothing and moved again, one small, soundless step at a time until he was at the door of her bedroom. It stood open and he waited in the doorway for her to move or speak or give any sign that she knew he was there.

The night remained silent and motionless, peaceful, except for the wild pounding of his terrified heart.

Owen walked into the tiny bedroom. In three steps he stood a mere two feet from her head. She slept with her face turned from him, her right hand beneath the pillow. How could she sleep so soundly when she had caused so much trouble? Did her conscience never bother her?

Without creating so much as a rustle of clothing, he slipped the pistol from his waistband. It seemed to weigh a thousand pounds. He pulled the pillow out from his shirt and snugged it against the barrel.

"Shannon?" he whispered.

She murmured in her sleep but did not wake.

He held the pillow and the revolver to the back of her head.

"You made me do this."

"Hmm?"

He squeezed the trigger.

OWEN

Owen stared at the damage he'd just done. One shot, straight into her crazy, sick brain. He thanked God for the lack of light; otherwise, the blood that poured out of his sister's skull would look like blood, instead of a merely rapidly spreading darkness. What he saw on the wall he ignored. He was pretty sure her face was gone. The smell was unpleasant to someone with his sensitive stomach. He breathed through his mouth.

At least she had not awakened and looked at him. He did not want the memory of her eyes looking at him in the last moment of her life.

He plucked away the bright white fibers of pillow stuffing that had not made it into the wound, put them into his pocket, then he crammed the pillow back under his shirt and tucked the shirt around it snugly. He patted it.

A regular ol' Santa Claus.

He wiped his fingerprints off the revolver, placed it in Shannon's left hand, and curled her fingers around the handle. He waited a moment, ticking off his agenda, then certain he'd taken care of everything, he left her room, shutting the bedroom door behind him and cleaning the knob with the sleeve of his jacket. He washed his hands in the bathroom, just in case he had blood on them, then he left the apartment, making sure the door was locked behind him.

Once he was home, Owen took a steaming hot shower and tried to wash away the stress of the day. For a moment, he found himself wishing he was a drinking man. Right then would have been the time to down a glass of whiskey, or maybe even a bottle. Then he caught the notion and was appalled at himself.

"Lord, forgive me. I know how you hate drunkenness."

Later, dressed in warm flannel pajamas and the robe and slippers his oldest daughter had given him for Christmas, Owen built a fire in the fireplace. When it was good and roaring, he shoved in the sweatshirt and mutilated throw pillow and watched the flames consume them in seconds.

He got the telephone handset and settled down in his recliner. He stared at receiver for a moment, wondered if he should wait to make the call. Instinct told him waiting spelled certain disaster, waiting gave someone else the opportunity to find then report her body.

He punched in the numbers and listened as the phone rang, once, twice, three times. It rang four more times before a groggy voice croaked, "Yeah. What is it?"

"Vernon. It's Owen."

"Owen! Godamighty, man, it's after three. What are you doing calling me at this time a day? Something wrong? Sarah Jean okay?"

"She's fine. Listen, something's happened and you have to help me."

"All right."

"My sister's dead."

"Donna? Oh my God, what happened? Heart attack?"

"No, not her. My other sister."

"Julie."

"*No*. Shannon! She's dead."

There was a brief pause. "She finally succeeded, did she?"

"You could say that."

"Well, buddy, I'm sorry. You knew she'd do it sooner or later. I'm surprised she pulled through that last time."

"Yes. Well, it's not that simple, Vern. What I mean is, when you go to her apartment…. Look, she remembered."

Silence.

"Do you know what I'm saying, Chief? She remembered that night with you and me and J.J."

"My God. Did she tell anyone?"

"I don't think so. She was going to. In the morning. The news-paper, the church, probably the TV and radio station. She was going to ruin me, Vernon. I had to stop her, so I did."

A moment's pause. "You stopped her." Silence again, this time long and bristling. "What's that mean, you stopped her?"

"Come on, Vern. I fixed it so she wouldn't tell anyone. Ever."

"Jesus Christ."

"You know I don't like that kind of language, Chief."

The other man laughed sourly. "You just murdered your own sister, but you don't like my language? Man, have you lost your mind?"

"Maybe. But you have to help me. You have to be sure you're the first cop on the scene. It's a suicide, you know."

"Except that it isn't."

"I didn't say that."

"You didn't have to. Owen, what do you want me to do? You've just confessed to murder—"

The recliner bucked as he sat straight up. "I have not!"

"Same as. What's to stop me from coming over there right now and arresting you?"

Owen swallowed hard and fought for breath.

"We've been friends for forty years. We've been through a lot together, and my family has done a lot for this town…. If it wasn't for me, you know you'd not be the chief of police right now."

The other man said nothing.

"Come on, Vernon. If I go down, Grady Wood Products goes down with me. Woodrow depends on me to keep this town alive."

"Aw, Owen. Man. Do you realize what you're asking?"

Owen smiled grimly. He'd won. "You know what you have to do."

Another pause, long, tense, unfathomable.

"Yeah," the chief said finally. "I know."

"Do it."

Owen received the call the next morning at work. When he rushed out of his office, his made sure his face was painted with alarm and concern, and he made doubly sure his vigilant and efficient secretary took notice.

"Mr. Grady!" she said as he charged through the outer office and passed her desk. "Is anything wrong?"

"It's my younger sister," he said, choking his voice. "She's…I have to go. Cancel my appointments today."

"What happened?"

"I'm not sure. The police think that maybe…maybe she killed herself." He closed his eyes, grimaced in mock grief.

"Oh, my God! What do you want me to do?"

He opened his eyes, looked at her as tenderly as a father would gaze at his baby.

"Keep things running this morning, then dismiss everyone at noon." He swallowed hard, took a deep breath as if it was hard for him to say these words. "And see if you can cancel that audit next week. I …I just…can't…."

She put her hand on his shoulder, bit her lower lip. Tears swam in her gray eyes.

"You leave it all to me, Mr. Grady. I'll take care of everything."

His heart lifted, and he swallowed back a smile.

"Thank you," he whispered, then hurried from the building.

In Shannon's apartment, Vernon said, "Her friend found her this morning. Said she got worried when she didn't come to the door, so she used her own key to get in. You'll have to make a positive identification."

All this for the benefit of the young deputy who hovered nearby.

Owen caught no more than a glimpse of his baby sister's destroyed face. For a moment he thought he had not gathered all the fibers from the blown-out pillow then realized the clots on the wall and bed were not the stuffing but Shannon's brain tissue. If he'd been able to eat breakfast that morning, it surely would have come up right then.

Holding back his urge to vomit, he told Vernon Fletcher, "Yes. That's her. That's Shannon Grady."

The deputy, standing behind the chief, studied the bed from a distance. Owen did not like the speculative look in the man's eyes. He met Vernon's gaze, sent an unspoken message and the man stepped between the body and his deputy.

"This was her third attempt, you know," Owen said. "She finally succeeded."

Vernon nodded. "Yeah. Of course the coroner will have to declare it, but it's obvious a self-inflicted GSW. With that old pistol."

They both stared at the revolver in her hand.

"Dad's old .38 Special. I'd wondered what happened to it." Still acting the part of a bereaved family member for the sake of the deputy, he sighed deeply and lowered his head. "She had every chance to live a good life, Vern. I gave her every opportunity I could, and she chose this way out. I just don't understand."

The chief laid a heavy hand on Owen's shoulder.

"I'm sorry, buddy. I know she caused you all kinds of grief, but you stood up to it real well. Your family ought to be proud of you."

Owen pulled in his lips so no one could see the smile that tried to form. He wiped his hand down his face and raised his head.

"I hope so. My family means everything."

"Chief, the coroner just drove up," the deputy said.

Vernon looked over his shoulder at the man, nodded. "I could use some coffee from the thermos in the car, Rick." The deputy left to fetch it. "You're laying it on a little thick, aren't you? Everyone knows you and Shannon had a strained relationship."

Owen swallowed hard. "I've never been any good at deception, Vern, but I'll take it down a notch. What about the coroner?"

"Jake's as crooked as a snake and has been for twenty-five years, but there's no way this looks like a suicide. Why didn't you use your brain, Owen? How can someone shoot herself in the back of the head? Jake, he'll want his palm greased for sure. Heavily. You know that."

"Fine. Whatever he wants. Just make it happen the way it has to happen."

Vern narrowed his eyes, and Owen knew a moment's chill from a perceived potential confrontation. "I know how to do this. Haven't I helped you before?"

"Yeah. Sure, you have. Of course. I just wanted to make sure…whatever Jake wants…."

"You better be glad J.J. Forbes got cancer and died last year. Otherwise, you'd have him to deal with, too."

"J.J. wouldn't have been a problem."

A small silence fell, and they heard the front door open.

"Must be nice to own this town," Vern muttered then turned to greet the Woodrow County Coroner.

EVIE

Evie Kendall slowly closed Shannon's third and final notebook and placed her palm on it, as if touching Shannon herself in benediction.

There it lay, Shannon's life coldly exposed like diseased entrails at an autopsy. So much misery hidden inside the fragile shell of her body, drawn out of her lost memories at last and recorded by her hand, without sentiment.

Evie shook, from the core of her being to the tips of her extremities. The first tremor had taken hold of her as she read the account of what had happened to five-year-old Shannon in the Gradys' basement. As she began to realize the magnitude of what had gripped her friend and scarred her mind, Evie's trembling grew more violent until she would have filled a tall glass with Wild Turkey and drunk it, straight up…if she hadn't emptied the bottle down the drain before she'd read the first word in the first line of the first notebook.

She fired up a cigarette and smoked it viciously.

In all her life, Evie had acted instinctively then pondered about those actions later. There had been times when she and Shannon were the quintessential Thelma and Louise, charging ahead and damning to hell whatever obstacles or results that might occur. But, as she had done frequently during her intensive, nonstop reading of Shannon's notebooks, she shoved aside the craving for a drink to soothe her raw nerves. If ever there existed a time for a clear head and logical thinking, this was it. She wanted to make sure Owen Grady's privileged soft life in Woodrow, Arkansas, hit rock bottom, down in the filth and muck and stink where nasty things rot.

She went to the housing office to use their telephone. The prune-faced, nasal-voiced woman behind the desk scowled at her.

"I wish you people would get your own telephones."

"I wish we would, too." Evie said. "Maybe one of us will win the lottery and we won't have to live here and bother you. Wouldn't that be the berries?" She gave the woman a goofy, put-on grin and dialed Dunn's number. She knew he was home because Owen had cut the factory hours to less than half.

"Hey, guy," she greeted. "I need to talk to you. Can you come to my place?"

"Right now?"

"Yeah. It's important."

"I have to come into town tomorrow. Can it wait until—"

"No, it can't," she snapped. "I need to talk to you about that box."

"The one Shannon left you?"

"Yes."

He was silent for a couple of seconds. "Okay. I'll be there pretty soon."

She hung up, looked at the woman behind the desk. "Have you cleaned Shannon Grady's apartment yet?"

The woman scowled at her over her glasses. "You said you did that."

"I mean, the carpets and painting."

The woman drew her lips together, but consulted a list posted on the small bulletin board behind her desk and said, "It's scheduled for tomorrow."

Evie's heart leaped. "Don't! I mean, don't do it tomorrow. You have to wait a few days."

The woman drew back. "We will not wait. Do you realize there's a list for these apartments and we—"

Evie had been without sleep or food for almost twenty-four hours. Her heart ached from reading the notebooks and her mind buzzed with the need to act. A snooty, low-level pen pusher was just one more obstacle, and a small one at that. She leaned across the desk until her face was inches from the other woman.

"Do not clean that apartment tomorrow. It's very likely Shannon Grady did not kill herself and proof might still be there."

The woman blinked and reared back even further. "Oh, for heaven's sake! The police have been here and gone. And you need to get away from me, or I'll call cops to cart you out of here. All of us have just about run out of patience with you, Evie Kendall."

Evie straightened, tried a different tactic. "I'm sorry. I don't mean to cause you any trouble. I'm just trying to make sure somebody guilty doesn't get away with murder."

"Murder!"

"That apartment won't get cleaned any earlier than tomorrow, will it?"

"No. But…but…murder. Of all things to come up with. Everyone knows Shannon Grady was always trying to kill herself."

Fury shot through Evie, but rage would cause more harm than good at this point.

"No, she wasn't," she said quietly. "And I'm going to prove it."

She hurried back to her apartment and waited for Dunn. As soon as he arrived, she threw open the door and yanked him inside.

"Good God, woman," he said. "You look like you've been hit by lightning."

"I feel like it. Dunn, Shannon did not kill herself."

"I don't doubt it. But what makes you say so?"

"Sit."

He did.

"Listen to me. When I emptied her apartment, I went through all her stuff, clothes, supplies, knickknacks, food."

"I know."

"She had a fresh gallon of milk in the refrigerator. She'd bought it that day along with a fresh bag of salad greens—"

"Shannon liked her salads and vegetables."

"Right."

"And she had a small beef roast thawing in the 'fridge."

"Evie, what are you getting at?"

"I'm not finished."

He held up one hand. "Okay. But I have to get home before dark to do the milking."

She scowled at him. "It's not even noon yet."

"I know. So stop beating around the bush and get to the point."

She glared. "Stop being a wise-ass and listen to me. Library books." She folded her arms and looked at him.

The confused expression on his face turned curious. "What about 'em?"

"Shannon had three library books on her table." She held up three fingers.

"Yeah. So she liked to read. C'mon, Evie. What're you driving at?"

"When I took them back, the librarian said, 'Oh, it's just so sad. She's been waiting weeks and weeks for this book to come in, and she was so pleased when she checked it out.'"

Dunn sat like a rock, then something flickered across his face. Like the sun coming up on a clear morning, understanding rose in his eyes and spread across his expression.

"Why would she buy milk and meat and fresh produce if she planned to kill herself?" he said.

Evie pointed at him in triumph. "Right! And why would she check out library books if she wasn't going to read them?"

"Exactly." He stood and paced the small room, his face like the wrath of God. "Have you told anyone else?"

"You mean like the cops? Are you kidding?"

"Well, we need to let someone—"

She picked up Shannon's notebooks off the table and handed them to him.

"Sit down and take a look. You don't have time to read it all this but at least look through them. Here. I'll show you where." She settled on the sofa next to him, guided him through the pages, the maze of secrets Shannon had hidden in her lost memories.

He grew angrier with every revelation. "My God," he said from time to time.

When they reached the last page, he jumped up from the couch, shouting, "I'll kill that bastard. I'll cut off his balls then skin him alive."

He strode toward the door, but Evie grabbed his arm.

"No, you won't. You wanna go to prison for the rest of your life?"

His face was dark with fury and she felt heat and rage radiating from his body.

"I gotta do something! She didn't deserve any of that."

"No, she didn't. None of it."

"That son of a bitch ruined her life while she was living then he took what was left and wasted it. He stole Shannon from the rest of us. He has to pay. I gotta do something."

She gave him a level gaze. "Oh, he will. He'll pay big time. And you know the cops aren't gonna help us. You saw for yourself the police chief is in his back pocket."

"He owns them," Dunn said. "The cops, the lawyers, the doctors…everyone in this goddam town, he owns it all." He slammed his fist into the wall, leaving a sizable hole. Evie seized his hand before he could do it again.

"We know that, but listen to me. We can do something."

He scowled. "Sure we can," he jeered. "People like us always can do something when the rich cats make a mess."

She ignored his sarcasm. "Woodrow is a small place, a dirty little smudge on the map. This pissant town ain't shit to the rest of the world and neither is Owen Grady. I tell you who he doesn't control. The state police."

As this sunk in, something other than wrath rested on his face. "You're right. You are one hundred percent absolutely right!" He grabbed her, planted a hard kiss right on her lips. "Evie, you are one terrific chick!"

Through her anger, a small, new light of hope flickered. It pushed aside her grief, nudged away the dregs of exhaustion, and began to burn with bright hope.

"You're a pretty cool dude yourself, Dunn."

Evie fixed a pot of strong coffee, and they sat at the kitchen table to discuss their strategy.

"We can't prove it, you know," she said, firing up a smoke. "I mean, he had her body cremated within twelve hours, and I'm not even sure that's legal."

"The law doesn't apply to the likes of Owen Grady."

"Not the local law. But we sure as hell have some circumstantial evidence to give to the state police. And here's something else. The morning I found her, the apartment was as neat and clean as ever. You know how orderly she was, nothing ever out of place. I think she always gave it quick straightening before she went to bed."

"That sounds like Shannon."

"Yeah, but I knew something was off the minute I went inside."

He frowned. "Something like what?

"It was the lamp. You know that lamp she had on the little table?" He nodded. "Well, it was on the very edge of the table and its shade was crooked. And she'd never have gone to bed leaving it out of place like that."

"Right." Dunn sipped his coffee. "Fingerprints."

She nodded. "I'll bet dollars to doughnuts, they didn't dust the place. When I cleaned, I didn't see any of that stuff they use anywhere. And I didn't wash off every little thing. Light switches, cabinet handles, doorknobs, closet doors. I didn't even think about something like that 'cause she always kept the place so clean. My fingerprints are all over the place, but I'll betcha Owen left his there, and maybe on that lamp."

"Don't you think he wiped everything off?"

"Oh, please." She lit a cigarette, took a deep drag, then spoke around the smoke. "Owen doesn't have enough sense to pour piss out of a boot."

He grinned. "So I've heard you say more than once."

"That's because it's the truth. Now, here's what we need to do. I'm gonna go talk to Mrs. Lawrence next door. Nothing ever happens around here that she doesn't see. While I'm with her, you call your sister at the beauty shop. And don't give me that look. You said yourself more gossip comes into that place than you have the stomach to hear. See if she's heard *anything*. No matter how insignificant."

"This is all well and good, Evie, but it still doesn't guarantee that Owen will get caught." He finished his coffee.

"I know. But we can still make him pay."

He took his cell phone out of his pocket. "In that case, let's get a move on."

"Amen, brother." She got to her feet, crushed out her cigarette, and took a final slug of coffee. "I'm off to talk with Mrs. Lawrence."

The old woman plied her with a steaming bowl of potato and cheddar soup, hot biscuits, and a hunk of chocolate cake so huge a starving farm hand couldn't consume it in three meals. When Evie smelled the food she realized how long it had been since she'd eaten. She sat at Mrs. Lawrence's tiny white dining table, and chowed down out of Blue Willow dishes.

"It's a shame about that poor girl next door. She was always so sweet and friendly-like. Here, honey, let me give you some milk."

"Thanks. This is great food, Mrs. Lawrence."

"Well, you were hungry. I can always tell by looking at folks if they're hungry. And I can always tell when they're troubled. Take Shannon. I knew she was troubled."

"Yes, ma'am. She was."

"I'm glad you were such good friends with her, Evie. Both of you needed that bond."

Evie nodded and the woman continued, "You were alone in the world until you moved here, weren't you? You got you some friends now, though."

How Mrs. Lawrence knew about Evie's loneliness was anyone's guess, but Evie didn't have time to ask. "I need to know something."

"Oh?"

"The night Shannon died, did you hear or see anything?"

The old woman cut a slab of cake, put it on a plate, shuffled across the kitchen floor to fetch a fork. She took her sweet time, stopping to wipe crumbs off the counter into her palm, then shambled to the sink and dusted off her hands. She sprayed a little water to wash the crumbs down. Before she came back to the table, she shook out a dish towel and dried every drop from the sink. Or so it seemed to Evie who watched all this with mounting impatience. The cake made the wait tolerable—it melted on her tongue the moment she took a bite.

Mrs. Lawrence finally sat down and cut into her own cake.

"Well," she said as she took a bite, "I'm not sure." She swallowed, frowned and said, "I b'lieve I'll get me some milk."

Evie jumped up as the woman started to scoot her chair back. "You just sit there, Mrs. Lawrence, and I'll pour you a glass of milk. Now, try to remember if you saw or heard anything that night that might have been out of the ordinary."

"Seems to me, I did."

In her eagerness to hear, Evie sloshed milk on the cabinet. She dabbed it off with her shirt tail.

She plunked the glass on the table, spilled a little more and wiped it with her hand. Mrs. Lawrence frowned. Evie grabbed a napkin and blotted up the rest.

"Tell me what you might've noticed that night, please."

"Oh, just her moving around in there, getting ready for bed, I guess. You know our bathrooms are back-to-back, so I always hear when she runs her shower."

"But what about anything unusual?"

She paused to take a leisurely sip. "I heard water running in the middle of the night."

"In the bathroom."

"Yes."

"I knew it wasn't Shannon 'cause she told me once that since she's been taking that medicine she sleeps like a rock all night, never wakes up, even to tinkle."

Evie said, "I see. Was there anything else?"

"Well, of course I got up, thinking she might be sick, and I was going to call her, but then I heard her door shut. Real quiet-like. So I snuck a look out and I saw a fellow cutting across the parking lot real fast."

Evie's blood quickened. "Did you see what he looked like?"

She shook her head. "No. It wasn't any of my business if she had a late night gentleman caller. I've had a few myself. Would you like some more cake, honey?"

Back in her apartment a few minutes later, Evie told Dunn what she'd just found out. "So all we know for now is that someone was there in the middle of the night, but that doesn't prove anything. What'd your sister say?"

He lit their cigarettes and said, "You're gonna love this. One of Tammy's regular customers is Rick Patten's wife, and Patten is one of Vernon Fletcher's deputies. According to her, Fletcher went to the scene by himself."

"Of course he did."

"There's more. Rick was in the vicinity when the call came in, so naturally he went to Shannon's apartment. He thought Fletcher acted strange, nervous, short-tempered. And Fletcher kept him out of the bedroom, but Rick did see the body once, just briefly and from the doorway. Pretty much all he saw was the revolver in Shannon's hand. Her left hand." He paused, then added, "Evie, you and I both know that Shannon was right-handed.

Their eyes met and they sat in silence until she said, "Let's take ourselves, our theories, and our 'circumstantial evidence' to the state police right now."

EVIE

Evie and Dunn rolled back into Woodrow past midnight. The notebooks, their statements, and all the information they had gleaned now rested in the hands of a higher authority.

"You think they'll move forward with this?" Evie asked as Dunn pulled up to her apartment.

He stretched his neck and rolled his shoulders. "We'll see. We've done all we can do, though."

Evie yawned, huge and jaw-popping. She was tired to the core and longed for a hot bath and deep sleep. But it wasn't over.

"Not quite all," she said.

Dunn interrupted his own yawn. "Huh?"

"You wanna make Owen Grady pay, don't you?"

"You know it."

"So tell me: what does he love more than anything else in this world?"

"You mean besides himself?"

She nodded.

"Well, I'd have to say he loves everybody kissin' his Grady ass and thinkin' he's the greatest thing that ever came down the pike. They won't be thinking that way about him once all this comes out."

"And if, for some reason, they can't prove he did it and he's never charged with her murder, or even investigated—"

He scowled and shook his head. "Well, surely they'll do something."

She held up one hand. "I'm just sayin'. All the business he did to Shannon might never see the light of day. No one may ever know, *unless…unless* you and me, Dundee, do it ourselves."

He narrowed his eyes. "Now who was it just a few hours ago carrying on about not wanting me to go to prison for killin' that shithead."

"We're not gonna kill him, Dunn. We're gonna do something worse."

At nine o'clock the next morning, Dunn Bradshaw and Evie Kendall pulled into the parking lot of Grady Wood Products. They sat in Dunn's old pickup for just a minute or so, taking in the huge steel warehouse that stored fencing, trusses, beams, lumber, and unfinished oak furniture. The offices were located on the second floor of the building.

Going on coffee, cigarettes, and very little sleep, Evie was jumpy as a cat, and Dunn's usual control teetered on the edge. But they had each showered and dressed in their best clothes for this event. For Dunn, it was clean jeans and a freshly-ironed white shirt. Evie was in her newest jeans and a blue sweater she'd picked up at the Share Center two weeks ago. She wore her long hair pulled back into a conservative ponytail.

"You look real nice," Dunn told her.

To her horror she felt herself blush. "Thank you."

"Ready for battle?" he asked.

She rubbed her hands together. "You betcha."

Owen Grady's easy life in Woodrow, Arkansas, was about to come to an end.

They entered the warehouse with its dusty men and noisy forklifts, their gazes going immediately toward the back where stairs led up to the offices. They did not want to confront Owen up there in privacy. Right where they stood, in the warehouse with workers all around, would do just fine.

"You ain't supposed to be in here," called out a wormy-looking, sallow-faced beanpole. He pushed his safety goggles up on his long, narrow forehead. The name stitched on his shirt front said he was Ron.

"I work here, Ricketts," Dunn said.

He glanced at Dunn then transferred to gaze to Evie. He grinned, showing a motley collection of unbrushed teeth.

"The boss don't like women in here."

"We're here to see Owen Grady," she said.

Ron Ricketts gave her a once-over. His wet-lipped leer made her skin crawl.

"What you want with 'im?"

"If you'll go get him," Dunn said, "you'll find out."

The man slammed him a mean look. "I ain't runnin' no errands for you."

"You're showin' your ass again, Ricketts. Why don't you just go tell Owen we want to see him?"

Ron's narrow face reddened. "Get out of here and take your ho' with you."

Dunn took a step forward, fists curled. Ron yelped like a kicked dog. Drawn by the ruckus and noise, other men stopped work and began to gather, doubtless hoping for a fight on the warehouse floor.

"What's going on here?"

At the sound of his voice, silence fell. Owen Grady, in his perfectly pressed brown slacks, tan oxford shirt and dark rust tie, approached with long swift strides from the back of the building. He held a clipboard in his right hand. Light glinted off the half-glasses perched on his nose and his middle-aged face was ruddy. Tension showed in his eyes and in every line on his face. Off to one side, Ron Ricketts smirked at Evie like a snot-nosed playground bully.

She made sure every person around them heard them and she met his eyes straight on. "You got a lot to answer for, Owen Grady."

His face paled and he swallowed hard. He gawped at her wordlessly then shifted his gaze to Dunn and made a shooing gesture. "You don't get paid to hang around the dock, Bradshaw. Get back to work."

"I'm not working today," Dunn said calmly. "Remember? You cut my days down to Thursdays and Fridays."

Ron moved behind Owen and goggled at Dunn and Evie like a pop-eyed frog.

"Then why are you here? Take that woman and get out." Owen turned, saw the pack that had gathered behind him. "Get back to work, or I'll have all your jobs!"

They started to scatter like roaches, but Dunn gave a piercing whistle that caught every ear and brought everyone to a silent standstill.

"Not yet," he shouted. "You men come back. We have something you need to hear." To Ron Ricketts, he said, "Go get Craig."

The man gave him a look of panic. "He ain't here. He's in Little Rock at that meeting."

Dunn pulled a pallet over and stacked it on another one. Evie stepped up on them so everyone could see her, and she faced the growing crowd. Watching her, Owen's left eye twitched. His lips trembled. Evie smiled at him grimly.

"I know what you did to your sister, you filthy slime," she said in a reasonable voice, as if she was talking about the weather. "You disgusting piece of shit. You rotten waste of human flesh."

Someone in the mob behind him laughed then immediately fell silent.

Owen gulped.

"You can't prove anything!" he yelled. "I stay home at night. I mind my own business. God will protect me!" He fumbled for the cell phone clipped to his belt. "Get to dock six right now!" he barked into the mouthpiece. To Evie he said, "Get off my property and don't come back here. And whatever fool thing you've dreamed up in your sick head, you better shut up about it."

She laughed, completely without mirth.

"My sick head. Oh, Owen, who are you kidding? It takes a real messed up, sick asshole to do to little girls what you did to Shannon. You and Vernon Fletcher and J.J. Forbes."

"Get out of here!" Owen squealed. He advanced, brandishing his clipboard like a sword. An overweight security guard trotted toward them, puffing as he halted.

"Get them out of here," Owen told him, gasping. "Get them out and if they ever come back, call the police."

"Yeah, Owen," Dunn said. "Tell him to call the cops. In fact, have him call the state police. Right now, they have three notebooks that Shannon wrote in. She wrote all about you, and how you used to creep into her room at night, and how you gave her to your buddies to play with…when she was only a tiny girl. No wonder you always treated her like shit. If everyone believed she was crazy, if everyone always thought she was a bad person, then no one would ever believe what you had done to her. You, with your holier-than-thou face."

"Throw them out of here!" Owen screamed. "Bradshaw. You're fired."

Evie spoke up. "They know about you sneaking into her apartment the night she died." Evie paused to let that sink in, watching his face grow paler and paler. "Someone saw you, Owen. Saw you hurrying away in the middle of the night. And guess what else? Soon everyone in this town will know all about the dirty little secrets you kept hidden behind your clean, white façade."

He looked from one face to the other, his eyes darting until they nearly rolled back into his head. He opened his mouth and nothing came out. The clipboard clattered to the floor. His face went from pale to gray. Owen collapsed and writhed on the dirty concrete of his warehouse.

The men who worked for him looked on without pity.

EPILOGUE

After their initial shock, the people of Woodrow began to speak freely. The name Owen Grady became a nasty taste in the mouth of anyone who'd ever known him.

All over town, conversations went like this: "I always thought there was something shady about him. He always seemed too good."

"When I was a little girl, he had a way of looking at me that made me feel dirty."

"I never trusted him."

"He wasn't the man his daddy was, and that's for sure. It was a dark day for Woodrow, Arkansas when Curtis Grady died, and a blacker day when Owen Grady tried to fill his shoes."

"Reckon he'll ever get out of prison?"

"Who knows? If he does, he better not come back here. There's them that would make quick work of 'im."

"Well, ol' Vernon Fletcher and his coroner buddy will keep each other company in the lock-up for a while, I reckon."

"I'm just glad Craig didn't have nothin' to do with any of that mess. He always tried to do what was best for the employees and the town."

The media settled like flies around the town and the Grady estate, and the internet bloomed with accounts and speculations. With their designer clothes and flashy jewelry, Sarah Jean and Donna became favorite targets. In the midst of personal and financial ruin, Sarah Jean somehow managed to elude the cameras and took off for parts unknown. Owen and Sarah Jean's two daughters, both in the university, refused to talk to anyone. They never returned to Woodrow

After twenty-three years of marriage, Craig Henson found his spine and his voice and he left Donna for a woman half her age. He moved with her to Little Rock. As for Donna, she shut herself away in their home and rarely came out. Her children were young adults by then. Their son left in the middle of the night, and no one was sure where he settled. Their daughter married and moved to Hawaii.

Julie stayed with Gwen in Los Angeles.

A month after Owen was sent to prison, the Reverend Randall Yeager and his faithful wife Patty accepted assignment for a mission in New Delhi. A young female minister took over the Woodrow Worship Center.

Grady Wood Products faltered for a time and nearly went under. It was saved by a conglomerate from North Carolina that changed its name, its focus and began making fine furniture that sold worldwide.

On Memorial Day, when the grass was lush and velvety in the cemetery in Champion, and the graves were ablaze with newly laid flowers, Dunn and Evie walked hand-in-hand toward Shannon's grave. Garrett was beside them, carrying a huge arrangement of daisies and sunflowers.

While they were still quite a way off, Dunn said, "I can see from here that the monument company hasn't put up the stone yet."

"They will," Evie assured him.

"Sure they will," Garrett said. "It's only been a little while since we ordered it."

"Yeah. But I hate to see nothing other than that little celluloid marker."

The breeze caught the voices of others who were strolling through the graveyard, pausing to read markers and remember loved ones. Above them the sky hung cloudless and bright blue. Sunlight gilded every tree, every blade of freshly cut grass, every stone.

Evie could not help but compare that day's glory to the bleak chill of the day Shannon's family had hidden her ashes in the ground. Tears blurred her vision and she stumbled.

Both men caught her.

"You okay?" Dunn asked.

"You feeling all right, Miss Evie?" Garrett asked.

She looked at them, one on each side, so much alike in body and spirit.

She wondered how much longer it would be before Dunn realized what she knew. No need to speculate long. These days there were tests to prove paternity beyond a shadow of doubt.

She smiled and wiped her eyes. "I'm fine."

They continued forward, then she stopped. "What's that on her grave?"

Dunn squinted, shook his head. "Someone's been here, left some flowers, but I can't tell what that other is…looks like a ball maybe." He glanced around. "There's a kid over there. Maybe he was playing with it and it got away from him."

"No," said Garrett. "It's not a ball."

They reached the marker and stopped. A mound of rich, red roses lay across Shannon's grave.

"Look!" Evie bent, picked up the snow globe. The oak base had a small V-shaped scratch. "It's Shannon's snow globe," she said faintly. "She bought it at a thrift store a few years ago. She said it looked just like the one that used to be in her folks' house. I saw Donna take it from the apartment on the day of Shannon's funeral."

For a little space of time they all gazed at the roses. Garrett knelt to add his daisies and sunflowers and stayed to gently stroke a rose petal.

"Maybe she had a change of heart," he said quietly.

"Maybe," Evie said. "I hope so."

She looked at the snow globe again. She shook it, watched the mini-blizzard envelop the tiny church on a hillside dotted with evergreens.

"Shannon once said if you had the ears to hear and the heart to listen, you could hear the people singing inside." She smiled. "I think I hear them."

ABOUT THE AUTHOR

Sydney Hope Archer is a devoted lover of the written word and spends her days spinning stories. She lives in the South with her husband, two dogs, and a spoiled cat.